CW01080678

i

Fourth Generation

by

Patricia Greasby

This is a work of fiction. Similarities to real people, places or events are entirely coincidental.

ISBN 9781300156321

Cover illustration courtesy of pixabay

FOURTH GENERATION

CHAPTER 1

Stephen Bryce hunkered into a padded anorak and looked up into the Abruzzo mountains with rising apprehension. They had two days in which to shoot a few advance publicity scenes in a remote area with minimal crew. The World War 2 khaki uniform he wore beneath a modern waterproof jacket was itchy and boots, styled for the same era, hurt his feet. Just a few bits to camera for background information, he'd been told, but now the stream that only yesterday had served as a scenic backdrop had become a raging torrent.

Arturo Morretti, their mountain guide, folded down the aerial of a satellite phone and was now speaking animatedly with assistant director Max Cavendish, drafted in at the last moment to manage the skeleton crew.

Seeing Yash Patel struggling to set up his lighting equipment in the howling gale, Stephen stepped from the cover of one of the Land Rovers to lend a hand.

'This is not working,' Yash shouted over the roar of wind and water. 'The weather people seem to have got it wrong; they said we'd get a two-day window.'

Stephen had worked under adverse conditions numerous times, it went with the job, but the situation here was bordering on dangerous and he was anxious to get on with the task and back down the mountain. He shot a glance to where, on a nearby gravel-strewn path, Max Cavendish seemed to be debating a point with their Italian guide.

Stephen left Yash to wrestle with the equipment and, leaning into the wind, joined Cavendish and the guide further along the path.

Arturo Morretti turned to Stephen and said, 'We must leave. There have been landslides above the gully.' He gestured over a ridge higher up the mountain.

1

Max Cavendish sighed, 'We only need two, maybe three, hours to get a few long shots.'

'We must go now,' Arturo insisted.

'Okay, we go back to the chalet and reassess the situation. Get the equipment loaded.'

*

Two fully loaded Land Rovers lurched down the track. Water running in a gutter between a steep slope and the road already overflowed in places, sweeping shale and pebbles into heaps.

Most of the crew squeezed into the first vehicle. Stephen, in the second, sat behind the driver, Louise, a production assistant. Cavendish and Arturo beside her on the front seat. Sitting beside Stephen was veteran cameraman Ethan Quinn and lighting man, Yash. Despite the seriousness of the situation, Stephen smiled as Ethan focused a handheld camera first on the peaks shrouded in cloud above then panned to the valley, lost in mist, below. At least if they went over the edge it would be recorded for posterity.

A chalet, huddled into the hillside, materialised from the gloom. Tension rose as they each craned forward. Stephen wondered if they were hoping, as he was, that they would not delay their descent by *reassessing* the situation.

Arturo called, 'Stop.'

Louise slammed on the brakes and they slewed on loose rubble to a shuddering halt.

Arturo stepped out of the vehicle and stood with head cocked, listening. After a moment he leaned into the Land Rover, grabbed the radio mike and tried to raise the driver of the other vehicle which was some way in front. Leaping back into the vehicle he ordered, 'Reverse, back up the track.'

Stephen lowered his window to peer at dark rain-laden clouds shifting across the mountainside.

Thunder rumbled, echoing from peak to peak. The ground trembled.

*

Ann Bryce sat at the table in the kitchen of Holly Cottage, a rambling, two storey, red-brick building, and tried to compose her thoughts. A couple of days ago she had been meandering through the streets of a small Italian lakeside town, hoping she and Stephen would have a few days

2

together to wind down before heading home but, as was often the case, plans change.

'I'll get a flight tomorrow,' she'd told Stephen. 'Nathan will be home in a few days and there's a good deal to be done.' Stephen would travel home the following week and still have a few days before setting off on a long-planned trekking holiday with his son, but late snow high in the Italian mountains had caused problems for the film crew. According to a phone call, rain and meltwater had created landslides.

*

'But Dad's all right?' Nathan queried.

'Yes, he's fine,' Ann told her adopted son's image on the screen of her iPad. 'They all are. They are hoping to helicopter them out when there's a break in the weather.'

'And he'll be back in time?'

'I was hoping he'd have a few days' rest before you both set off.'

Nathan scowled and put his head down so all Ann could see was a mop of loosely curled fair hair. 'Your dad will be home as soon as he's able, so Grandad and I will come down to collect you and Matthew from school this evening.'

Nathan lifted his head and without smiling, said, 'Okay, Mum. See you later,' adding, 'love you,' before breaking the connection.

Ann's concern for her husband's health vied with the knowledge that Nathan had been looking forward to the hiking trip with his father, along a section of the Grand Canyon, for such a long time. They had carefully planned schedules to allow Stephen time off before and after Nathan's two-week Easter break.

Stephen's father, Peter, put a hand on her shoulder. 'It would be sensible to postpone the hiking trip, or at least delay it a week or so.'

'Nathan has to be back at school for exams, and Stephen has a date for the start of his next film.'

'You should have made Nathan wait for a holiday. If he's having a year off before starting university there'll be plenty of time in the summer. No such thing as *a year off* in my day,' Peter chided as he stalked back to his own rooms in the annex.

'Yes, Peter,' Ann muttered. She loved her father-in-law; still standing straight, with that firm step and determined aspect, he'd been through a lot over the years, but his upbringing had been hard and he tended to see things in black and white, right and wrong, with nothing in between.

3

CHAPTER 2

Nathan straightened from searching his desk in the study he shared with his cousin, Matthew, at Edgehill School.

'Lost something?' enquired Matthew.

'I can't find my notes from this morning's IT class.'

'You can borrow mine.' Matthew skimmed a notepad onto Nathan's desk.

Nathan didn't bother to look at the pages before flinging the notebook back. 'I can't read your writing.'

'What's the panic? We won't need it until next term. And old Thompson's only temporary; he might have moved on by then. He's weird, anyway.'

'You think everyone's weird.' Nathan slammed a drawer shut. 'And there's more in there than notes. Thompson's so involved with technicalities, I didn't understand half he was rambling about.'

'Not the greatest technophile, are you?' Matthew said amiably. 'Bet you were writing a few lines of poetry when you should have been listening.'

'No.' Nathan threw his cousin the famous Bryce grin. 'I was making a list of what I need for my holiday with Dad. Maybe I left it in the computer room.' He headed for the door.

'Don't be long, you need to finish packing,' Matthew called after him.

Nathan clattered down a wide, uncarpeted staircase, into the grand entrance hall and across the courtyard to one of the more modern school buildings. He pushed open a door leading to a high-ceilinged room lit by large windows.

Sitting at one of the many computer terminals was Mr Thompson, the IT master, whose spindly fingers stilled abruptly above the keyboard. Rimless spectacles making him appear older than his thirty-three years, he speared Nathan with an icy stare. 'Bryce. Where's your tie?'

Nathan's hand shot to his open collar.

'As it's the last day of term,' Thompson said begrudgingly, 'I'll let it go. What do you want?'

4

'I may have left something when I was here this morning, sir.'

Thompson lifted a notebook from the corner of the desk. 'Are you going home for Easter?'

'Yes, sir.'

'Who's collecting you?'

'My mother and grandfather.'

'Your father is the actor Stephen Bryce.' It was a statement not a question and Nathan remained silent.

Mr Thompson shifted on the chair. 'My mother was an avid fan of his.'

'Dad's not that old.' The words spoken before he realised.

'Neither was my mother,' Thompson retorted. 'I didn't know my mother until I was in my twenties. My real mother that is. I think it's important to know one's birth mother, to treat them like precious gems.' He cocked his head. 'Don't you?' He held out the notebook.

Nathan stepped forward and took the book. 'Thank you, sir.'

*

'You're right,' Nathan told Matthew when he returned to their room. 'He *is* weird.

5

CHAPTER 3

The buzzer for the front gates of Holly Cottage sounded and Ann glanced at the screen as Nathan wheeled his bicycle into the garage.

A small black and tan mongrel greeted him on his entry into the kitchen and he stooped to rub its ears before tossing his cycling helmet into a utility room.

'Hello, Mum. Is Dad on his way back?'

'Nathan, I—'

'Don't tell me the flight's been delayed.' He took a tumbler from a cupboard and downed a glass of cold water.

'Sit down, Nathan. I need to talk to you.'

Nathan remained standing.

'The weather has turned bad,' she explained. 'There have been more landslides, and they can't get a helicopter up for another couple of days.'

'I don't mind if we're a day late. We can join the trekkers further along.'

Ann calmly took a seat at the table and waited whilst Nathan perched on a stool opposite.

'Do you remember about nine years ago, your dad was in hospital for a while?'

'Yes,' replied Nathan, suddenly frowning.

Ann knew immediately her words had released a childhood memory from a compartment of Nathan's mind normally locked and bolted.

'That man's dead,' he blurted.

Anxious not to stir memories of the dreadful episode that had scarred them all, Ann said, 'Don't worry, darling, that's all over, I promise.' She moved to sit beside him and gave her son's hand a reassuring squeeze. 'You remember it took your dad a long time to get better and there was a certain amount of damage to vital organs that, over time, might get worse. That's why we arranged for him to have a break before and after your trip.'

'You're saying he won't be able to go.'

'I'm saying we don't know how long it will take to get them off the mountain and, though Dad would probably disagree, I don't think he

6

should immediately go on a gruelling trek along the Grand Canyon or anywhere else. Perhaps Matthew would like to go with you? Or someone from school?'

'Matthew is going on a camping trip with school, and it was supposed to be just me and Dad.'

'I know, but we can make arrangements for later in the year—'

'He'll be working later in the year, and I've my own plans for the summer,' He shoved back the stool and stormed from the kitchen. Ann heard the back door slam and a moment later the buzzer on the front gates as they opened. She watched on the screen as immediately the gap was wide enough, Nathan sped through the gates on his racing bike.

'He's not wearing his helmet,' Ann yelled.

Her cry brought Peter into the kitchen. 'Let him go. He'll get over it,' he said calmly, giving Ann's shoulder a reassuring squeeze.

*

Nathan cycled through the village, bouncing his bike over kerbs, moving from road to pavement and back on to the road. On Common Road, he slowed, coming to a halt at the gates of Elliston Spa. His former home stood square and imposing at the end of a long circular drive. Restored and refurbished following a destructive fire, the new owners were doing good business. Although Nathan was unaware of the circumstances of the fire, the house was a reminder of events which, despite his best efforts to lock away, occasionally escaped to haunt him. It wasn't so much that his father had almost died, though that alone chilled him, it was that whilst Stephen lay sedated and on a ventilator, there were people willing to put his and his mother's lives at risk. A terrible lesson for a child.

Nathan considered going through the grounds, over The Common and through the trees. He should have used his all-terrain bike; best stick to the road.

*

Nathan propped his bike beneath the kitchen window of The Rookery: a barn conversion his uncle had been working on for as long as Nathan could remember.

Matthew didn't seem surprised at his return, merely saying, 'Aunty Ann rang.'

'Did she?'

'My mum and dad have gone out for a couple of hours, left Lizzie with me,' Matthew explained.

Nathan took Lizzie's hands and jiggled them. The nine year old gurgled at him through a lopsided grin. She rocked back and forth, supported by a frame similar to an oversized baby walker.

'She's no bother,' Matthew said. 'And it gives them time to themselves.'

Nathan helped himself to a cola from the fridge whilst Lizzie rattled some plastic keys attached to her frame.

'No more cola for you, Liz,' Matthew told her. 'It makes you hyper.' He filled a spouted mug with blackcurrant juice and handed it to her before turning back to his cousin. 'Sorry about the holiday, but from what my dad said, Uncle Stephen isn't fit. I'd go with you, but this school trip has been arranged for ages.'

Nathan sank onto a kitchen chair. 'Wish I was going on the school trip. Don't suppose there's any room at this late stage.'

'Not unless someone drops out. I bet there're lots of lads from school who'd go with you.'

'I was supposed to be going with Dad.' He was aware he sounded petulant.

'Well, your dad won't be going. I think the situation is more dangerous than your mum let on.'

Nathan shrugged.

'Come on.' Matthew gave him a nudge. 'I'll put Lizzie in her chair; we can walk round to the stables. She likes to look at the horses.'

*

Matthew pushed Lizzie in her wheelchair along a tarmac path to the paddocks and stable block.

A few ponies were turned out into the paddocks and the yard was quiet. The half-dozen horses in residence poked their heads over stable doors and pricked their ears at the sound of visitors.

Gill, a young woman newly qualified in stable management, came out of the office. Since Matthew's mother's time was taken up caring for her daughter, Gill had been employed to take care of the animals. 'Hello, Matthew,' she said, smiling. 'Brownie is in the far paddock. I'll need to get her if Lizzie wants to ride.'

'No, we've just come to see the horses, perhaps give them a few titbits.'

'Sure. Grab a handful of carrots from the store.' She cocked an eyebrow. 'Hello, Nathan.'

Nathan gave her a quick smile, hiding his blushes by quickly disappearing into the feed store. He emerged a few seconds later with a handful of carrots.

Matthew elbowed his cousin in the ribs. 'You'll be all right there if you fancy an older woman.'

'She's not that much older,' Nathan pointed out. 'Jealous?'

'Nah, I've got my eye on that girl working at the pub in the village.'

Nathan held Lizzie's hand open and placed a small carrot on her palm. Her obvious delight at the feel of soft equine lips tickling her hand a joy to see.

Nathan showed Lizzie the last carrot, the rest having been shared among the stabled horses. 'We'll save this for Brownie.'

When Lizzie had first seen the placid Exmoor pony bought for her by her parents, Julian and Fiona, she'd babbled with delight. Matthew had declared, 'She's trying to say Brownie.' So Brownie it was.

The pony whinnied and trotted up to the rail when they called her. The last carrot gone, they headed back to The Rookery.

'Do you think she knows Brownie is her pony?' Nathan asked.

'Sure she does. Lizzie knows more than anyone thinks,' Matthew affirmed, and with a note of conspiracy, said, 'I tell her all my secrets.'

'Yeah,' Nathan smiled. 'I expect she can keep a secret.'

'So can I,' Matthew told him with a sidelong glance. 'If you've got any secrets you want to share.'

It was the opening Nathan was hoping for. Only six months his senior, his cousin always seemed more worldly wise. 'Not a secret exactly, but ...'

'But what?'

'I spoke badly to Mum this morning. I muttered as I left but I don't think she heard.'

'Well?'

'I said...' Even now a couple of hours later, Nathan felt his shame. 'I said she wasn't my real mother and had no right to make decisions for Dad.' Matthew remained silent and Nathan added, 'I didn't mean it. As long as I can remember I've called her Mum. I hardly remember Lisa. I don't even think about her as being my mother, just Lisa from somewhere in my past. And it's not Mum's fault Dad's trapped halfway up an Italian mountain. I should have known filming always

9

overruns or something else turns up. I suppose I wanted someone to blame. I don't think she heard me.'

'She wouldn't bear a grudge if she had.'

*

In the kitchen of The Rookery, Nathan glanced at a magazine open on a worktop. He did a double take. An interview with Lisa Brookes disclosed she was acting as the figure head for the charity Ann and his father had set up in memory of Andy Roberts. A contemporary of Stephen's, Andy was an innocent victim of events now a dark cloud hovering just beyond the scope of Nathan's recollection.

The article mentioned she had been touring America in a play but now had a part in a period drama to be filmed in Derbyshire.

Nathan turned to find his cousin at his elbow, and quickly flipped the publication closed. 'Have you got any money, Matt?'

Matthew put a hand in his pocket and pulled out a few coins.

'I was thinking nearer a couple of hundred pounds.'

'You're joking. But I expect Dad will have some stashed somewhere. Why?'

Nathan didn't answer but said, 'Would you be a mate and fetch my cash card from Holly Cottage?'

Matthew pulled a face. 'Why can't you go?'

'Because Mum would ask what I wanted it for.'

'What *do* you want it for?'

'Don't be offended, Matt, but if you don't know you can't tell.'

'I won't tell.'

'Maybe not, but this way, if Mum or Grandad ask, you won't need to lie. Please, Matt; I'll look after Lizzie.'

Matthew reversed his small Peugeot hatchback from the garage, Nathan, leaning in the window, said, 'The card is in my room, the top left-hand drawer with my passport.' Matthew zoomed off in the direction of Elliston Village.

Nathan returned to the kitchen and chucked Lizzie under her chin, making her giggle. 'I wish I'd applied to take the driving test at the same time as your brother.'

Whilst waiting for Matthew's return, Nathan made several phone calls to his dad's agent but failed to get the information he needed. 'Never mind,' he told Lizzie, 'I'll cycle to the station, get a train into London. I know someone at Dad's agency who'll tell me where the cast are staying.'

10

Lizzie gave her lopsided grin, the equal of any charming Bryce smile.

Nathan leaned in close. 'You won't tell anyone, will you Lizzie?' Her eyes shone and Nathan smiled, confident she understood.

CHAPTER 4

Stephen twisted to look through the rear window of the Land Rover as Louise reversed erratically back up the mountain path.

Thunder reverberated, the ground shook, the side of the mountain shuddered and heaved. Stephen's last view of the chalet was of it sliding, almost intact, over the edge of the road and down the slope beyond.

Ethan lowered the handheld camera. Mouths hung open. A river of slag and rubble followed the chalet down the mountain – no sign of the leading Land Rover.

Louise was first to speak. 'Did they get through?'

Ignoring the question, Arturo said, 'The road further up is wide enough to turn around. We must go up the mountain before the whole lot comes down.'

'But what about them?'

'We should look,' Stephen suggested, making a conscious effort to sound calm. He opened the vehicle door a fraction but a shower of pebbles, cascading from above, rattled on the side of the Land Rover forcing him to slam the door.

Cavendish leaned across Louise and pulled on the steering wheel. 'Reverse. NOW.'

'Get your hands off,' Louise snapped. 'I can do it.'

She reversed further up the road and, after a few careful manoeuvres, put the vehicle in a low forward gear and proceeded cautiously along the higher mountain track.

Rain battered the windscreen. Slurry trickled over the road, gathering gravel and taking it over the edge. Concerned to tell Ann he'd be late, Stephen pulled out his mobile. No signal. Late! Nathan – trekking holiday. He had more immediate problems.

*

At Bridgford Station, Nathan locked his bike into a rack before taking a ticket from the automatic dispenser. He tucked his cash card into the inside pocket of his jacket and waited for the London train.

From St Pancras, Nathan hopped on the Tube to Camden and walked the short distance to his father's agent. The receptionist was

12

explaining that Lynn Ryder was not available when a voice behind exclaimed, 'Nathan, what are you doing here?'

'I tried to phone.'

'I've had meetings all day,' Lynn said. 'Have you news of your father?'

Taken off guard, Nathan stuttered, 'Nothing definite.'

'Come in,' Lynn invited and, after instructing the receptionist to hold her calls, led him into her office. She gestured to a chair, settled behind her desk and said, 'We're supposed to be kept informed about the situation in Italy, but we've heard nothing all day.'

'The Italian authorities told mum it might be a couple of days before they get a helicopter up, but that's not why I'm here.'

A few moments passed, Lynn obviously waiting for an explanation.

Nathan shifted nervously in his chair before saying, 'You have people from the agency involved in shooting a film in Derbyshire.'

'Yes,' Lynn said cautiously. 'Were you interested in anyone in particular?'

'I wondered if you could tell me the location and what hotel they're likely to use.'

After some thought, Lynn reached across the desk for a notepad. She made some jottings, tore off a sheet and handed it to Nathan. With a knowing smile, she said, 'I hope you find the young lady.'

He grinned in relief. 'Thank you.' So, she believed he was chasing a girl.

In the street Nathan's phone pinged. A text from Ann asking, *Where are you? Are you okay?* But, in no doubt Lynn would have told her his whereabouts, he ignored the message. His first task was to check train times from St Pancras. He supposed Derby would be the best destination, but it was getting late, so deciding on an early start next morning, his thoughts turned to food and somewhere to stay. Pulled up sharply, he wondered where his dad would be sleeping tonight.

13

CHAPTER 5

Ann put down her phone and opened her iPad. Aware of Peter at her elbow, she said, 'I can't keep up with all the enquiries and emails, so Lynn's put out a brief statement on all the usual media platforms. I suppose, now, we just wait.'

Peter humphed and paced around the kitchen.

'Lynn said Nathan called in to the office,' Ann continued. 'She believes he's on his way to see a girl.'

'And what do *you* believe?'

Ann twisted around to face her father-in-law. 'He asked for details of the filming in Derbyshire, and we know who is involved in that production.'

'You think he's looking for Lisa?'

'She *is* his mother.'

Peter humphed again. 'She's shown hardly any interest in him for the last ten years.'

'Stephen and I have given her every opportunity to keep in touch. Perhaps Nathan needs to come to some understanding of his relationship with her.'

'It could wait until we get Stephen home. Nathan should be here, with us.'

'Peter—' Ann hesitated to remind him of his chequered history with his own mother and said instead, 'I know he's worried about his dad, but there's nothing he can do. Lisa's obviously been on his mind and he's at an age where he feels the need to assert his independence.' She turned back to the iPad. 'He's quite capable of looking after himself, though I wish he would text.' She sneaked a look at her phone. Nothing. 'I'll transfer some money to his account, then I'll walk into the village, take these envelopes to the post office.'

Yvonne, the long-time housekeeper, paused on her way through the kitchen. 'I'll take them for you.'

'Thanks, Yvonne, but I need some fresh air.'

Yvonne still hovered. 'The press were gathering in the village when I came through this morning.'

14

Ann grimaced and handed over the mail. 'Thank you, Yvonne. Are you all set for your holiday?'

'Yes, we're off tonight, but with Stephen missing and Nathan … Perhaps we should—'

Ann picked up a bowl of potatoes. 'We'll be fine, Yvonne, go home, James will be waiting. Where are you off to? Did you say Greece?'

'Yes. But what if you need a chauffeur—?'

'If we need a chauffeur, there's a taxi in the village.' Ann searched in a drawer for the potato peeler. 'This will give me something to do, maybe take my mind off other things.'

*

Nathan strolled past cafés and restaurants in the station complex, plenty of places to eat but he needed to eke out his money. There was a limit on his cash card and another week before his allowance was paid. There was one place he could go. He'd hoped it wouldn't be necessary but … he headed for the Underground.

Twenty minutes later, Nathan looked up to the top floor apartment of Park View. He could barely remember the previous caretaker, Mrs Mitchell, who had lost her life in an explosion that wrecked the apartment block almost ten years ago. Ann and Stephen referred to her as Rosa Klebb. He couldn't remember why, only that it was used as a term of affection.

Relations between Ann's elder son and Stephen had been uneasy from the start and Nathan hesitated before entering a code which let him into the grounds. At the main entrance, he pressed the intercom button for flat 5.

'Hello?'

'Hello, Richard, it's Nathan.'

The locking mechanism clicked and Nathan pushed the door. Ignoring an elevator across the hall he took green-carpeted stairs two at a time.

Richard waited on the top floor landing, his greeting, 'Are you on your own? Is Mum okay?'

'Yes, she's fine.' Nathan followed his step-brother into the sitting room.

'It's been on the news about a film crew being stranded on a mountain in Italy.'

'Yeah, Dad's with them.'

'Bad luck.'

'Yes.' Nathan agreed. 'Where's Keely?'

'She's on a late shift.' Richard frowned. 'Does Mum want the apartment back?'

'No. She doesn't like coming here after what happened.'

'We've been looking for a place of our own but everything is so expensive. Would you like something to eat? I'm just about to put a ready meal in the microwave. There's another in the freezer.'

Nathan's stomach rumbled. 'Yes, please,'

'Make yourself at home, then you can tell me what this visit is about.' Richard disappeared into the kitchen only to stick his head around the kitchen door a moment later. 'Beef in black bean sauce or sweet and sour – any preference?'

Nathan, pleased at the prospect of being fed, said, 'No. either will do fine, thank you.' He picked up a motor magazine while Richard rattled about in the kitchen.

After eating, Richard handed Nathan a mug of tea and they settled in the lounge. 'What are you up to, when you should be with Mum waiting for news of your father?'

Nathan wrapped his hands around the mug and leaned forward. 'I suppose I should, but there's nothing I can do. The film company promised to keep Mum up to date and perhaps fly her out if necessary.'

Richard nodded his understanding before saying, 'And?'

'Dad and I were supposed to be going on a trekking holiday. You know, a father-son thing.'

Richard gave a wry smile. 'I wouldn't know about a father-son thing. The Grand Canyon, wasn't it?'

'Yeah, well, that's obviously not going to happen, so I'm at a bit of a loose end. I'm heading north in the morning and wondered if I could stay here tonight.'

'It's Mum's flat, not mine.'

Nathan knew it was his father's flat and it was Stephen who'd suggested Richard should use it until he and Keely found their own.

'What's so attractive up north?' Richard's flat Midlands accent reminiscent of Ann's.

Unable to tell a blatant lie, Nathan said, 'Someone I'd like to see,' and hoped Richard would jump to the same conclusion as Lynn.

Richard pulled a movie periodical from under the coffee table and dropped it open at the article about Lisa Brookes.

16

Nathan's face and ears gave the game away and he wasn't surprised when Richard said, 'Does Mum know?'

'Not unless she's guessed.'

'She's probably too busy worrying about your dad.'

Nathan waited for the inevitable question.

'Why?'

He sought the right words. 'I don't know. Mum ... Ann, your mum, has always been just that, Mum. And I wouldn't want it any other way.'

*

After thirty tortuous minutes, the Land Rover hit more solid ground. Stephen pointed into the misty distance as the dark shape of a shepherd's hut emerged from a murky dusk.

The immediate danger over, questions rattled round Stephen's brain: how long before they could get back to the town? *How* would they get down? Was this squalid hut any safer than the chalet? And what about the rest of the crew?

Max Cavendish, Louise, Ethan, Yash and Arturo must have felt the same, but their thoughts, like Stephen's, remained unvocalised.

Leaning into the wind, Arturo and Max crossed a grassy area to inspect the hut. They disappeared inside, Arturo reappearing a moment later to beckon the others in.

Louise slid a dozen bottles of water, shrink wrapped on a cardboard tray, across the tailgate of the Land Rover to where Stephen waited. He put out a hand to help her down but she ignored it and jumped down, landing with a squelch on sodden ground. She was about to lift the water bottles but Stephen beat her to it, leaving her to carry an armful of spare coats and rugs to the hut.

Arturo lit a paraffin lamp, the glow flickering in a draught from the ill-fitting door. He placed a case containing the satellite phone onto a rickety table, lifted the lid and fiddled with the keyboard.

Stephen plonked the tray of water bottles in a corner before standing at Arturo's elbow. 'Problem?'

Arturo slammed the lid. 'We have lost connection. 'Tis temporary. I try later. There should be emergency food here; someone make a fire, please.' He indicated a blackened hearth and logs stacked alongside.

17

Max laid his clipboard on the table and turned to Louise. 'See what food you can find and, Ethan, can you get the folding chairs from the Landy so at least we have something to sit on.'

Stephen unclipped the first few sheets from the clipboard. 'I assume, Max, these notes are no longer relevant.' He screwed the paper into a ball, crouched before the fireplace and settled the crumpled paper onto long cold ashes. From a nearby box he gathered kindling and struck a match along rough stone. He waited until flames licked the sticks before carefully placing a couple of logs.

Louise held up an iron cooking pot with a chain dangling from it. 'What am I supposed to do with this?'

'I believe it fits on here.' Stephen jangled a hook attached to a beam over the fire. He sorted through a box of emergency supplies stashed in the hut. 'See if you can find a tin opener and we'll put soup over the fire.' He examined some tins. 'These are past their sell-by date, but I guess we can't be too fussy.'

*

Yash sat on a blanket and leaned against the wall of the hut, hands wrapped around a mug of hot soup.

Max and Arturo used the folding chairs to sit at the table and, through steam from the soup, perused a detailed map. Stephen sat beside Louise on a wide wooden bench. She rested against the wall, her legs curled beneath her.

Ethan stood and leaned over the map. He voiced the concern of everyone. 'Is there another way down without going over the top?'

All eyes rested eagerly on the three at the table, ears on stalks.

Max folded the map. 'Don't panic, Ethan. They'll get a helicopter up if we can't get through.'

'Who's panicking? I don't know why there was such a rush to get this done,' Ethan told Max. 'There should have been more preparation.'

Getting to his feet, Max said, 'Since when have you been in charge?'

'I've been on more shoots than you've had hot dinners,' Ethan retorted.

Stephen forced himself between the two men. 'Arturo, do you believe we'll be safe here for the time being?'

'I believe so,' the guide confirmed. 'In any case, we can't go anywhere in the dark.'

18

Stephen went on, 'So we have to make the best of a bad situation.' His glance encompassed them all. 'We're warm, dry and have food.'

Ethan looked as if he would protest and Stephen put a hand on his chest. 'It's okay, we can take up any complaints when we get back.' Ethan stepped away, and Stephen turned to look hard at the young assistant director before resuming his seat beside Louise. Ethan wasn't the only one who had doubts about the wisdom of this excursion and who had authorised it.

*

Wind and rain battered the shelter. Stephen watched Ethan patting his pockets as if looking for something. Yash, sat on the floor of the hut, head over his mobile, the screen lighting up his face. Stephen glanced again at his own phone. No connection. Best switch it off, save the battery. Most of the heat from the fire blazing in the hearth seemed to be going straight up the chimney, smoke occasionally billowing into the room. Max and Arturo remained huddled over what appeared to be the blank screen of the satellite phone.

A blast of wind rattled the shutters and Louise, on the bench beside him, her back against the wall of the hut, flinched before shuffling into a more comfortable position. A log in the hearth burned through and crashed in a heap of ashes. Stephen stood and retrieved a spare blanket. He wondered if his gesture of help as Louise disembarked the Land Rover had been misconstrued. One had to be careful but he risked offering her the blanket. She took it from him and put it over her legs, drew her knees up and hugged them. Stephen turned up the collar of his anorak and folded his arms surprised when Louise hitched closer, lifted a corner of the blanket and said, 'Share?'

Stephen pulled up his knees and loosened the laces of the army boots, the most uncomfortable part of the khaki uniform. Louise unfolded the blanket and stretched it across them both. She leaned towards him. 'I'm sorry.'

'Sorry?'

'Sorry for being a little prickly, and ... well, I've wanted to apologise for a long time.'

Stephen racked his brain for an incident worthy of an apology. An attractive brunette, in her late twenties, he recalled he'd had a few dealings with her on previous productions. She'd brought him coffee and copied scripts, carried messages, scurrying about doing the one hundred

19

and one things necessary to keep things running smoothly. He'd been surprised to see her on this extra-curricular jaunt.

She kept her voice low. 'Nine years ago, at the Apollo Studios, I was on work experience from college.'

Stephen frowned in concentration. 'My memories of that time are a bit hazy.'

'Sophie—'

'I remember Sophie.'

Louise winced. 'It was me who Sophie sent out to get cough medicine. The next thing I knew there was an ambulance and paramedics …'

Stephen recalled the fuzzy world he woke to. His sense of being but not knowing. Familiar faces he couldn't name. He knew them now and wanted to be with them.

Louise intruded on his thoughts. 'It's one of the reasons I took this job, to say sorry for all you suffered.'

He found a smile for her. 'It wasn't your fault, nor was it Sophie's. I asked her to get something for a cough. Even the experts couldn't determine whether it was a reaction to one of the ingredients or because of the medication I was already taking.'

'You nearly died.'

'Yes, well …' To change the subject he said, 'And the other reason … for taking this job?'

'I was hoping to get on the camera crew. After some studio work experience I did a degree in cinematography.' She shrugged. 'But I've no experience and I'm a woman.'

Stephen detected a note of bitterness and thought it wise not to comment.

She went on, 'I have worked on other projects. The last one with a friend of yours.' She shot him a sideways glance. 'Lisa Brookes.'

He knew it was impossible for their paths not to cross from time to time and after a few moments' consideration, he said, 'And how is Lisa?'

Louise studied her hands for a long moment before saying cryptically, 'A woman shouldn't have to choose between a career and a family.'

Stephen tensed, an inner voice telling him to take care. To what was she referring? Seventeen years ago Lisa had all but rejected her son, initially leaving him in the care of her parents, then when her mother

20

suffered a stroke, she consented to his adoption by himself and Ann. She had shown little interest in his upbringing from the start.

After a few moments' thought he hoped he was on safe ground by saying, 'It requires sacrifices from all concerned.'

CHAPTER 6

Pleased to find his next month's allowance already in his bank account, Nathan texted, 'Thanks, Mum. I'll be in touch soon.'

He took an early train to Derby where Ann's younger son, his step-brother Christopher, was waiting on the platform. A phone call from Richard had explained the circumstances, so he was spared further inquisition.

Nevertheless, he was greeted with, 'I spoke to Mum earlier; there's no more news about your dad.' His disapproving look prompted Nathan to say, 'I *will* ring later.'

Over a late breakfast at a nearby McDonald's, Chris said, 'I'll drive you to Crich, but I'm on shift tonight so I must get back for some sleep.'

'Thanks, Chris, but there's a train to—' Nathan checked his phone. 'What ... stand ... well, then it's only about a mile.'

'Whatstandwell,' Chris corrected. 'I'll give you a lift anyway. It's only a twenty-minute drive, but you'll need to make your own way back. You can stay at my place tonight if you like. I'm on duty at six, so,' he fiddled with a key ring, 'if you're any later, here's a key. I've got a spare.'

Overwhelmed with affection for a step-brother he saw perhaps, only twice a year, Nathan said, 'I might not get back tonight. It's a tourist area, so I'm sure there'll be lots of hotels.'

'Take it anyway. Mum will kill me if I let you wander the streets.'

*

'And make sure you let Mum know you're okay,' Chris added as twenty minutes later he let Nathan out on the outskirts of the Derbyshire village of Crich.

'I will,' Nathan conceded sheepishly. Hitching a borrowed rucksack onto his shoulders, he surveyed the steep hill and village streets and wondered where the cast and crew might be billeted. Lunch was the next thing that came to mind. *You're always hungry* were Ann's words. A nearby pub offered food and would be a good place to make enquiries.

'Are you one of that crowd?' a young waitress asked. 'You're a bit late if you're after a job as an extra. I understand they're almost finished.'

'I'm related to one of the cast, Lisa Brookes. She's my aunt,' he added in explanation, aware Lisa might not appreciate the disclosure of personal details.

'Is she really?' was the sceptical reply.

Nathan smiled. He noted its effect as she leaned over to collect his plate, and said, 'We're not supposed to say, but I think she's among the group staying at the New Bath Hotel in Matlock. Right now, they're filming at the Tramway Museum.'

'Is it far?'

'A good walk.' She eyed the half pint glass at Nathan's elbow. 'Are you old enough for that?'

'Almost,' he grinned, guessing the girl's age to be not much more than his own. 'It's only shandy.'

'I finish in half an hour,' she told him. 'Take your time drinking that and I'll show you the way.'

*

Nathan sat on a bench outside the pub, and shortly after three o'clock, he was joined by the young waitress. Dark hair hung over the collar of the gold-coloured quilted jacket she wore over her working gear of black T-shirt and short black skirt. Shapely legs encased in black tights terminated in black ballet shoes.

She introduced herself. 'Jessica.'

'Hello, Jessica, I'm Nathan.' He liked her smile.

'The tram museum is this way.' She led him uphill, past stone-built houses, the path eventually overlooking hills, dales and fields bounded by drystone walls.

'It's beautiful countryside. It reminds me of Wales.'

'Is that where you're from?' Jessica asked. 'You're obviously not from around here.'

'No.' He grinned. 'I live about thirty miles outside London, but we sometimes stay with family in Wales.'

'Southerner.' She laughed. A merry sound, without malice.

They walked on until a lane branched to the left and followed a sign to the car park of the Tramway Museum.

Jessica strode over a grass verge to look over railings fixed at a slant in old British Rail style.

Nathan rested his hands on the fence to lean over. 'It's like a 1930s city street with tramlines. I can see scaffolding. Looks like it's for camera equipment but I can't see much happening.'

Jessica tugged his sleeve. 'The big trucks and trailers are parked further down the lane.'

Around a bend, the usual traffic associated with a film shoot filled the large car park. A couple of men were loading equipment into the back of one of the vans.

Jessica called to them. 'Where is everyone?'

'Hello, Jessica,' the younger man said. 'They've gone to the Bath Hotel. Bit of a party before we pack up tomorrow.'

'Are you finished?'

'Still some shots for tomorrow, I believe, so I'll see you again before we leave.'

'Justin and his mates are staying at the pub,' she explained to Nathan before turning her attention back to Justin. 'Will Lisa Brookes be here tomorrow?'

'No good asking me, luv. I merely do as I'm told.   'Why? Has laddo here got a crush on her?'

'No,' Nathan cut in. 'She's my … aunt.'

'She expecting you?'

'No,' Nathan admitted reluctantly. 'It's a spur of the moment thing … I heard she'd be here.'

From the tailboard of the truck, Justin put hands on his hips and studied the youngsters. 'Why don't you come back tomorrow, and if she's here, she might see you.'

*

Nathan and Jessica walked back towards the pub. In frustration, Nathan kicked a loose stone. It skidded across the path and thunked against a drystone wall. 'I was hoping to head home tomorrow. My dad's in trouble and I should be with my mum.'

'What sort of trouble?'

Nathan bit his lip, he should know better than to volunteer too much information. 'Nothing much. Mum's just worried about him.'

'Is it important you speak to Lisa Brookes?'

'Only to me.'

'Let's get the bus to Matlock.' She grabbed his sleeve and pulled him towards a bus stop just as a yellow single decker came around the corner.

24

Nathan used the remainder of his cash to pay the fare for them both before settling in the seat beside her.

'It's not far,' Jessica told him, 'but further than I'd care to walk in these shoes. And we shall need to make sure we're at the bus stop outside the hotel before seven for the return journey because that's the last one.'

Nathan had given no thought to what he would say to his mother, but assumed he would know when the time came, but now he wondered if he'd even recognise her.

CHAPTER 7

In the lounge bar of the New Bath Hotel, Lisa stood, drained a glass of white wine and said, 'Well, everyone, I must leave. I have a date.'

'Another six o'clock call tomorrow', Claire Hammond reminded her.

Lisa rolled her eyes, picked up a light jacket and left, just as a group of the other members of the cast and production team arrived to join them for an evening meal. She caught a glimpse of heads bent in conversation and assumed she was the topic of their conversation. She'd long since given up being one of the crowd, one of the 'family' of movie people.

A red Jaguar car drew up outside the country hotel; Lisa opened the passenger door and slipped onto the leather seat.

'Your friends have been very generous,' Dean told her. 'All the cheques are banked and a few applications received from local schools. Andy was a popular young man.'

'Yes,' Lisa agreed. 'I still miss him.' What, she wondered, would life be like if Andy had survived? She imagined them being the perfect celebrity couple. Something else to lay at the door of Stephen Bryce.

*

Jessica pushed open a heavy swing door into the reception area of the New Bath Hotel. 'Come on,' she called to Nathan.

'Perhaps we shouldn't. I don't want to bother anyone.'

'You're the one anxious to see your aunt. If Lisa Brookes *is* your aunt, then surely she'll be pleased to see you.'

'I wouldn't be too sure,' Nathan muttered before following Jessica inside.

Soft sounds of conversation drifted from the restaurant, punctuated by an occasional ripple of laughter.

Jessica stood back allowing Nathan to face a man, slightly overweight, white shirt and tie beneath a waistcoat, who looked up from sorting papers on the reception desk. 'And what can I do for you, young man?'

'Can you tell me if Lisa Brookes is staying here, please?'

'I don't think Miss Brookes or anyone else wants to be bothered tonight, son. If you want to write a note, I'll make sure she gets it.'

'I'd really like to see her, if I may. Could you tell her—?'

The receptionist drew himself up to his full height. 'This is a private party. If you don't want to leave a note, I must ask you to leave. We don't want any trouble now, do we?'

Nathan felt Jessica tug on his sleeve, but he'd come this far and persisted, 'If you could tell her I'm here, I'm sure she'll see me. Tell her it's—'

'Nathan?'

All eyes turned to an attractive young woman framed in the doorway of the hotel lounge.

'Aunty Claire!'

'It's okay, Ralph. I know this young man.' She addressed Nathan. 'You can drop the aunty, you're old enough to call me Claire.' She led the way into the lounge. 'Come in and introduce me to the young lady, then you can tell me how things are with your father.'

Settled in the lounge, Jessica gazed around at the famous, and the not so famous faces.

'What's happening with your father? Claire asked. 'Are they safe?'

Safe? The thought gave him a jolt. He didn't know. 'Last I heard, the authorities are waiting for the weather to break so they can get a helicopter off the ground.' A quick glance at his phone showed no further message from Ann.

'Well,' Claire said, 'will you tell me why you're here, or shall I guess.'

Nathan felt a surge of warmth and knew he'd blushed.

'She's not here,' Claire told him. 'Her boyfriend called for her earlier. She didn't say where they were going, but I hope she remembers we have an early start tomorrow.'

Jessica, who'd been struck silent, nudged Nathan with her foot and tapped her watch.

Nathan understood, and said, 'We have to get back to Crich, the last bus goes at seven.'

Claire touched his hand. 'Stay and have dinner with us, they'll be serving soon.'

Nathan and Jessica exchanged glances, and Claire said, 'Are you staying in Crich? I'll arrange a car to take you back.'

27

Jessica fumbled for her phone. 'I shall have to tell my dad. I'm supposed to be waiting on table tonight, but we're not very busy, most of our customers are eating here.' She made to go into the reception area to make the call, but leaned across to Nathan. 'Have you anywhere to stay? We have a small room to spare.'

'Thank you,' he said sincerely.

Whilst Jessica was away, Claire said, 'I was surprised to see Lisa fronting Andy's Drama in Schools charity.'

'I don't think it's official,' Nathan told her. 'At least, Mum and Dad haven't mentioned it.'

'She seems to be quite involved with one of the charity's administrators and has elicited a great many donations.'

Nathan considered the statement for a moment and wondered if it was a criticism, before saying, 'That's good, isn't it?'

Claire smiled. 'Yes, of course it is, dear.'

*

Outside the pub in Crich, Nathan helped Jessica from the taxi, slammed the door and leaned in to pay the driver who merely nodded and said, 'Paid for, mate,' before driving off.

Jessica led him into the empty lounge where the landlord was wiping the bar and generally tidying up.

'Sorry, Dad,' she said. 'It was a last minute thing and I guessed it wouldn't be busy with all the film crew eating at the New Bath.'

'Good thing we've only had half a dozen of the regulars in then, isn't it.'

Undaunted she went on, 'We've had a lovely time. Nathan knows all the stars. We sat next to Claire Hammond, she's lovely, and Guy Gilliard spoke to me.'

'That's as maybe, but I'd appreciate a bit more notice the next time you decide not to turn in for work.'

'Sorry,' she repeated a little more contrite.

'Aye, well. Go and make me a cold meat sandwich for supper, and I'll bring a nightcap, and perhaps one for your friend here.'

Jessica grimaced at Nathan before leading him into the family kitchen.

Nathan said, 'You should have said if you knew you'd be in trouble.'

'Don't worry about that. Would you like a sandwich?'

28

Jessica's dad put two whisky tumblers on the table beside a plate of cold beef sandwiches. He pushed one glass over to Nathan. 'Well in with the showbiz crowd then?'

Nathan gazed at the contents of the glass, wondering how he could say he didn't like the taste, without causing offence. He said, 'My dad knows them.'

Jessica, who after working at a gas hob, put a mug of hot milk beside the tumbler. 'Nathan's dad is Stephen Bryce.'

The landlord looked blank.

'You know.' Jessica reeled off the titles of a string of movies whilst stirring the whisky into the milk.

'Might have seen one on the telly,' he conceded. Then leaning forward he said, 'It's been on the news. They're still looking for them. What are you doing here whilst your dad's missing?'

Nathan gave a brief rundown of events.

'And what's so special about this Lisa Brookes?'

'She's my mother.'

'Mother?' Jessica piped through a mouthful of sandwich.

*

Jessica showed Nathan to a small bedroom high in the roof space. 'The bathroom and toilet are on the floor below.' She hesitated before going on, 'Sorry my dad went on about loyalty to the folks who brought you up and looked after you. My mum left about five years ago. Long story.' She grinned.

Nathan's head, fuzzy from the whisky and milk, felt his mind clearer now than for the last few days. 'I've decided,' he said. 'I'm going home in the morning.'

She raised a questioning eyebrow.

'Your dad's right. I should be with my mum, Ann.'

'Oh.'

'I was disappointed after planning this holiday for so long, and I suppose it was selfish of me to just leave and look for Lisa on a whim. She's obviously not bothered about me. But the time has not been entirely wasted, everyone has been good to me. Lynn, Dad's agent; both my step-brothers …'

Jessica, hands on hips, scowled at him.

Nathan put a hand on her shoulder. 'And you.' He lowered his head and kissed her lightly on the lips. 'Thank you.'

Jessica stepped back and, still frowning, headed towards the staircase.

Nathan took a step towards her. 'Would you like to ... I mean ... when I know Dad's safe ... would you like to come to Elliston, where I live? Or when I've finished exams I shall have a year off before university, I'll come back.'

Jessica smiled. 'Of course you will.' She approached to return his kiss. 'There's a bus at eight in the morning. I'll go with you to Ambergate; you should be able to get a train from there. Goodnight.'

CHAPTER 8

A rolled knitted blanket served as a makeshift pillow which Stephen shifted around in an effort to get comfortable. Rain slammed against the window of the hut; wind searched out and rattled every loose slat. Yash had elected to sleep in the Land Rover whilst Ethan, curled in a corner and wrapped in his coat and a blanket, tossed and turned. Max Cavendish and Arturo each occupied a director's chair, feet propped on the table. Louise had stretched out to occupy most of the bench, and Stephen shifted awkwardly, pleased when the first pale light of dawn filtered through a small window. He eased from the ledge, pulled up the zip of his anorak and picked his way to the door. No en-suite facilities at this five star hotel, he went outside and made his way round to the back of the hut.

On his return he met Louise, and together they looked towards the east and lengthening fingers of pink and gold trickling between banks of dark clouds which threatened more rain.

Louise shifted her gaze to the track they'd driven along yesterday and voiced a question no doubt on everyone's mind. 'Do you think the other vehicle got through?'

It was all Stephen could do to murmur, 'I hope so.'

Louise went on, 'If they did, they would have got down the mountain before dark and let everyone know where we are.'

Stephen ran a hand through his hair. Cut shorter than usual, it showed only a hint of curl, not quite the short back and sides military style expected in the 1940s, but then his character had been a prisoner of war for six months before making his escape in the days between the capitulation of the Italians and the arrival of German troops to take over the running of Campo 78. The weather then, according to research, included heavy snow in the mountains and he had an inkling of how it must have felt.

Movement from inside the hut prompted Stephen to say, 'I'll keep the others out of the way if you want to—' he inclined his head indicating the rear of the hut.

Just inside the door he intercepted Max. 'Hang on a few minutes, Max; Louise is out there.'

Max nodded his understanding and turned his attention to fiddling with the satellite phone.

31

'Any signal?' Stephen asked.

Max shook his head. 'Nothing. It must have been damaged.'

'Damaged?' Yash, who'd stirred from the confines of the Land Rover, snapped. 'How the hell did it get damaged? Whose bloody stupid idea was this anyway?'

'Okay,' Stephen cut in. 'We're all anxious. There'll be time for recriminations when we get back.'

'Recriminations?' Max's head shot up. 'It's not my fault if the weather people got it wrong.'

Stephen felt his patience ebbing. It was in no one's interest to be at each others' throats and he turned to their guide. 'Arturo, what's our best move?'

'If we went back,' Arturo pointed out, 'the track is blocked and the ground above is unstable.'

'It's not so good here,' Stephen commented as loose shale rattled against the side of the hut.

Even as the group loaded the Land Rover, rivulets from above trickled across the path carrying mini landslides.

'I know this area,' Arturo said. 'I suggest we continue along the track, get from under these cliffs.'

*

In the office at Holly Cottage, Ann listlessly shuffled papers about on the desk.

A tap on the door announced Peter bringing a mug of coffee. He searched under the paperwork for a coaster and found a clear corner of the desk to rest it.

Aware of her father-in-law's excessively tidy habits Ann made an attempt to gather the papers into some sort of order before slapping them down again and saying, 'I can't concentrate. I'm going to ring Lynn and ask her to get me on the first plane to Italy.'

'Make that for the both of us.'

'I know it's awful just waiting, Peter, but I was hoping you'd be here when Nathan gets back.'

'Are you sure you trust me not to wring his neck?'

'One of your *looks* should be sufficient.'

Peter, humphed.

'And,' Ann reminded him, 'we promised to look after Lizzie for a couple of hours. Jules has to work and Fiona is dropping Matthew at the coach station. He's off on the school trip.' Ann again turned her attention to the papers on the desk. 'I've had a letter from a girl I knew at school thanking me for suggesting she apply to Andy's charity for help setting up a music and drama group at the school where she teaches...and—' Ann picked out the letter. 'She says a cheque for £2,000 will go a long way towards the purchase of instruments and ... other things ...' She scanned the letter. 'And the pupils and staff will be holding cake sales, sponsored runs and the like ... to raise more money to help with the refurbishment of the school theatre. The upshot is that she's asking if it's possible for Stephen to talk to them or open the theatre when it's ready.'

'I'm sure he will if it can be arranged conveniently.'

'We'll sort it out as soon as we know he's safe.'

A buzzer sounded and a picture of the front gates flicked up on a TV screen. 'It's Jules.' Ann pressed a button to admit Stephen's brother.

Peter indicated the paperwork on the desk. 'Leave this for now, Ann. I'll look at it later.'

*

Ann opened the door to her brother-in-law, Lizzie in his arms. 'Hi, have you heard anything?'

'The weather has improved marginally. I'm trying to get a flight out later today.'

'Perhaps you'd rather not have Lizzie today.'

'It's fine. Your dad will be here and I'll get a taxi to the airport as soon as I get the time of the flight.'

Peter stepped up to take his granddaughter. 'Come on, beautiful.' He settled her in an armchair and wedged cushions either side while Jules went back to collect her wheelchair.

'If it's not too muddy on The Common, we'll take Toby out later,' Peter told Lizzie.

'Have you heard from Nathan?' Jules asked.

'He texted late last night to say he'd be home soon.' Ann checked her mobile. 'Nothing since.'

Jules reached towards the phone. 'You should be able to get a location if you—'

'I know,' Ann said, quickly returning the phone to a pocket in her jeans. 'If I considered him to be in any danger or in trouble I wouldn't hesitate.'

'Matthew still insists he doesn't know where he's gone or why. Or at least,' Jules gave her a sceptical look, 'he says, Nathan didn't *tell* him but it doesn't take a genius to guess.'

'Yes, well,' Ann flustered. 'If he wants us to know, he'll tell us when he gets back.'

Jules handed over a holdall of Lizzie's essentials. 'Fiona should be back in a few hours.' He headed back to his car, calling, 'Let me know if you hear any more from Italy.'

Ann waved him off, made sure the gate was secure and returned to the sitting room.

Lizzie seemed as if searching the room, struggling to control her head movements.

Ann took both Lizzie's hands in her own, waited for the girl to focus and said, 'Are you looking for Nathan? He's not here, Lizzie, darling.'

It seemed to Ann that the returned lopsided smile was sad and jiggling the girl's hands again, she said, 'I bet he told *you* where he was going, eh?'

Ann's mobile jangled.

*

'Have you got everything?' Peter asked.

'Passport and plenty of clothes for a couple of days,' Ann told him. 'Yvonne left plenty of food in the pantry before she went away. Are you sure you'll be okay with Lizzie?'

'I'll put her in her chair and we'll take Toby on The Common. I've got my phone in case Nathan calls, and yes,' he smiled knowingly at her, 'it *is* switched on.' He glanced through the window. 'That's the taxi now. You'd better get off.' He carried her case to the door and handed it to the driver who stowed it in the boot.

Ann kissed Peter's cheek. 'I'll keep in touch.'

*

At the pub in Crich, Jessica was in the kitchen before seven. The film crew were already up and out, a catering van at the transport museum would take care of their needs. She popped a couple of slices of bacon into a pan and assumed the smell of cooking drifting upstairs would rouse Nathan, and she expected him to enter the kitchen any moment.

The bacon crisp, she put it between a couple of slices of bread, poured out a mug of tea and took it upstairs, surprised to find the door to the attic room slightly open.

34

She called, 'Morning, Nathan. If we're to get the eight o'clock bus, we'll need to get a move on. Nathan?' She pushed the door open with her foot. The room was empty, the bed roughly made. She left the plate and mug on the bedside table, went down the narrow stairs to the bathroom and put an ear to the door. 'Nathan? Are you there? If you want breakfast you'll have to hurry.' Silence. She pushed open the door.

CHAPTER 9

Nathan stood at the gates of the Tramway Museum. Shivering in pre-dawn cold he scrolled through the messages on his phone. One to his mum, last evening, saying he would be home today. And one received half an hour ago that said merely, '*what do you want?*'

The text was from Lisa. Claire must have told her he was here. Nathan remembered Ann suggesting he text Lisa once a week when he was younger, but in the absence of regular replies, he'd let the habit slip.

The museum was coming to life. In the grounds, movie personnel went about their business, erecting rigs, mounts for cameras and other equipment. Nathan wandered between trucks and lorries, making his way towards the trailers.

'Oi,' someone hailed. 'You're back then.'

'Hello, Jason.' Nathan recognised the young man Jessica had spoken to the previous day.

'She's not your aunt, is she? Lisa Brookes.'

Nathan remained silent.

'I didn't know she had a kid. People were talking about it last night,' he explained. 'And your dad is Stephen Bryce.' It was a statement, not a question. 'I worked with him a couple of years ago. Well, I was still an apprentice technician then. I hope he's okay.'

'I hope so too.' Discomfited, Nathan lost his tongue and looked around until Jason said, 'It's that end trailer.'

Nathan nodded his thanks and moved on.

Jason called, 'Good luck.'

What had been said last evening after he and Jessica had left? The last thing he wanted was to cause Lisa any embarrassment.

Nathan lingered around the side of the trailer. He stood back as the door opened. Two women stepped down, one in late-nineteenth-century costume, skirts brushing the ground, lace around the neckline. The other threw a shawl around the shoulders of the first and arranged it neatly. The actor walked smartly along a wooden boarding path laid over grass. Was it Lisa?

The other young woman returned to the trailer. The door had slammed back against the side of the trailer and locked into the catch which held it open. She leaned out to grasp the handle, caught sight of

Nathan as he tried to retreat and halted in the act of pulling the door closed.

'Who are you? Some sort of peeping Tom? Clear off before I send for security.'

'Sorry,' Nathan stuttered. 'I was looking for Lisa Brookes.'

'Well, she's not ...' The young woman, perhaps twenty-five, hesitated. After studying him for a moment, she said, 'Are you Nathan?'

He nodded.

'You'd better come inside and wait.' She indicated a sitting area with well upholstered benches. 'Everyone was talking about you last night.'

Nathan winced. What had he started?

'I need to change.' She yanked a curtain which divided off a section of the vehicle and cut him off from the door.

From behind the curtain she called, 'My name is Julie.' Her head appeared again. 'Lisa's your mother, isn't she?'

'Will you tell her I didn't mean to embarrass her and—' he had given the matter some thought. 'And that I've decided to go home?'

'You can tell her yourself. They'll be finished soon.'

Nathan felt trapped and cursed himself for not leaving when he had a chance. He sat on the padded bench, pulled earphones from his pocket and connected them to his phone in order to drown the noise of undressing from the other side of the curtain. He brought up the text from Lisa. He'd replied, *'I'd like to see you.'* Her response, *'I'm busy. Go home.'*

Julie again stuck her head around the curtain. 'Your father is Stephen Bryce.'

Nathan pulled out the earpieces.

'Have they been found?' she asked. 'I heard some of the crew got off the mountain.'

Nathan paid attention. He didn't know. He said, 'I'm still waiting for news.'

'Well, I hope he's okay. Everyone here is worried.' She withdrew her head and whilst the rustling of clothes continued, she called, 'Lisa's helping raise money for the Theatre in Schools project. It's a Bryce charity, isn't it?'

'My dad set up the project in memory of Andy Roberts.'

Julie went on, 'I wasn't very old when it happened, but I remember people talking about Lisa being kidnapped by gangsters or drug dealers and Andy Roberts being killed.'

'I remember very little about Uncle Andy except he was a friend of my dad.'

A tap on the door. Someone called, 'They're ready for you, Julie.'

She partly opened the curtain. Clad only in a linen bodice and lacy drawers tied just below the knee she retrieved a dressing gown from the floor. 'I have to go.' In the doorway she turned back to Nathan, 'You make sure you're here when Lisa gets back, even if she doesn't want to see you.'

As the door slammed, the implication of Julie's parting shot hit home. Nathan blinked back tears. He shouldn't have come. He wanted to go home.

*

Yash took over the driving of the Land Rover from Louise. Once out from the shadow of the cliff, the terrain opened to gently sloping grassland, and the road dwindled to a track which eventually narrowed to a footpath.

Louise leaned over to Stephen. 'Where are we going?'

Though grateful to be away from the shadow of overhanging and dangerous cliffs, Stephen felt he should voice what he assumed were also the concerns of the others.

'Surely we're getting out of the search area.'

Arturo called over his shoulder, 'We need somewhere to shelter. My family's village is some kilometres further on.'

The vehicle lurched over steepening grassy slopes with rocky outcrops, driver and passengers leaning against the angle of incline until the Landy ground to a halt.

Arturo addressed Yash. 'We must leave the vehicle here.'

Bottles of water and extra clothes stuffed into rucksacks, the party set off on foot. Stephen gazed down the steep pastureland dotted with an occasional copse of beech, ash and pine. He judged that they had travelled to an area above the location of the town nearest to the old POW camp. He'd already toured the camp in preparation, seen the huts, spoken to daughters, sons and grandchildren of some of the men who had been prisoners and who had chosen to take their chances in the mountains instead of waiting for German troops to arrive and take over from the Italian guards who had fled. Filming would take place on similar slopes

38

but with easier access, though he suspected the schedule would be gruelling.

How much more gruelling for real? He felt in his coat pocket for a blister pack of tablets. On medication for a blood disorder for many years he usually carried a three-day supply.

'Signor Bryce.' It was Arturo. 'Signor Bryce, we need to go on.'

Stephen took stock of the steady uphill climb, slung a rucksack on his shoulder and strode after the others.

Louise slipped on wet grass. Stephen put a hand under her elbow. 'How much further?' she muttered.

Stephen wondered the same thing. The genuine 1940s army issue boots had plenty of grip on soft ground but were heavy. Yash, young and fit, strode on in front; Arturo, an experienced mountaineer, didn't falter. Working under difficult conditions, Stephen would pace himself, take regular breaks. He cursed the day he'd taken a swig of cough medicine which had reacted badly with existing medication. Twenty days in an induced coma before vital organs recovered and resumed their functions had left an inevitable legacy.

Another hour tramping high, steep slopes led to a sparsely wooded area, mist hanging between scraggly trees and a weird, deathly quiet.

The terrain levelled and Stephen exchanged a relieved glance with Louise.

Arturo pointed to a row of pylons in the distance. 'Just a few kilometres to my village. They have electricity,' he boasted. 'And maybe a working telephone – but not all the time.'

A watery sun breaking from leaden clouds encouraged the group to pick up the pace. Further on, a few ragged sheep looked up from cropping short grass and gazed stupidly at the intruders.

Another hour trekking and they came across a shepherd. Standing on a rocky outcrop he waved his crook and called out, 'Hey, Arturo.'

Stephen, with a smattering of Italian, deciphered the rest as, 'Who have you brought with you?'

Arturo waved at his companions and Stephen raised a hand in acknowledgement when he heard his name included in Arturo's rapid fire response.

'This is Marco, my cousin. He will go to the village; they will prepare food. We can rest here for a while.'

Stephen sat on the rock vacated by Marco and put his head in his hands. He was dog-tired; he wanted to tell Ann he was okay and not to worry, tell Nathan he was sorry he was missing the holiday. And what about the rest of the crew? Had they made it through the landslide?

Louise sat beside him. 'You okay?'

He straightened. 'Yes. I was thinking about Nathan. We were doing a father-son holiday. But,' he gave a wry smile, 'I wonder now if I could manage to do a trek along the Grand Canyon.'

'Is Nathan Lisa's son?'

He nodded.

'I got to know Lisa last year,' Louise told him. 'She'd split from the guy she'd been living with in Canada and had been doing theatre in the southern States. Then a job came up with a schools' programme and I was part of the camera crew.'

'You know her well?' Stephen was wary of what Lisa might have disclosed.

'We shared a flat for a while—'

'Shall we move off?' Arturo called.

'Come on,' Stephen levered himself from the rock. 'I hope it's not far: I shall be pleased to get these boots off.'

40

CHAPTER 10

Nathan remembered Lisa from when he stayed with her parents. She was glamorous, with thick dark hair similar to her photo in the movie magazine, but his recollection of helping Grandpa Reg in the garden was more vivid than the memory of his biological mother. Nor could he remember seeing her at Nanna Peggy's funeral, though she must have been there.

Nathan checked his phone. A message from Ann said she was flying to Italy. There must be news of his dad. Good news? She didn't say. Was there still time to get a bus and train? He stood, intending to leave.

Voices. The trailer door opened. His heart thumped. Lisa and a man. Still concealed behind the half-drawn curtain, they didn't see him.

'You have to understand,' the male voice said, 'you can't just walk away. This is only a small part of a larger organisation and they might not take kindly to our, shall I say, extra-curricular activities.'

'But it makes a bit extra for a good cause,' Lisa protested.

'You knew what you were doing, and I noticed you didn't object to the perks.'

'That's not right. I did it for Andy. He loved going into schools and getting the children involved.'

'Unlike you,' was the retort.

Nathan heard an intake of breath from Lisa before the man continued, 'I need to get back to the office; there are things to be done. As soon as you're finished, get back to Birmingham, go to the Regency Hotel.' The man paused at the door. 'And we can do without that boy hanging around.'

'Don't worry, I'll get rid of him.'

Nathan stood, juggled with his phone. It clattered on a table under the window just as the trailer door slammed shut.

The curtain whooshed back on its runners. Nailed in Lisa's startled glare, Nathan felt as if he was being weighed and measured.

Lisa eventually said, 'Nathan? What do you want?'

His 'I came to see you,' sounded lame, and he added, 'I thought you might like to see … me.'

'Well, it's …' Lisa chewed her lower lip. 'It's not convenient.'

Nathan rocked back on his heels.

Lisa reached towards him. 'I didn't mean …'

Nathan clamped his jaw, took a ragged breath. 'Yes, you did. Even when I was small, you didn't want me around.'

Indignant, Lisa said, 'I saved your life. You fell in the river when that man was chasing you. Don't you remember?'

'I remember you pushing me away.'

'What chance did *I* have when Ann was happy to have your sticky fingers all over her?'

Nathan blinked back tears and swallowed. He wound up the cord to the earphones and stuffed them in his pocket before heading for the door. A hand on the handle he paused. 'Was that man referring to Uncle Andy's charity?'

'Dean's an administrator. I've been helping to raise money.'

Nathan pulled the door open, and slammed it behind him. He hurried between trailers and trucks, saw someone winding cable onto a reel – probably Jason, but Nathan ignored the shout and blundered on until he was at the main gate. A security man glanced in his direction, but there to prevent unwanted entry, he didn't hinder Nathan's exit.

Nathan didn't notice Jessica's approach until he became aware of her sitting beside him on a bench at the side of the road leading into the village.

She slipped a hand through his arm. 'I guessed you'd be here.'

Unable to trust his voice, he remained silent.

After a while she said, 'It didn't go as well as you hoped, then?'

Nathan sat back and on a sigh, said, 'I shouldn't have come. She never had time for me when I was small, so why should she now? I only came because I was disappointed about the holiday. I saw an article about how she was raising money for the Theatre in Schools project. Mum and Dad set it up in Uncle Andy's name after he was killed, and I thought perhaps she'd be … different.' His memory of Andy Roberts hazy, Nathan was grateful Jessica didn't pursue the subject.

'There was a man with her,' he told Jessica. 'Dean something. They were arguing about donations made to the fund. I suspect he's up to no good.'

'You mean, like fraud?'

Nathan was suddenly alert. 'Exactly like fraud.' He fished out his phone and after a few minutes googling, said, 'There's a Dean Henderson, administrator of the charity for the Midlands.'

'Surely they're all vetted.'

Nathan considered the statement. 'Yes, I suppose so. Jessica?'
He stood, took her arm, guiding her along the lane towards the village.
'Do you have access to a car?'

'My dad occasionally lets me drive his. Why?'

'That man, Dean, mentioned a hotel in Birmingham. He told
Lisa to meet him there.'

Jessica faced Nathan. 'What are you saying?'

'If Lisa is involved in something with Dean Henderson, I think
it's against her will.'

'Bearing in mind what you've said about her, why should you
care?'

'If there's anything illegal going on, it would reflect badly on
my dad.'

'So?' Jessica said warily.

'Ask your dad if we ... *you* can borrow his car.'

'You'll be lucky! Besides, I've never driven in the city.'

'Drop me somewhere on the outskirts and I'll get myself there.'

They reached the pub in the village, and Jessica went in search
of her father. She returned within a few minutes and jangled car keys at
Nathan.

'Great.'

'Not so great, actually. Dad's gone out.'

'Oh.'

The two swapped a knowing glance, before Jessica said, 'Come
on, I'll ring him when we're on the way.'

*

A man stepped forward to meet Ann as she disembarked at Abruzzo
airport. He stretched out a hand. 'Owen Wyatt, Key7 Productions. I'm
afraid we have no further news of your husband.'

Waved through Customs, he stowed her small bag in a black
Mercedes. 'You're booked into a local hotel.'

Owen drove off the main thoroughfare, through narrow streets
and past stucco buildings, to a pleasant square. Fringed canopies sheltered
the hotel's arched windows.

Owen collected a key from a marble-lined reception area and
showed Ann to her room. Before entering, she turned to face him. 'There
must be someone who can tell me exactly what has happened.'

'There's a meeting for relatives in the lounge at two o'clock.
The head of rescue services will be there to bring everyone up to date.'

Ann nodded, 'I'll be there.' She closed the door. In the silence of the room she felt utterly alone. Perhaps she should have asked Peter to come with her. But she needed someone at home when Nathan came back. She checked her phone. Nathan should be on his way home by now. But where was Stephen?

In the restaurant, Ann picked at a light lunch. Confident Peter would let her know if there was any news from Nathan, she took a coffee into the lounge and settled in an easy chair. Still an hour before the meeting, Ann could no longer resist and snatched up her phone to ring home.

'Hello, Peter. I wondered if Nathan was home.'

A momentary silence caused some concern, before Peter said, 'No.'

She could almost hear the cogs whirring and knew he was deciding what he should tell her. She reminded him, 'I told you he texted last night to say he was heading home. Has something happened?'

'I've heard from Brian Foster, the landlord of the pub where Nathan stayed last night. Mr Foster rang Stephen's agent and Lynn thought it important enough to let me know, so I rang him back.'

'And?'

'It seems his daughter, Jessica, went with Nathan to see Lisa on set at the Tramway Museum this morning.'

'Yes, and?'

'Mr Foster had to go out on business and when he came back his car was gone.'

Ann's brow creased. 'So?'

'The car keys were kept in the kitchen at the pub, and the only other person with access was his daughter.'

'So his daughter borrowed the car.'

'Well, Mr Foster would have been happy to leave it at that until his daughter rang him to say that she and Nathan were halfway to Birmingham.'

'Bir …? Is she giving him a lift home?'

'It's hardly on the way. Brian Foster was at pains to point out that Jessica has only just passed her test, has only driven in the immediate area and never in a city. He's obviously worried and was considering informing the police, in which case he'd have to tell them she took the car without his permission, with all the attendant implications.'

Ann felt sudden heat in her face. 'What the hell is he playing at?' People drifted into the lounge in ones and twos. 'Peter, I don't know what to tell you, but there's a meeting with rescue services in a few minutes.'

'Okay. I'll try again to get in touch with Nathan. Will you let me know what's happening with Stephen?'

'I'll ring as soon as the meeting is over.' Ann took a long, shuddering breath before returning her phone to her bag.

She became aware of someone with a clipboard moving among the thirty or so people now gathered in the lounge of the hotel. It seemed some were being selected and asked to move to an anteroom.

A young woman asked her name.

'Ann Bryce.'

'And your husband is Stephen Bryce?'

Ann nodded.

'Would you like to come through?' She indicated the room adjoining.

As if in a dream, Ann stood and, with a feeling of dread, joined a dozen others in the other room.

A murmur from others voiced her own opinion. 'Good news for one group, not so for the other.'

*

An hour later, Ann rang Peter.

'What exactly did the Italian authorities say?'

'The convoy was on the road heading down the mountain. There was a landslide; the driver of the first Land Rover put his foot down and managed to get out of the way. They said it seemed as if half the mountain crashed down behind, took the road and the chalet that was their base over the edge. The other vehicle was a good way behind. Ashley, one of the crew, said he looked back and saw the other Land Rover start to reverse.'

'So ...' Peter hesitated, 'they could have reversed out of danger?'

'Yes,' Ann, shut out all other possibilities. 'Ashley said they must be having trouble with the satellite phone and there's no mobile signal.'

She gave Peter a moment to digest the information before saying, 'Anything from Nathan?'

'Calls are going to voicemail. He'll know about it when I get hold of him. Christ, if he'd pulled a stunt like this in my day—'

45

'Yes, I know, Peter. Right now *I* could knock his block off. Have you heard any more from Brian Foster?'

'No. Leave it with me for now. I'll check in with you this evening, but if you hear anything about Stephen in the meantime—'

'I'll let you know. And you, if you hear from Nathan.'

*

'How much further,' Ethan wheezed.

'Just over the next rise,' Arturo called back to the single file of weary trekkers.

'Take a minute,' Stephen suggested.

Whilst Ethan sat upon a nearby rock, Stephen wandered to another pile of stone enclosed in metal railings. An inscription on a plaque brought home what he had already learned when researching in preparation for the film.

'A memorial for one of the farms burned during the war?' Louise asked.

Stephen nodded. 'The price for helping escapers.' He looked back along the track. 'I wonder if that was the wood where the massacre took place.'

The rest of the ragtag party stood for a moment, each with their own thoughts.

Arturo pulled off his woollen head gear. 'I lost an uncle and a cousin who was merely a child.' The moment stretched, until Arturo said, 'We must get on.'

Stephen tried his phone. Still no signal. The sun warm on their backs, they moved off.

A little later, Yash, a good way in front, turned and called back, 'I can see the village. And power lines as well.'

'Thank God for that,' Max Cavendish muttered. Raising his voice, he informed them all, 'As soon as we get in touch, the authorities will get a chopper up.'

On cresting a rise, Stephen saw Marco together with a number of other villagers emerging from a collection of small stone built houses and coming to meet them.

A dark haired youth, about Nathan's age he guessed, relieved Stephen of the padded anorak he now carried and beckoned him towards one of the houses.

'Nonna,' the boy called.

46

The boy's grandmother met them in the rustic kitchen. Stephen considered she would have done credit to the costume department: long black skirt, black top, headscarf tied at the back of her head, Nonna barely reached Stephen's shoulder. A dish of food, stew of some sort, was placed on a table, Nonna gesticulating for him to sit and eat. Stephen needed no second bidding. Mutton stew he guessed. And bread, still warm.

Whilst he ate, Nonna pulled at his khaki blouse and emitted a stream of rapid Italian.

'No, Nonna,' Stephen tried to explain. 'I'm not a real soldier. We were shooting a film, a movie.'

'She doesn't understand,' the boy said in good English. 'When she was a girl, soldiers came to the village from the prison camp.'

'Please tell her I'm not a real soldier,' Stephen insisted.

The youth again spoke to the old lady, who muttered and returned to a back room. The boy grinned and said, 'My name is Francesco.'

'I'm very pleased to meet you, Francesco. I'm Stephen Bryce.'

They shook hands.

'Please thank your grandmother for the food.'

'She is pleased to help. The others in your party are being taken care of by other families. The same way her parents helped the escaped prisoners many years ago.'

'They were very brave, at some cost,' Stephen agreed.

'I have been brought up on these stories. When you have eaten and have cleaned up, my grandfather has many things he would like to tell you.'

Nonna returned, scooped a jug of hot water from a vessel heating above the fire and poured it into a bowl. She shook a towel at Stephen before laying it over a chair.

Stephen said, 'Grazie, Nonna.' To Francesco, he said, 'You're very kind, but do you know if Arturo has been in touch with the authorities? We need to get a message to our families. Our party was separated and we don't know what happened to the others.'

'Our power lines are down, but someone will go down to the next village tomorrow, maybe have more luck there.'

With nothing to be done until tomorrow, Stephen said, 'Thank you.'

'Perhaps,' Francesco said, 'when you've cleaned up and rested you'll allow my grandfather to show you ...'

47

'Show me?'

'I know you are not a real soldier. It's just that my grandfather, his name is Giuseppe, has always believed they would come back. There are things he would like to show you.'

CHAPTER 11

At a McDonald's in services on the motorway, Nathan collected a couple of burgers, fries and cola. He slid the tray on to a table and took the seat opposite Jessica. She looked a little flushed. 'Trouble?' he asked.

She grimaced. 'Not half.' She picked a couple of chips from the carton and munched them before explaining, 'I've just phoned my dad. He says we stole the car and threatened to call the police.'

The news dampened their enthusiasm and they ate in silence for a while before Nathan said, 'Go back. I can get a lift into Birmingham; there must be plenty of trucks going into the city.' When she made no comment, he went on, 'I shouldn't have asked you. I don't want you to get into trouble. Blame me – it was my idea.'

'I suggested taking the car and it seemed exciting, but I should have asked. I didn't realise Dad would be so angry. He's worried because I've never driven in a big city.' She shifted uncomfortably. 'I've never driven much further than the next village.'

'Then I'll go with you. I'll drive if you like. I've passed the written test and should have applied to take the practical ages ago.'

'But I'm still classed as a novice driver. I can't "accompany" a learner. Besides,' she said, 'you need to get into Birmingham.'

'I need to ring my mum,' he said thoughtfully. 'She and Grandad will be expecting me home. And I should find out if there's any news about my dad.' He turned his phone over in his hand. Now fully charged whilst travelling, there was no excuse. Instead, he googled the address of the Regency Hotel then laid the phone on the table. 'When I left home the other morning, I was determined to do this on my own. I just wanted to see Lisa. I didn't expect her to hug me and say this is what she's always wanted.' He ran a hand through his hair. 'I don't know what I was expecting, but she's obviously in some sort of trouble and I can't ignore it, especially if it's going to create problems for my mum and dad. The last thing I want is to get someone else into trouble.'

'Dad said I should start back as soon as I've had a rest and something to eat.'

Nathan put a hand over hers. 'That's okay, you go. I'll get a lift.'

Jessica added her other hand to the pile. 'What then?'

'I know where Lisa is staying. I'll try to talk to her, find out what's going on. If this Dean what's-his-name is taking money from the charity, perhaps she'll help expose him.'

'What makes you think she'll be any more helpful than she was earlier?'

Nathan shrugged. 'I wasn't prepared this morning, but now I know a little of what's going on …' He grinned. 'I shall have to use all my powers of persuasion.' He was aware of the effect of his smile, it having got him out of trouble, or at least lessened the consequences, on previous occasions. He'd also learned there were certain figures of authority on whom it did not work. He noticed Jessica's eyes soften, her face relax for that fraction of a second before she was again composed. He hoped she realised it was genuine affection.

They drained their cartons of cola, sharing an amused glance as the straws noisily slurped the dregs.

Jessica frowned in concentration. 'Have you enough money to pay for 24 hours' parking?'

'Sure.'

'Then I'll go with you. We'll hitch a lift into Birmingham together on condition you ring your mum so she won't worry.'

'Okay,' Nathan readily agreed. 'Provided you tell your dad so he doesn't think I've kidnapped you.' After second thoughts, he said, 'Unless, of course, he decides to tell the police.'

'Wait here.' Jessica picked up her phone and went outside.

Nathan watched from the window as she paced the car park, phone to her ear. She ran a hand through her hair, turned on her heel, did another circuit of the car park before halting in mid stride. Her body language changed, she lowered the phone, slipped it into her pocket and marched towards the automatic doors.

'Okay,' Jessica announced with a wide smile. 'We've got 24 hours. Let's hitch a ride.'

Nathan matched her expression before saying, 'Let's sort out the parking first. The last thing we need is for your dad to receive notice of a huge fine.'

*

Ann paced her hotel room, mind flicking from one problem to another. She'd been invited to join the others who were also waiting for news in the lounge but, for the moment, felt she needed to be alone. She went onto the balcony and looked up and down the street. Her mobile phone rang and she dashed back into the room. 'Nathan.' Overwhelmed with relief, Ann sat heavily on the bed. 'Are you okay, sweetheart? Where are you?'

'I'm fine, Mum.'

'You may well be fine, but where are you, and what are you up to?'

'Any news about Dad?'

'I'm in Sulmona and still waiting for the rescue services to get back to me.'

'Mum …' His voice cracked. 'I love you, Mum. I want to be with you, waiting for Dad, but there's something I have to do.'

'If you want to see Lisa, we can arrange—'

'It's not just that – I should be home tomorrow.'

'That girl's father said you took his car. He threatened to call the police.'

'That girl's name is Jessica.'

Ann repented. 'Jessica.' The hotel phone jingled. 'I'll have to go; there may be news. You'd better ring Grandad and explain yourself,' she switched off her phone and picked up the hotel handset. 'I'll be right there.'

*

Peter placed Lizzie's spouted mug on the kitchen table and wiped her mouth with a tissue before reaching for his phone. The missed call message showed it was Nathan. He listened to the voicemail.

'Hello, Grandad. I've spoken to Mum. I'm sorry … well, Mum will explain. I'll be home as soon as I can.'

Peter sighed and laid down the phone. 'What is he up to?' he asked his granddaughter. It wasn't her usual smile she turned upon him. 'What's the matter, princess, not feeling well? Anyone would think you were worried about Nathan. Perhaps you are. Who knows what goes on in that mind of yours?' He tweaked her pointed chin. 'Come on.' He lifted Lizzie from her chair, carried her into a roomy sun lounge where he settled with her on his knee to read a story.

*

Nathan breathed a sigh of relief when the call to his grandfather went to voicemail. He kept the message short.

To Jessica, Nathan said, 'They look like truckers over there.'

A man in a white T-shirt, hands wrapped around a mug of tea, looked them up and down. 'Runaways,' he grinned at his companion.

51

'No,' Nathan said, a little too quickly. 'No,' he repeated. 'We're on our way to Birmingham to meet my mother.' No reason not to tell the truth.

'Any chance of a lift?' Jessica added.

*

The driver dropped them at a transport café in Solihull and found them a ride with a van driver into the centre of Birmingham. Nathan googled the postcode of the hotel Lisa had mentioned and entered it into the navigation programme on his phone. 'We can walk from here.' They watched the progress of the green dot on the map on screen as they walked along a busy street, newsagents and vape shops beneath towering office blocks.

Jessica glanced around. 'Cities frighten me.'

Nathan took her hand. 'Avoid eye contact.' He took a swift look at his phone then slipped it into a pocket. 'And look as if we know where we're going. There's a crossing just ahead, then turn left and the hotel is a couple of hundred metres along the road.'

They walked smartly, looking neither left nor right, until they halted opposite the Edwardian frontage of the Regency Hotel.

'Have we enough cash between us for a coffee?' Jessica asked.

'What?' Nathan, jolted from thoughts of what they should do next, looked surprised.

'There's a coffee shop in the hotel foyer.' She pointed across the road. 'I doubt they'll tell you her room number, and if they ring her to ask, and she really doesn't want to see you, I suppose they could throw us out. We should plan our next move.'

CHAPTER 12

Francesco put a hand under his grandfather's arm and together they led Stephen out of the village and across an expanse of grassland where sheep grazed. In the distance, dark clouds hid snowy peaks.

The boy made a sweeping gesture to encompass stones, overgrown with moss and grass, which marked the outlines of buildings. 'These are the ruins of the old village. See, much of the church still remains'

The old man shrugged himself free of Francesco's hand and, resting on a smooth rock, began to speak.

'My grandfather says,' Francesco translated, 'that he was sent to take cheese and bread to his father who was on the hillside with the sheep. He say, "Hey, Poppa. Where you find these soldiers?"'

'His poppa tell him, "El Duce is finished and the Germans are taking over the prison camp in Sulmona. We must help get these three men over the mountains." Grandfather looked up into a tree and said, "Poppa, the sheep!"'

'One soldier, the older one, tells Poppa he haul the sheep carcass into the tree to keep it safe from wolves. He say, they will pay for the sheep.'

Francesco's grandfather gave a throaty chuckle and Stephen turned to Francesco for explanation. 'The older soldier say, "Winston Churchill will pay for sheep." On paper torn from a notebook, he write, "I.O.U. the cost of one sheep." and signed it, "Tom Mix."'

Francesco waited whilst his grandfather spoke again before taking up the story. 'The soldiers were starving; before they killed the sheep, they had been eating molasses put out for the animals. There was a German patrol in the distance so he took the soldiers, hid them. The patrol searched every house in the village.'

Giuseppe moved on through the ruins, pointed out his family's house and that of his uncle. He gestured to a set of stones slightly apart from those of the ruined village.

Francesco continued, 'Here was the barn. This is where we kept the wine press. They put the British soldiers inside the wine press and covered the lid with turnips and hay.'

Giuseppe moved inside the foundation stones of the barn. He gestured a stabbing motion.

Stephen imagined himself in the dark confines of the press. The smell of sour wine, bodies sweating in fear of discovery. The thud of bayonets splitting wood only inches overhead.

Francesco translated, 'Grandfather prayed the British would not give themselves away. The German soldiers didn't find them but knew they were here. They came back.'

*

Nathan pushed open the heavy glass door of the hotel and led Jessica across the tiled floor of the foyer to the coffee lounge. He indicated an upholstered chair beside a low table and took a seat opposite. A couple sat at a table in the window and two well-dressed ladies had their heads together over a table nearby. A waitress about Jessica's age approached. She hesitated slightly before taking their order for two lattes.

Jessica leaned forward, whispered, 'I feel a little travel stained.'

'You look fine,' Nathan answered.

'Flatterer!' she hissed.

The waitress returned, coffees balanced on a tray. She dipped to place a tall glass before each of them, a biscuit in the saucer. She left the bill in the centre of the table.

Nathan said, 'Thank you,' and returned her smile. 'What?' he asked Jessica, who was failing to hide a grin.

'Have you decided how we can find out which is your mother's room?'

'I could ask at reception. She is my mother.'

'And if she doesn't want to see you?'

Nathan leaned forward. 'I'm sure she does, but she's afraid of that man.'

'If they're sharing a room, she's definitely not going to invite you up.'

'I could ask her to meet me down here. Say I'm someone else.' His fair brows drew together in thought. 'I can't say it's Dad – she knows he's in Italy. I can't think of anyone else she'd come down for.'

After a moment's thought, Jessica said, 'Do you like that girl?'

'What?'

'The waitress, do you like her?'

Nathan was bewildered. 'I don't know her.'

'But she likes you. I can tell.'

54

Nathan took a quick look over his shoulder, made eye contact with the girl and immediately turned back. 'She's nice. So?'

'Last year I worked in a hotel for a few months as a receptionist. I know how to operate the computer system. We need to distract the man at reception.'

Nathan shot a glance at the desk and the suited young man in attendance. 'How?'

She leaned towards him. 'When you go to pay, talk to her. Chat her up.'

'That's not going to distract *him*.'

'Pinch her bum. Get her to make a fuss so he'll leave the desk and come over.'

'You'll get me arrested! Or he'll thump me. *You* make a fuss – faint or something. *I'll* sneak a look at the computer.' Nathan caught the movement of someone entering the foyer and snatched up the menu to hide his face.

'What?'

'Lisa has just come in.'

Jessica stood, said, 'Leave this to me.' She casually walked over to the reception desk, picked up a leaflet from a nearby stand and pretended to study it.

Lisa, wearing a short cream skirt and matching jacket, strode across to the lift, high heels clacking on the tiled floor. She pressed a button on the panel beside the lift, her dark hair swishing about her shoulders as she glanced around.

Nathan squinted over the menu, horrified to see Jessica step into the lift after his mother. Forcing himself to stay calm and wait, he became aware of the waitress hovering nearby.

'Can I get you anything else?' she asked sweetly.

'Err.' He couldn't follow Jessica. So said, 'Yes, another coffee, please.'

She glanced at the empty chair opposite. 'Just one?'

'Yes, please.'

She gave him an uncertain smile before leaving to fill the order.

Nathan ran a hand through his hair and shifted in the armchair.

The waitress returned and placed the coffee on the table with the bill. 'Your girlfriend left?'

'Yes, err, no. She'll be back shortly.'

With, 'Oh, right,' she collected the empty glasses and moved away.

Nathan ignored the coffee and continued to fidget.

Within a few minutes, the lift doors pinged open and Jessica emerged. She strode confidently across the foyer and retook her seat opposite Nathan making no attempt to hide a wide smile.

'Well?'

'I followed her to the second floor. She stopped to rummage in her handbag outside room 217. I went further down the corridor, and to make sure that was the room she went into, I pretended to search my pockets for a key. When she went in I nipped back into the lift, and here I am.' She spread her hands palm up to emphasise how pleased with herself she was.

Nathan bit his lip and looked across the foyer where the lift doors stood open.

'Don't change your mind now,' Jessica chastised.

Nathan pushed the coffee across the table towards her, stood and headed for the lift. A man stepped into the lift before him and the doors closed. Knowing if he hesitated he'd be lost, Nathan walked smartly towards the stairs, taking them two at a time.

On the second floor, Nathan pushed a fire door which opened on to the corridor. It swung closed behind him. He vaguely registered the lift door sliding closed, it wafted a vague whiff of perfume. Lisa's perfume.

For a second Nathan considered turning around, but took a deep calming breath. It was a long corridor, doors set well apart: the rooms must be spacious. He counted them off. 213, 215 … and 217. The door stood slightly ajar. Nathan eased the door a little further. 'Lisa. Mother? It's Nathan, can I come in?' He stepped inside.

*

Jessica watched Nathan cross the foyer. As the lift doors closed, he veered left and took the stairs, her sense of satisfaction now shot through with apprehension. She sat back in the chair and tentatively sipped coffee whilst awaiting Nathan's return.

A few moments passed. The lift doors opened again and Lisa emerged; apparently in a hurry, she threw the narrow strap of her bag over her head, clutched her jacket tightly around herself and marched out of the hotel. Jessica looked for Nathan following, perhaps from the stairs. When he didn't appear, she stood, grabbed her own coat and followed

Lisa. She heard a shout from behind. She ignored it and followed Nathan's mother into the street.

*

Mesmerised by what he saw, Nathan stood just inside the door of room 217. He didn't hear a door opposite click shut, nor a woman, on her way to the lift, come to a halt outside. Not until she screamed.

CHAPTER 13

Stephen looked from the ruins of the buildings into the mountains. 'And did they?' he asked. 'Did the German patrol come back?'

Francesco translated for his grandfather who nodded and plunged into a stream of rapid Italian.

Stephen waited patiently until Francesco translated. 'The patrol was spotted in the valley. My grandfather was sent to the barn to tell the soldiers they must go, go quickly. Neither spoke each others' language, but they understood. They took no food and the weather was closing in. There was snow in the mountains.' Francesco looked up into the same mountains, the higher slopes shrouded in clouds which crept down the valley filtering into every rocky crevice. 'Grandfather says we should go back; another storm is gathering. We may need to wait another couple of days before power is restored.'

The temperature dropped, dampness permeated the atmosphere. Stephen turned up the collar of the anorak he'd put on over the khaki uniform. On the walk back to the village he again checked his pockets for the blister strip of tablets.

*

A woman screamed. Nathan turned on his heels.

The woman let out another scream and backed away. She scuttled along the corridor and rattled frantically on the call button for the lift.

Nathan raised his hand. There was blood. He couldn't remember touching the body sprawled on the bedroom floor. He moved, at first as in a dream, then he ran to the service door and thundered down the stairs.

*

Jessica looked up and down the street outside the hotel. Again she heard someone call, but she'd spotted Lisa rounding a corner and scampered after. She came to a pedestrianised area and, across a slabbed square, caught sight of Lisa entering a shopping precinct. Jessica followed her into a department store. Lisa seemed in a hurry, her face flushed. Jessica squeezed past shoppers on an escalator only to see Lisa halfway up the next flight. At the head of the second escalator she saw Nathan's mother going into the Ladies, and keeping an eye on the door, she fished her phone from her coat pocket and rang Nathan. 'What happened? What did you say to her?'

Nathan sounded breathless. 'I didn't see her. Where are you?'

Jessica gave him directions.

A woman strode from the toilets. Jessica took a second look and snapped off her phone. Lisa's hair was damp and arranged to conceal much of her face, a scarf around her shoulders, posture altered.

Jessica stepped into Lisa's path. They almost collided. Lisa put her head down and sidestepped, but Jessica again blocked her way. 'Miss Brookes—'

Lisa withdrew sunglasses from her handbag and made to walk on.

Jessica, a hand on Lisa's arm, said, 'What happened with Nathan?'

'Nathan?'

'Your son, Nathan.' Jessica slipped her arm firmly under Lisa's. 'He needs to talk to you.'

Again Lisa tried to pull away. 'I haven't time right now.'

Jessica's grip tightened. 'Let's find a seat in the café.' She steered Lisa to a corner seat in the restaurant of the department store. Jessica sat opposite, on a seat with a view of the entrance.

Lisa rubbed her arm. 'You're a very forceful young lady. What's Nathan to you?'

'We're friends.' Jessica leaned across the table. 'You've no idea what trouble he's been to so he can talk to you. The least you can do is listen.'

Lisa's turn to lean forward. 'If you are his friend, you'll keep him well out of my way.' She huddled into the corner, head down.

Jessica noticed the older woman's hands tremble. This was not how she expected an actor, even of moderate fame, to behave. Or was it an act?

*

Nathan remembered clattering down the stairs and into the foyer – no sign of Jessica. Someone shouted, he ignored them and ran outside, dodging pedestrians in the busy street before ducking into a doorway to answer his phone.

He followed Jessica's directions to the department store and spotted her bright-gold-coloured jacket in the corner seat of the café, someone sitting opposite. It took a moment for him to recognise his mother, but he was confident it was her who had entered the lift, the doors closing as he looked for her room. The room where the body of a man oozed blood onto a pale carpet.

He sat beside her. His 'What have you done?' almost inaudible.

'Nothing, Nathan. I've done nothing.' Lisa's voice, shaky.

'What?' Jessica interrupted. 'What's happened?'

'There is a dead man in my mother's room,' was Nathan's harsh whisper.

Jessica's eyes widened. Her mouth snapped shut. She leaned forward and said, 'A couple of policemen have just walked in.'

Lisa gathered her bag, straightened her jacket and looked about to make a run for it.

Jessica put a hand on Lisa's arm. 'Wait. Give me your jacket. Here's mine. Hide in the toilets, you too, Nathan. I'll distract the police.' She leaned closer to Lisa. 'Just to give you time to talk to Nathan. Sort things out between you. Then you must go to the police and tell them what's happened or we'll all be in serious trouble.'

Lisa stood, pulled on Jessica's jacket and grabbed Nathan's arm.

'I'm not going into the ladies' toilets.'

'There's no one in there, Nathan. Come on.'

CHAPTER 14

Peter hitched Lizzie into a more comfortable position on his knee. The girl had closed her eyes, so Peter shut the story book and sighed. Another hour or so before Fiona would be back to collect her daughter. He wondered if Ann had any further news of Stephen and what would happen if Nathan caught up with Lisa. The boy's birth mother never seemed to have time for him in the past. He was bound to get hurt. Peter stifled a yawn. A walk on the Common, something to eat, the warmth of the sitting room, Lizzie secure on his knee, her head safely in the crook of his arm, he let his eyes drift closed.

Lizzie shifted and he again hitched her higher on his knee. Something felt wrong and he roused himself. Her eyelids flickered with rapid eye movements. Recognising the signs, Peter slid from the settee, knelt and placed Lizzie on the floor. As she began to convulse he grabbed cushions from the settee and placed them around her.

He stroked her forehead. 'It's okay, Lizzie, darling,' he soothed. 'It will soon be over.' He glanced at his watch. Three minutes extended to five, still her weak muscles contracted with irregular spasms, heels drumming, elbows rattling. Peter patted his pockets, searching for his mobile phone. 'Where the—' He spotted the phone on a nearby coffee table and stretched across to retrieve it.

An ambulance on the way, he rang his elder son, Julian, and daughter-in-law Fiona – Lizzie's parents.

*

Stephen flicked up the hood on his anorak and followed Francesco and Giuseppe back to the village. Huge drops of rain, at first intermittent, increased to a deluge and the youth put a hand under his grandfather's arm to hurry him along. The path from the ruins of the old village, worn through meadows and over steep slopes, quickly became muddy. Stephen's legs felt heavy and he was glad when they reached the village.

Max Cavendish stood in the doorway of one of the cement rendered houses. 'There you are, Stephen. Come in, and I'll update you on the situation.' Max gestured for Stephen to join the others sitting around a rough wooden table. 'This house is no longer occupied,' Max explained. 'It seems many of the villagers have chosen to live further down the mountain or in the city, so it's been placed at our disposal.'

Stephen shook the drippings from his coat before hanging it on a hook behind the door. He slipped onto a chair between Yash and Louise and glanced around at roughly plastered walls; dust and cobwebs hung from the rafters, but it was dry and a fire glowed in a stove in the far corner.

Max stood by the door whilst a woman placed a wooden platter of freshly baked bread on the table. She fetched a jug of red wine and tumblers which clinked as she lay down the tray.

There were murmurs of 'grazie' from the film crew, and after pulling on a headscarf, she slipped out of the door into the rain.

Experienced cameraman Ethan, nearing sixty and the eldest of the group, folded his arms and said, 'Okay, Mr Cavendish, just what is our situation?'

Stephen glanced around the table. He'd had a sense of unease from the start of this venture. This wasn't a happy crew. It had been hastily assembled to get publicity shots ahead of the main circus, but not, Stephen suspected, with the usual thorough preparation. He was acquainted with Ethan, had worked with him previously; Louise, he'd seen around at various preparatory meetings. With a recent degree in cinematography, she'd been pointed towards this job by Lisa, not difficult, he imagined in view of her being indirectly responsible for the misfortunes of nine years ago. Accustomed to being *directed*, Stephen wondered when he had slipped into accepting being *told what to do*. He became aware Max Cavendish was speaking.

'I feel it's my responsibility, and as there appears to be little chance of power being restored within the next few days, I'm willing to go with Arturo to try and find a way through, let the authorities know our position and get help.'

Stephen dragged his mind back to what had been said – swollen river, unstable ground, no communication even with villages further down the mountain.

'Well,' Ethan said. He leaned across the table, poured wine into the tumblers and pushed a glass towards Stephen. 'What do you say, Mr Bryce?'

Stephen gave the matter some thought before saying, 'I assume the decision to be made is do we all try to get to the next village? Or do

Max and Arturo go in the hope their communications are still intact and send help?'

Louise reached for her glass of wine and took a sip. 'I understood someone from the village was going down the mountain.'

Arturo stepped from the back room. 'I know the area as well as anyone. We will get help.'

Yash piped up, 'What about the satellite phone?'

'The battery is flat,' Max told him. 'Arturo and I have discussed it, and we'll start first thing in the morning.'

'I'm younger and fitter,' Yash said, 'and willing to go with Arturo.'

'No,' Max insisted.

Ethan said, 'I'm sure we will be well looked after here until rescue arrives, but there are pressing reasons we should get help as soon as possible, apart,' he shrugged, 'from being anxious to get back to our families.' He looked meaningfully at Stephen before pulling an empty tablet blister pack from a pocket and placing it on the table. 'I have a heart condition and I had the last of my medication last night. I imagine Mr Bryce is in a similar situation.'

Stephen shifted in his seat, uncomfortable in the knowledge that others knew of his condition. It was necessary to clear his throat before he could say, 'I don't wish to be responsible for others making any rash decision. I assume a search will start at the scene of the landslide. Will they know in which direction to look? Neither Ethan nor I can afford for rescue to be delayed too long.'

'As you know,' Ethan interrupted, 'the on-set doctor was in one of the other vehicles.'

Arturo spoke again. 'Max and I will leave in the morning. I know a shepherd's hut to stay overnight and we should be at the next village by noon the day after, and if telephone lines are still standing or we can get a mobile phone signal, we can get the authorities to send a helicopter.'

'Very well,' Max said. 'We had better get some sleep. There are a couple of rooms upstairs. I believe the people across the way have a bed for you, Stephen.'

Louise stood. 'And I'm staying with a family down the road.'

'Me too,' added Yash.

Ethan said, 'I'll sleep here.' He gestured to a bed set up in the downstairs room, near the stove.

63

Yash gathered his coat into a bundle and followed Stephen and Louise outside.

Stephen again flipped up his hood against the pelting rain. Louise pulled her coat over her head. At Giuseppe's house, Stephen pushed the door open. 'Louise, I need to talk to you.'

Yash called, 'Can *I* come in?'

Stephen held the door as they almost fell inside in a splatter of raindrops. Nonna was there to shake wet coats and hang them on the door, scolding the young man in rapid Italian for not wearing his. She gestured for them to sit at the table then bustled around fetching cheese and bread.

Giuseppe appeared from a back room holding aloft a dark bottle, brandy, Stephen guessed – proved correct when Giuseppe poured a good measure for each of them.

Nonna flew into a tirade of what seemed like admonishment. She took a saucepan of hot milk from the stove and half filled three earthenware mugs before tipping the measures of brandy into each of the mugs. Nonna put her hands together, tipped her head to one side and rested it on her hands.

Stephen smiled at the others. 'I think she means this will help us sleep.'

Yash grinned back. 'Personally, I'd rather just have the brandy.'

They were joined by Francesco. 'Nonna, Nonno.' He spoke kindly as he ushered them from the room. He turned back and shrugged apologetically. 'They are so pleased to be helping you.'

'Yes,' Stephen said. 'I know.'

The youth made to follow his grandparents from the room, but Stephen called, 'Francesco.'

'Si?'

'Did a messenger set off for the next village?'

'No. Signor Cavendish said not to bother; he and Arturo will go.'

'Okay, Francesco. Thank you.'

Francesco nodded. 'There is a room in the back with a bed. I hope you will be comfortable.'

'I'm sure I will,' Stephen reassured. 'Thanks again.'

CHAPTER 15

Ann closed her eyes, tummy churning. She took a moment to compose herself before leaving her room to meet with the rescue organisers and other authorities. She would be joining a group of people separated from the main party of relatives and guessed it wasn't to receive good news.

'Ah, Mrs Bryce.' Owen Wyatt, the senior representative of the film company approached. 'Please come through.' He showed her into a small lounge where half a dozen or so others waited. Owen introduced Angelo Russo from rescue services.

Angelo marked the whereabouts of the chalet used as a base on a map displayed on an easel. He pinned some aerial shots of the landslide to the board. Photos taken hastily before a second storm moved in and made it too dangerous for any rescue attempt. 'This is the road,' he pointed out, 'the first Land Rover took down the mountain. You can see above where the road is washed away, but a little higher it's still intact. If the second Land Rover was lagging as far behind as they say, I'm sure it could have reversed out of any immediate danger. What we propose, as soon as the weather clears, is to cover this area,' he tapped the map, 'and maybe get a team on the ground. I'm sure your guide,' he addressed Owen Wyatt who had taken off his jacket and loosened his tie, 'is experienced enough to know what to do.'

'Yes,' was the reply. 'We only hire the best.'

Ann thought he looked distracted as he concentrated on skimming through an iPad, flicking up page after page.

Angelo's presentation concluded, he said, 'There is nothing more I can tell you. Please make yourselves comfortable, and you will be informed immediately we make any contact with the missing group.'

A waitress entered with a tray of tea and set out cups on a low table.

Owen Wyatt tore himself away from his iPad to say, 'I've asked the management to bring sandwiches. Dinner is at seven and, of course, is at the expense of the production company, as is your stay here, for as long as—' he hesitated. 'As long as necessary.'

65

The waitress returned with a colleague and a selection of refreshments. Owen returned to his place at a desk in the corner of the room and resumed perusal of his computer.

'My name is Marion Quinn.'

Ann looked into the face of a woman of perhaps sixty, a few years older than herself, who lifted the silver teapot and gestured towards a cup. 'Oh, yes. Thank you.'

'My husband, Ethan, is the senior cinematographer on this shoot.'

Ann said, 'Thank you,' as Marion poured tea. 'I'm Ann Bryce. My husband is—'

'Yes, I know who your husband is. I believe he and Ethan have worked together previously.'

A couple sitting opposite introduced themselves as Sarah and James Austin. 'Our daughter, Louise, is the production assistant,' Sarah told them.

'Adrian Bowler,' a young man announced. 'I'm Yash's partner. He's the sparky on this caper.'

Ann wished she had Stephen's knack for remembering names and faces and of putting people at ease. She smiled sympathetically at the others, knowing they were just as worried as herself.

'What do you think?' Marion appealed, indicating the map.

Ann examined the photos before turning to Ethan's wife. 'I think there's a good chance they reversed back along the road and they'll be found safe and well.'

'Is that the official line?' It was Yash's partner, Adrian. He glanced at the sandwiches. 'I can't eat whilst there are lives at risk.'

Ann put a hand on Adrian's arm. 'We're all worried. There's not much the rescue services can do until the weather clears.'

Ann moved over to where Owen Wyatt was sitting, still earnestly searching through his iPad. 'Can you have a word with Adrian, Yash's partner? He's a bit concerned that there might be more that can be done.'

Owen put down the iPad. 'Oh, Mrs Bryce. I didn't realise it was you.'

She gestured to the iPad. 'Something wrong?'

'I'm having difficulty identifying all the members of the crew. It was put together hastily, hoping to get the shots before the weather closed in.'

66

Ann merely said, 'Mm,' before indicating Adrian should join Owen at the table in a corner of the room.

If, she wondered, the crew had been put together hastily, what else was not planned properly?

Sarah said, 'I don't know why Louise was so keen to join this production. She's already spent time as a production assistant and now has a degree in cinematography. She did work experience at Apollo Studios around the time your husband was taken ill.'

Ann frowned in concentration. 'Yes, Louise. She ...' Perhaps Louise had not told her parents that it was she who bought the cough medicine for Stephen. It was an accident, no one would know it would react badly with his prescribed medication. Ann said, 'Yes, I remember Louise.'

'I hope the weather clears soon.' Marion Quinn joined the conversation. 'Ethan has a heart condition, and I'm not sure if he was carrying his medication.'

*

Later in the dining room, Ann picked at a salmon salad. She glanced across the table at Marion Quinn and Louise's parents. Their appetites mirrored her own. Yash's partner was at the bar. He'd declined when asked to join them.

Sarah Austin leaned towards Ann. 'What was Owen saying to you?'

'He's having difficulty finding details of Max Cavendish.'

'But he's among the missing,' James Austin, Louise's father, stated.

Ann shrugged. 'So it seems.'

'I spoke to the first aider who was with them,' Marion Quinn chipped in. 'He was drafted in at the last moment to deal with emergencies or injuries during filming and not responsible for existing medication. Ethan takes tablets morning and evening, and as they were supposed to be back before nightfall, there would be no need to keep a supply with him.'

'Stephen told me the day's filming should only take a few hours,' Ann confirmed. 'They were using the chalet as a base then going further on to the location. According to Owen Wyatt, they checked the weather and this belt of rain wasn't expected so soon, but they didn't take into account rain and snow in the mountains, which you would expect an experienced guide to do.'

Marion looked forlorn. 'I've spoken to a doctor here, and he believes Ethan missing one or even two days' tablets wouldn't be too much of a problem, but any longer and it could be serious. I do hope the weather clears tomorrow.'

Despite their mutual concern, Ann felt a need to be alone, and said, 'I have some calls to make. Owen promised to let us know if there's any news before morning.'

Ann paced around her room, phone to her ear. 'Come on Peter, where are you?' The call went to voicemail. 'Just checking in,' she told the automated response. 'Things are a bit of a muddle here, but there's no news of Stephen or the others. Let me know if you've heard from Nathan.' After a moment she rang their home number. Peter sometimes forgot where he'd left his mobile, – most unlike the Peter of a couple of years ago. Still straight backed and alert, it could not be denied that age was catching up with him. 'With us all,' she muttered, before leaving the same message on the home answering machine. She tried Nathan's phone, 'Hope you're okay, Nathan. Let me know where you are.' Then Julian and Fiona. Perhaps Peter had gone back to The Rookery with his elder son's family. 'Where is everyone?' she begged the darkening room. In a desperate hope, she pressed the speed dial for Stephen, throwing the phone on the bed in frustration on hearing, *We are unable to connect your call, please try again later.*

Ann opened double doors and stepped onto a small balcony. Heavy rain had abated to a fine drizzle leaving a warmer, damp atmosphere. The moon struggled from behind clearing clouds and glinted on the cameras of the media circus gathering outside. Ignoring the hum of voices below Ann gazed again at the moon now clear, bright and almost at its fullest. 'Please let the moon that shines on me shine on the ones I love.'

CHAPTER 16

A few crumbs left scattered on the breadboard, Stephen offered Louise the last chunk of cheese Nonna had provided.

'I shall have nightmares,' she grinned, popping it into her mouth.

Yash poured a drop more brandy into his cup. 'Why do you think Cavendish doesn't want anyone else to fetch help?' He retrieved his coat, which was folded in a bundle, and placed it on the table. 'I offered to look at the satellite phone; I'm good with electronics. Cavendish said it was beyond repair, waterlogged and the battery flat—' he unfolded the coat. 'So I decided to have a look.'

'You stole it,' Louise said as Yash revealed a metal case containing a handset and keyboard.

Yash produced a small screwdriver and removed several tiny screws from the back of the keyboard and poked about, finally saying, 'No wonder he couldn't get a signal, there's no bloody battery.'

'He could have taken it out to dry it,' Louise suggested.

'There's no way to charge it here, but the built-in solar sensor should have put a bit of life in it.' Yash's chair scraped the floor as he stood. 'I'll go and see Mr Cavendish.'

Stephen, quickly on his feet, caught Yash's arm as he staggered. 'I think you've had a little too much brandy for a sensible discussion tonight. Leave this here—' he gestured to the phone console, 'and we'll tackle Cavendish and Arturo tomorrow before they leave.'

'Yeah, okay,' Yash slurred. 'I could do with a good night's sleep.' Yash slung his coat around his shoulders and opened the door. 'It's even stopped raining.'

Stephen stood at the door and watched Yash weave his way down the rough road and enter a house on the other side. 'He's okay,' he told Louise. 'And you should be going. Which house has your bed for tonight?'

'It's next door, but you wanted to speak to me.'

'It'll keep until morning.'

She made no move to leave. 'There are things I should have told you earlier.'

69

They sat at the table and Louise made to pour more brandy but Stephen put a hand over his cup. 'I think we've had enough – *I* certainly have.'

'What did you want to ask me?'

'Did you join this shoot so you could—' he hesitated to use the word, 'apologise. Or did Lisa suggest it?'

Louise picked at crumbs on the table. 'Lisa said she'd done something she was beginning to regret, and if I could warn you, it would make up for me buying that cough medicine that ... almost killed you.'

'It was an accident. No one knew it would react that way with the medication I was taking.' He gave an exasperated sigh. 'So like Lisa to use it as a lever to get you to do something.'

'No.' She leaned forward. 'When she explained, I was pleased to do it. Okay, it's a step backward in my career, but that's only temporary.'

'What is it Lisa wants you to do?'

'She was in love with your friend, Andy Roberts, who was killed.'

Stephen shook his head. 'It was around the time I was out of it. I could never get my head around Andy with Lisa, though I can't deny she's worked hard for the charity.'

'She told me he loved working in schools.'

'Yeah,' Stephen said softly, remembering his friend. 'He liked to name drop.'

'After Lisa came back from Canada, we shared a flat and it was then, when she was fundraising, she became friendly with a man who worked for the charity. Dean ... something, an executive or trustee.'

'Yes?' Stephen encouraged her to go on.'

'I'm not sure how it came to light, but Lisa said something was wrong. Don't ask me what or how,' Louise declared. 'But she was worried enough to ask me to warn you.'

'Warn me?'

'You set up the charity in memory of Andy. If some fraud or scam comes to light, it's bound to reflect badly on everyone concerned.'

Stephen sat back in his chair, struggling to take in what she said. He put his hands to his face and rubbed his eyes. Wine followed by brandy fuddled his brain. 'Louise, you must know of Lisa's reputation for being ... melodramatic. This can't be right. People are vetted before being appointed trustees.'

Louise's face hardened. 'She said you wouldn't believe her. But she was genuinely frightened.'

'If there's any suspicion of wrongdoing it will need to be investigated, but there's nothing I can do right now.' Stephen stood and lifted her coat from the hook behind the door. 'Our main concern is getting off this mountain and home safely.' He slipped the coat over her shoulders and made to follow her outside.

Louise turned to face him. 'I don't need escorting less than ten metres.' Swivelling on a heel she continued towards the house next door.

'Louise,' Stephen called.

She turned back.

'Why tell me now?'

'Before we began this little adventure, I was waiting for a call from Lisa telling me who else was involved.'

'She had a name?'

'She was close to finding out. But he's someone important.' She shrugged. 'Maybe more than one person. Maybe someone here.'

She spun round and continued to the next house. Stephen watched the rough wooden door close before returning to his own billet.

The fire in the stove still glimmered, warmth lingering in the room. Stephen lifted the lid on the satellite phone. Before this last belt of rain there had been a few hours of sun. The solar sensor would surely put some life in the battery. He pushed the case aside and searched his jacket pockets for his medication. The blister pack was empty. To go without for a couple of days, surely wouldn't do much harm. He picked up a paraffin lamp and took it through to the back room. Resting the lamp on the floor he sat on the bed to untie his bootlaces and eased off the uncomfortable footwear. As he lay on the bed, the crudely plastered ceiling began to spin. He shouldn't drink – he'd feel rough in the morning. Morning – Cavendish and Arturo – phone. Forcing his eyes open he found his mobile. *What time will it get light?* He concentrated carefully to set the alarm. '6.00 a.m.,' he muttered. 'Should be early enough to see them before they leave.' Through a high window, a big moon shed silvery light. Stephen thought of Ann and a melody filtered through his dulled brain. *Please let the moon that shines on me, shine on the one I love.*

CHAPTER 17

A couple of women on their way into the ladies' toilet in Jacob's department store looked startled as they met Nathan and Lisa coming out.

Nathan glimpsed Jessica at the entrance to the restaurant. She was speaking to a uniformed policeman, another officer nearby. Lisa moved to the fire exit and slipped through the door. Nathan caught the door before it closed and followed her to a landing at the head of a flight of stone stairs.

From a few steps down Lisa called, 'Go back, Nathan. You've done nothing wrong. Go back and explain to the police.'

'Come with me. Tell them what happened.'

Lisa went back up the steps and said urgently, 'No. There's something I must do.'

'I'm coming with you.'

'You can't come, Nathan. It's … it's not just the police.' She descended a few steps before looking back. 'I don't want you with me.'

Nathan heard the clack-clack of shoes as she again trotted down the stairs. 'Wait.' He leapt down the first four steps and caught her at the next landing, his trainers squeaking on stone steps. 'This concerns my dad.'

She halted again. 'It concerns everyone connected to Andy's charity, but you can't help, so clear off. I don't want you.'

Momentarily stung, Nathan stopped in his tracks. He recovered, followed. 'You can't get rid of me that easily.' He followed her into a basement car park, heard the beep of a car being unlocked and sprinted to where lights flashed in time to see Lisa slipping into the driver's seat. 'Wait', he called again. 'Mother, wait.' His plaintive cry echoed around the cavernous parking area.

A silver Honda pulled from a row of parked cars and rocked to a halt allowing him to open the door and fall into the front passenger seat.

Lisa snapped, 'Didn't your father teach you to do as you're told?' She drove out of the dim car park and into the street.

Nathan ignored the remark. *Doesn't she know being a parent is more than telling people what to do?* He scrabbled at the seatbelt and managed to click it into place. 'Where are we going?'

A screaming siren drowned her reply. The flash of a police vehicle on an adjoining road – Lisa nipped through traffic lights a fraction before they turned red.

'Lisa.' Nathan put a hand on the dashboard as she drove round a sharp corner. 'Who is the dead man in the hotel room? Is it your boyfriend, Dean? You know who killed him.' It wasn't a question. 'We should go back, tell the police what happened.'

Lisa stamped on the brakes. A blue car sounded its horn and swerved around them. 'Get out and go back.'

'Not without you.'

'There's something I must do.'

'Then I'm coming with you.'

'Then shut up and let me think.' Her attitude softened. 'Just shut up, Nathan. Please.'

Nathan sat back and tried not to flinch as his mother navigated city streets, eventually turning into an alley at the rear of a row of shops where she parked next to a Fiat 500 and switched off the engine.

She indicated the smaller car. 'Ellie is in the office today.'

Nathan followed Lisa across the yard to an external wrought iron staircase with a small, square landing. He noticed a small plaque, *Registered office* and *Charity number* on the fire door. From a dingy corridor, Lisa opened a door, half glazed with frosted glass. The office inside housed a couple of desks and computer screens. On the wall was a portrait photo of Andy Roberts, looking young and handsome, just as Nathan remembered.

A young woman, who Nathan assumed was Ellie, looked up and said, 'I wasn't expecting you today, Miss Brookes. I'm afraid Mr Henderson isn't here.'

'He won't be coming in today,' Lisa told her. 'Will you nip to the café across the road and get two coffees.'

'I can make coffee,' Ellie said, indicating a door to a back room.

'I'd prefer a latte,' Lisa said pointedly.

'Certainly.' Ellie crossed the office, unhooked her coat from a stand and slipped it on. 'Latte and—?' She cocked an eyebrow at Nathan.

'Oh,' Lisa exclaimed. 'This is … this is Nathan.'

Too much to expect her to own him as her son, Nathan smiled and said, 'Not for me, thank you.'

Ellie glanced again at Lisa but getting no reaction sighed and made to leave.

Nathan understood. He rummaged in his jacket pocket, dragged out his last £10 note, and handed it to Ellie. As the office door closed, he said to Lisa, 'I've just remembered; Jessica and I didn't pay for our coffee at the hotel.'

'Don't fuss about that now.' Lisa had opened a desk drawer, pulled out a notebook and was flicking through. 'Ah, here it is.'

'What?'

'Ellie writes down passwords and ... yes, here it is.' Lisa moved to the back of the office and opened a cupboard door to reveal a safe. She entered a series of digits into a keypad, it peeped and the door swung open. From its depths she withdrew a memory stick. Lisa switched on the computer, entered the password and repeatedly rattled the 'enter' key. 'How do I do this?'

Nathan moved to her side. 'What are you trying to do?'

'I need to see what's on this.'

Nathan inserted the memory stick and pressed a few keys. 'It's an accounts programme, showing donations, payments to various schools. It's—'

'Never mind that, what else is there?'

Nathan found some other files and imported the information. 'Looks like holding accounts. Wow, some huge sums.'

'Okay,' Lisa snapped. 'Is that all?'

'There are some files I can't open.'

'Never mind. Can you print off what there is?'

Nathan stood back. 'This can't be right. There's never been that much money donated.'

'I know, Nathan. Print it off before Ellie gets back and I'll explain, but not here.'

'But—'

Lisa slapped the desk. 'Do it, Nathan.' She stood and indicated the seat she had vacated.

Nathan had seen his mother hysterical and angry but this was a new experience. He wanted to walk away, find Jessica and go home. Instead, he took a shaky breath, sat at the desk and hit the print button.

The handle to the office door rattled. Lisa snatched the flash drive from its slot and was gathering the last page of the half dozen printed sheets as Ellie entered.

'Sorry to be so long, there was a queue,' Ellie explained. She handed a paper cup to Lisa and pushed a handful of change at Nathan.

74

Lisa, now more composed, put the cup on the desk. 'We have to go.' At the door, she turned. 'Ellie, lock up early and go home. You won't be needed for a couple of days.'

The girl halted in the act of taking off her coat. 'I'm in the middle of—'

'There's nothing that can't wait. Lock up now and go home.'

Nathan followed his mother back down the external stairs to her car. He sat quietly while she skimmed through the printed sheets and flinched when she thrust them at him. 'We need to find somewhere where I can study these.' She started the engine and drove out into the street.

Shops, dirty streets, high rise buildings and junctions flashed by until Lisa was forced to halt at traffic lights.

'Is it fraud?' Nathan asked. 'This?' He held up the papers. 'Are you and your boyfriend taking money from the charity?'

Lisa shook her head, put her foot fiercely on the accelerator and screeched off at the first hint of amber.

'Where are we going? You can't keep running away.'

Lisa negotiated a traffic island and turned into a more residential area eventually pulling up outside a house in a Victorian terrace. 'I used to share a flat here and still have a key.'

Nathan followed his mother to a front door set between stone-mullioned bay windows. In the hallway, doors to apartments on either side were secured by Yale locks. Lisa went upstairs to rooms at the front of the house. They made a generous living area with two bedrooms at the rear.

Lisa pushed some magazines from a coffee table and spread out the printed pages.

Nathan sat next to her on the settee and studied the pages. 'It looks like money paid in then transferred elsewhere.'

Lisa ran a finger down the lists. 'I need to know if my account is here but there are no names, only numbers.'

'Have *you* been taking money from Uncle Andy's charity?'

'It's not money that belongs to the charity. It's ... it's commission.'

Nathan's indignation rose. 'For what? Is your boyfriend taking money and you know about it?'

'No.' She sounded tearful. 'Dean bought me gifts that were more and more expensive, and when I asked him, he said he was being paid for doing bookkeeping for other people.'

'What other people.'

Lisa raised her head, tears brimming her lashes. 'Important people,' she whispered. 'People who won't be happy knowing we have this information.'

Nathan rubbed his eyes. 'Dad always said—'

'What did your father say?' Lisa snapped.

'Just that ... trouble always finds you.'

'He should know.'

Nathan rolled his eyes. What he'd not overheard from the family, he'd worked out for himself. 'If you've done nothing wrong there's nothing to be afraid of and we should ring the police.' He fished his mobile from his jacket pocket and skimmed through the messages.

'Any news of your dad?'

'Mum's flown out to be nearer the rescue site.'

'Does she know who else is missing?'

Nathan shrugged. He noticed Lisa's gaze travel to a photo propped on the mantelpiece. 'Is that the girl whose flat this is?'

'Louise. She's working for the same film company as Stephen, and I've not heard from her.' Lisa shuffled the papers together. 'I hope she's okay and that she's managed to speak to him.'

Nathan again let a finger hover over the screen of his phone, hesitating to instigate the trouble he knew would be in store. It was inevitable the police would catch up with them before long – and it was the right thing to do. Lisa again distracted him.

'You wouldn't remember Louise.'

'Should I?'

'Do you remember when your dad was very ill?'

Nathan bit his lower lip. His mother was rattling on a door behind which those memories were locked and bolted.

'Maybe not,' she went on. 'You were only a child. It was Louise who fetched the cough medicine which reacted badly with your dad's medication. The silly girl has been tormented by guilt thinking she almost killed him. An opportunity arose, and I persuaded her to take the job as a production assistant.'

'Dad doesn't blame anyone.'

'No, but hearing Stephen say it wasn't her fault will make her feel better. And besides, I wanted her to warn him.'

'About this?' He gestured to the papers now scattered across the table.

'Well, *he* set up the charity. The police could think he's involved.'

'Dad has nothing to do with the running of the charity, that's down to the trustees.'

'That may be, Nathan, but while Stephen and I are under suspicion, these people are distancing themselves and if they know we have this information—' she collected the papers.

Nathan heard a distant thud.

Both froze, eyes locked. Lisa whispered, 'That was the front door. The two girls downstairs should be at work.' She quickly folded the printed sheets.

'Give them to me,' Nathan demanded. When she hesitated he added, 'You have the flash drive, give me the papers.' He zipped them into his jacket pocket.

Nathan followed Lisa onto the landing and peered over the bannister.

She beckoned him along a corridor, past what he presumed to be bedrooms and bathroom and, handing him a pole with a small hook on the end, pointed to a hatch in the ceiling. 'There's a fire escape leading from the loft,' she whispered in explanation.

Nathan hooked the latch, the trapdoor fell open allowing him to lower a ladder.

Lisa pushed past, he followed her through the open square and heaved up the ladder. He leaned back through the hatch, intending to pull it closed but glimpsed a figure moving in the corridor. The catch just out of reach, he withdrew into the loft to see Lisa already climbing out of a dormer window.

About to scramble after his mother, Nathan recoiled from the dizzying drop of three storeys. A shout drifting through the still-open trapdoor spurred him on. Narrow metal steps led to a second landing, and below this, his mother clung to a vertical ladder, secured from the small metal platform.

'I can't move,' she called up. 'The ladder is loose.'

'Keep still. I'll come down.' Nathan clattered down the steps then, avoiding Lisa's fingers, carefully stepped past her until he was two rungs below. 'I think it's okay. It just rattles a bit.' Clinging with one hand he placed the other around his mother's waist. 'I've got you; step onto the next rung.' A noise from above. She slipped – let go.

Her weight dislodged Nathan – he hit the ground first, broke Lisa's fall, but had jolted an ankle.

Lisa gained her feet, ran along the alley past wheelie bins lined up against the wall and into the street.

Nathan limped after in time to see his mother throw herself into the driving seat of her car. He watched in wonderment as the vehicle did a grand prix start and sped along the road.

A second later the front door to the house containing the converted flats opened. Nathan snapped closed his gaping mouth and pressed against the wall. A man in dark clothes ran into the road and gazed after the speeding car. He wrenched open his car door and roared after.

In gathering dusk, a street light pinged on, and Nathan looked skyward, tears stinging. He sighed, looked up and down the road. What to do now? He had no idea where he was, or how to get back to Jessica. His phone jingled. 'Not now, Mum, please.' He ignored the text and rang Jessica.

CHAPTER 18

An ambulance arrived in response to Peter's emergency call. Paramedics checked vital signs. 'You say she's had these attacks before.' 'Yes,' Peter told them. 'But she's always recovered after a few minutes.' He stood back, allowing them room to work. Relieved when Lizzie's body visibly relaxed, he let go a breath he didn't know he had been holding. Her little body remained limp.

The paramedic met his gaze. 'She's not responding.'

*

Fiona and Julian were already at the hospital when Peter arrived in the ambulance with Lizzie. He followed them into A&E, and whilst Lizzie and her parents were taken into a treatment room, he sat with other patients' relatives in a corridor. Never a patient man, he stood and paced the length of the passage before returning to his seat. He read the direction signs on the wall: notices of various clinics, advice on how to recognise symptoms of stroke or heart attack.

The treatment room door opening distracted Peter from another turn along the corridor.

Fiona beckoned to him, ruffling her usually immaculate blonde hair by dragging a hand through it. 'Take me for a coffee, Peter.' She linked her arm in his.

Peter inclined his head towards the door of the treatment room.

'Jules wants to stay with her. Come on, I'll fill you in.' She led him out of the department and to a volunteer café where they sat either side of a table.

'As soon as I realised she wasn't coming out of it, I called for an ambulance.'

'You did the right thing.'

'Perhaps I should have rung sooner.'

'It's happened before, and you had no reason to think she wouldn't recover after a few minutes.' She laid a hand on his arm. 'I'd have done the same, Peter.'

Peter took a shuddering breath before saying, 'How is she?'

'Still unresponsive. They're admitting her and will do a brain scan. Why don't you go home? Jules and I will stay until she's settled. I suppose I ought to fetch some clothes … but …' Fiona looked a little stunned. 'I don't suppose she'll need clothes but a nightdress and toiletries. And I need to tell Gill, the girl who runs the stables, to keep an eye on things.'

'I could do that,' Peter suggested. 'I came with Lizzie in the ambulance, so I'll get a taxi home. '

'I'll drop you at Holly Cottage then go home, speak to Gill before picking up some things for Liz.'

'I'd rather be doing something,' Peter countered. 'I've had enough of waiting for the phone to ring.'

'I should have asked. Is there any news about Stephen?'

'Not as far as I know. I should ring Ann.'

'Don't tell her about Lizzie, 'Fiona appealed. 'She has enough to worry about. And I won't tell Matthew until we know a little more. No need to ruin his holiday.'

'If that's what you want. There's no need to bother Nathan – he won't even answer his phone.' Peter spoke with some exasperation.

'Give him a bit of space, Peter.' She stood and came around the table to kiss her father-in-law's cheek. 'Let me take you home and then I won't need to worry about you. I promise I'll call you immediately if we know anything.' A sadness came to Fiona's eyes.

Peter stood, gave her a hug and said, 'Lizzie has great spirit.'

*

Fiona dropped Peter outside Holly Cottage. It crossed Peter's mind that after the fire and other tragic events at Elliston House, Ann and Stephen were lucky to find such an attractive house in the same village. *Lucky there's room for me. And that they want me here.*

He didn't press the remote for the gates but unlocked the small gate at the side. Before he reached the turning circle outside the front door to the main house, the separate door to his single-storey extension opened. His heart swelled as it always did when he saw Kathy. He should have married her years ago but the moment had passed, overtaken by tragic events, and now they spent time at both her house in the village and here at the annex to Holly Cottage.

Kathy ran to meet him and, throwing her arms around his neck, said, 'When a neighbour told me she'd seen the ambulance, I thought it was you.'

Peter hugged her. 'It's Lizzie.' His voice, hoarse. 'She had a seizure and hasn't come out of it.'

'I'm so sorry, and on top of the other problems.' She took his hand. 'Come on, I'll make you a coffee.'

By the time Kathy and Peter sat at his kitchen table, dusk was settling. Peter felt a stab of guilt. In light of Fiona's request not to tell Ann about Lizzie, he had resisted returning Ann's calls.

In the office, Peter found the message from Ann. 'Just checking in. It seems to be a bit of a muddle here. No news of Stephen or the others. Let me know if you hear from Nathan.'

It was a repeat of the message she'd left on his mobile.

Muttering, 'No news is good news, I suppose,' he returned to the kitchen and sat with Kathy until gathering dusk prompted him to switch on a light and ask, 'Will you stay tonight?'

She touched his hand. 'Of course.'

After a while Peter said, 'Perhaps I should get in touch with the police in Birmingham, or at least that girl's father, Brian Foster.'

Peter and Kathy fell silent as the landline telephone rang.

81

CHAPTER 19

Nathan sat on a wall outside the flats and waited. A squad car arrived and a uniformed officer alighted. Nathan slipped from the wall and, with the officer's hand on his arm, was led to the car and instructed to sit in the back beside a woman who identified herself as Sergeant Carlton.

Sergeant Carlton, dark shoulder-length hair hooked behind her ears, rested an arm on the back of the seat the better to look at the youth in her custody. 'The young lady at the station tells us your name is Nathan Bryce.'

'Yes.'

'And your mother is Lisa Brookes?'

'Yes.'

'Would this be the same Lisa Brookes I may have seen in gossip magazines?'

'Probably.'

'And she's your mother?'

Nathan nodded, cringing at the police officer's sceptical tone.

'Bryce?' Sergeant Carlton pushed a lock of hair from her face and pouted in thought. 'Why do I know that name?'

Nathan shot her a glance. 'How often do you go to the cinema?'

The uniformed officer returned and slipping into the driver's seat said, 'There's evidence of a hasty exit round the back. I've made things secure.'

'My mother used to share a flat with the girl who lives here, and she still has a key,' Nathan said quickly, anxious they shouldn't think he and Lisa had broken in.

'And where is your mother now?' Sergeant Carlton asked.

'A man followed us into the apartment, so we got out by the fire escape ... and she drove off.'

'Leaving you here? That's not very motherly.'

Nathan gazed at the back of the seat in front.

'Get traffic on to it,' Carlton instructed the uniformed other officer, 'then we'll get this young man back to his girlfriend.'

'Is Jessica okay?'

'She's in as much trouble as you are.'

'I can pay for the coffee,' Nathan pleaded. 'We just forgot.'

'Fasten your seatbelt,' was the sergeant's only reply.

*

'I can manage from here,' Sergeant Carlton told the driver of the patrol car before leading Nathan towards the entrance of the police station. A sign blazed above the door which, together with street lamps, created a concrete-lined, bright zone in the darkness of early evening.

Half a dozen people were in the reception area. A couple held hands, looking anxious; a man remonstrated with an officer at the desk whilst others sat on chairs set in a row, looking either bored or apprehensive.

Nathan spotted Jessica sitting at the end of the row, arms folded, head down. He called her name and she stood and ran to him. 'Are you alright?' they chorused.

'This way,' Sergeant Carlton instructed. Indicating Jessica should stay, she led Nathan into an interview room.

The sergeant introduced Inspector Ishir Varma. Small of stature, dark intense eyes, he threw a folder onto the table and motioned Nathan to sit. Sergeant Carlton pulled up a chair and sat behind and slightly to the side.

'How old are you?' Varma asked.

Nathan tried not to fidget. 'Seventeen.'

'You understand you can be treated as an adult with all that entails?'

The information did nothing to alleviate Nathan's apprehension. 'I do now,' he muttered.

'What happened in room 217 at the Regency Hotel?' the inspector continued. 'From the beginning.'

Nathan took a breath and explained how Jessica followed Lisa to the room and seeing Nathan's mother enter returned to the coffee shop to tell him. 'I'd missed the lift so I took the stairs to the second floor. The lift doors were closing as I got there. I assumed someone was on their way down.'

'Did you see who it was?'

'No, but ...'

'But what?'

Aware of the implications of his answer, Nathan ignored the question, instead saying, 'The door to the room was slightly open so I pushed it. I might have called her name.'

'Her name?'

83

'Lisa. My mother.'

'Do you always call her Lisa?'

'I don't know what else to call her. I haven't seen her for—' Nathan shrugged. 'Ten years. I live with my father and step-mum.'

'Okay,' the inspector said. 'What did you see when you opened the door?'

Nathan inhaled deeply. 'I saw a man, lying face down, on the floor. There was a lot of blood.'

Inspector Varma leaned back in his chair. 'And what did you do then?'

'A woman in the corridor behind screamed. I stepped out of the room ... and ...'

The inspector again leaned forward. 'I'll tell you what you *didn't* do.'

Nathan felt his heart rate increase.

'You didn't report the incident. Not to the police, or the manager of the hotel, or anyone.' The policeman paused for effect. 'Instead you ran from the hotel after the person you suspected of having killed the man.' Another moment's silence. 'Your mother, Lisa Brookes.'

'No,' Nathan almost shouted. 'I knew it must have been Lisa going down in the lift, I could smell her perfume on the landing, but she didn't kill him. She told me she didn't kill him.'

Inspector Varma again leaned back in his chair. 'Maybe not,' he mused.

Nathan rubbed a hand across his mouth and closed his eyes. 'I've never seen a dead person...'

'Do you know who it was or why your mother was there?'

Caught in a quandary, Nathan said, 'I was hoping to speak to my mother.'

'You obviously caught up with her before you were picked up at the flat at Oakfield Terrace. After the incident at the hotel, I don't suppose she was interested in what you've been doing for the last ten years.'

Nathan rankled at the insensitive remark but remained silent.

It was the inspector's turn to sigh. 'Okay, Nathan, perhaps that was below the belt. Your girlfriend told me you wanted to track down your mother, and I don't suppose this is how you expected it to be. What did Lisa tell you about the incident at the hotel?'

'I don't know if she saw what happened.'

'Did *you* see anyone else, perhaps leaving the room or in the corridor at the hotel?'

'Only the woman who screamed. She must have thought that I ... had ... but he was there when I opened the door.'

'Do you know your mother's boyfriend?'

'I had a glimpse of him when I saw her on the film set in Derbyshire. His name is Dean.'

They were interrupted by a knock at the door. An officer entered and handed a paper to the inspector who took a moment to read its contents. He put the paper aside and said, 'Dean Henderson and your mother are involved with people who have connections to organised crime.'

Nathan, shaken from dwelling on being snubbed by his mother, remembered the printout in his pocket. 'Lisa suspected Dean of defrauding Uncle Andy's charity. That's why I followed her from Derbyshire. My dad set up the charity and it's bound to reflect badly on him even though he's not involved. Dean is a trustee.' He pulled out the papers and straightened them out on the desk. 'Lisa took me to the charity's office; she took a memory stick from the safe and we printed this out. It shows sums of money going in and out of various accounts.'

Detective Inspector Varma searched among the papers in the file. 'This charity has already been flagged as of interest.' He extracted a sheet. 'It does seem a little out of your mother's and her boyfriend's league. They must have upset someone further up the ladder. We believe someone confronted Dean Henderson at the hotel. Dean must have had time to give Lisa Brookes some information, and she retrieved the evidence. The question is, does she still have the stick and what does she intend to do with it?'

'She gave me this.' Nathan tapped the print off he had handed over. 'You can find these people and arrest them.'

'This is a series of numbers that could relate to anything. We need to know what's on that memory stick, and before these thugs catch up with your mother.'

Nathan's head shot up. 'Then you have to find her. She intended to hand it over to you but—'

'But what, Nathan? Why did you and she go to her friend's flat?'

'She wanted somewhere quiet to examine the printout, to make sure they weren't using an account in her name, but like you say, it's just numbers. Then a man came in the front door and we—'

85

'Went out the back.'

Nathan took a shuddering breath, he could hardly believe it, even now. 'And she drove off.'

'And you've no idea where?'

Nathan shook his head. 'I don't know where she lives. She wouldn't take money from Uncle Andy's charity. She loved him. You have to find her before this gang do, even if she doesn't care about me.' In his eagerness perhaps he had blurted the truth. Lisa didn't care about him. He knew the probable outcome from the outset and had hoped to be prepared, but it still stung.

The inspector stood. 'It's too late for Dean Henderson, but we'll find your mother, Nathan. The information on that flash drive will help put an end to a big international crime syndicate. Somewhere, at the heart of this web, is a very clever spider. A pity you got involved. The best thing now is to get your father to take you and your girlfriend home.'

'He's missing somewhere in the Abruzzo mountains in Italy. Mum's flown out to be near.'

'Excuse me, Inspector,' the sergeant interrupted. 'It was the boy's grandfather we spoke to. He's extremely concerned about him. The girl's father wasn't too pleased either.' The sergeant took Nathan to where Jessica was waiting. 'Now,' she said seriously. 'There's the matter of avoiding payment at the Regency.'

'We can pay,' Nathan and Jessica chorused.

DS Carlton smiled, softening her hard lines. 'I had a word with the manager; he's not taking the matter any further.'

Nathan and Jessica gave a joint sigh of relief. They looked at each other and grinned.

'Nice double act,' Detective Sergeant Carlton commented. She showed them to the exit. 'You'd better ring your grandfather. Tell him where you're staying tonight? And you, Miss, your father's worried. You *have* got somewhere to stay?'

Both youngsters shrugged.

'There's a hotel down the road,' DS Carlton pointed along the street. 'It's where we put up personnel seconded from other areas. Nothing posh but it's clean.'

In the pool of light outside the Police Station, Jessica said, 'So what do we do? I didn't expect to be away from home this long and haven't any money or clothes. I haven't even got my bank card.'

'My account has been topped up,' Nathan told her. 'And,' he sighed. 'I didn't want to do this but,' he pressed the speed dial for his grandfather. Whilst waiting for it to connect he said to Jessica, 'You'd better ring your dad.'

Peter answered almost immediately.

'Hello, Grandad.' Nathan heard Peter's intake of breath.

A few tense moments passed before Peter said, 'Are you alright, Nathan?'

'Yes.'

'And the girl, Jessica?'

'Yes, she's okay.'

After a few more anxious moments, Peter said, 'Where are you?'

'Still in Birmingham. We got caught up with—'

'I know what you're caught up with. I had a call from Birmingham Police, but for now, let's just get you home. I'll drive up—'

'No. I'd like to stay at least until tomorrow. There might be news of ... of Lisa.'

'For goodness' sake, Nathan.' Peter let go an exasperated sigh. 'Have you somewhere to stay?'

'Yes.'

'Is there enough money on your card?'

'Yes, thank you.' Another pause. 'Any news about Dad?'

'Nothing.'

Silence extended a while longer before Nathan said, 'Is anything else wrong?'

Another pause. 'Make sure you come home soon, son.'

'I will, Grandad. I will.'

Nathan slid his mobile into his pocket and turned around in time to hear Jessica saying into her phone, 'I *am* eighteen, Dad.'

A few minutes later Jessica slipped a hand through Nathan's arm. 'At least Dad didn't tell the police about the car.'

'I hate to be the cause of trouble between you and your dad.'

'He'll be okay. He's recruited one of the girls from the village to give him a hand in the pub.'

They walked to the Fern Guest House and rang the bell on the small reception desk. A woman, small and neat appeared and looked them up and down before saying, 'Did Sue Carlton send you? I shall have to ask for payment up front. As much as I'd like to help, we're not a charity. If you haven't any money there's a hostel round the corner.'

'We can pay,' Nathan said, extracting his card from an inside pocket. 'Two single rooms please.'

The woman gave him a questioning look before scrolling down a computer screen. 'One night? You can have two singles for £200 or a small twin for £125.'

Nathan handed over his card.

'We'll take the twin,' Jessica said, before the woman had time to key in the amount.

The receptionist handed over a receipt and keycard but before releasing her grasp on the documents, said, 'There's a café round the corner and a late night shop that sells anything else you might need.'

Nathan and Jessica exchanged a glance. Was their plight so obvious? Nathan felt compelled to say, 'We weren't expecting to—'

'I know, my lovely,' the receptionist interrupted. 'Second floor, to the right.'

*

An hour later Jessica emptied a carrier bag onto one of the narrow beds in the hotel room. She found some sheets of headed hotel notepaper and a pen in the top drawer of a chest and began making notes.

Nathan looked over her shoulder. 'What are you doing?'

'I'm working out how much I owe you.'

'You don't owe me anything.'

'There are these.' She indicated toothpaste, toothbrushes, pants and T-shirt. 'And half the cost of the room.' She looked up at Nathan. 'That's why I asked for the twin room. It's cheaper.'

'I didn't think … you meant anything else.'

Jessica grinned at him. 'If I *had* intended anything else, I'd have asked you to get a double.'

Nathan's ears burned. 'Yes, of course you would.'

Jessica's grin widened as she gathered the toiletries. 'I'll use the bathroom first.'

Nathan couldn't decide if he was relieved or disappointed. He sorted out his own clothes and threw them on the other bed before going to the window to close the curtains. The room faced an enclosed yard, and away from the glare of street lights, an almost full moon hung over the rooftops. 'I hope you're safe, Dad.'

CHAPTER 20

Ann looked from the hotel window to where the press gathered below in a pool of light. Were they anticipating a happy outcome or waiting for photos of bodies being recovered? She yanked the curtains closed and turned away. Perhaps she should go downstairs, spend a little time with other relatives of the missing, a bit of moral support all round.

Ann collected a cardigan and was about to head for the door when someone knocked. She opened the door to Owen Wyatt. He was in shirtsleeves, his tie was askew and he clutched the iPad Ann had seen him using earlier.

'Mrs Bryce, may I speak to you?'

'Of course. I was on my way down.'

'In private.'

'Yes,' she said tentatively. When he didn't move she stood back and allowed him to enter the room.

Owen set down the computer on a table near the window and, pulling up a chair, indicated Ann should join him.

She placed a second chair so she could see the screen and watched Owen scroll through a series of emails.

'Mrs Bryce, where were you when you received details of this publicity shoot?'

'Stephen had just finished filming and we were having a few days holiday near Lake Garda. He was supposed to have at least three weeks free before starting his next film. He had a holiday with Nathan planned, but this job was supposed to only take a couple of days.'

'And how were you contacted and by whom?'

'Stephen had an email from Lynn, his agent, saying George Deacon from Key7 Productions wanted Stephen to do a scene in WW2 costume, telling how the film would demonstrate how POWs tried to escape over the mountains. He's already done some research but was asked to meet with an assistant director, Max … err…'

'Max Cavendish.'

'Yes, that's it. He had a skeleton crew and said it would only take a couple of days, but our son was due home from school, and I needed to get things ready for his and Stephen's trip, so I went home.'

Owen rubbed his chin. 'It didn't strike you as unusual?'

With a wry smile, Ann said, 'Most things concerning Stephen's profession strike me as unusual. Stephen wasn't exactly pleased but he's always amenable, and I've had to accept that it's part of his job.'

'Do you still have the emails on your phone?'

'They were sent to Stephen's phone, but I can access them on your computer. I know the password.' After rattling a few keys, Ann sat back and said, 'You think something is wrong? I mean apart from Stephen and half the crew being missing.'

'I just need to check a few things.'

Ann hit the enter button. A list of emails filled the screen. She scrolled down to the message from Lynn and opened it, following suit with others.'

'They look genuine,' Owen said.

'But you don't think they are?'

It was Owen's turn to shrug. 'I'm waiting for some further information but—' he lowered his voice though there was no one to overhear. 'If I have a word with some of the crew who managed to get back, will you speak to the other relatives of those still missing? I mean, just chat, see if anything doesn't sit quite right?'

'I can do that.' As Owen was about to leave, she called, 'When do you think they'll start the rescue?'

'Angelo Russo has a team ready to start out at first light and a helicopter will cover an area higher up the mountain. The crew's mountain guide may try to take them further up and maybe over the top, or perhaps they've managed to get to one of the villages.'

'I hope so.' Ann took a calming breath and said, 'I'll come down and spend time with the others, if you think it will help.'

*

In the hotel lounge Ann joined Marion Quinn and Louise's parents.

'They're going out in the morning,' Marion told her enthusiastically. 'I've made sure the medical team has Ethan's medication.'

'Yes,' Ann wondered if Stephen had more than one day's medication with him. 'They have details of whatever is needed.'

'Ethan needn't have come on this job. George Deacon, a coordinator for Key7 Productions, emailed saying he'd been let down and asking if Ethan could help. He said the chap directing would appreciate Ethan's experience.'

'Did you speak to George Deacon?'

'He emailed to say everything was organised for Ethan to meet a director he'd brought in specially, Max Cavendish.'

Jim Austin added, 'Louise's friend Lisa persuaded her to join the crew. I told Louise it wasn't a good idea, all those years at college and a degree and now she's back where she started.'

'She was anxious to see your husband, Mrs Bryce,' Sarah Austin added.

'Call me Ann, please.'

Sarah glanced at her husband. 'Louise said she was there when your husband was taken ill and she felt responsible.'

'Why on earth should my daughter feel responsible?' Jim exclaimed.

Ann explained, 'Louise bought the cough medicine that reacted badly with Stephen's medication. But it wasn't her fault. If anyone is to blame it's Stephen; he should have known better than take anything until he'd checked it was safe. Though even the experts weren't certain that was the cause.'

'Whatever,' Louise's mother shrugged. 'She felt responsible and was anxious to apologise, and it was only supposed to be for a couple of days.'

'Yes,' Yash's partner, Adrian piped up. 'Two days' work, easy money, and now they're stuck up that damn mountain.'

Ann wandered away in search of Owen Wyatt. She found him at a corner table in the dining room again hunched over his computer and slipped onto the chair opposite.

'All arranged rather hurriedly by email,' Ann told him. 'And agreed as a favour to George Deacon at Key7. I remember now, Stephen said that if it was for anyone else he wouldn't have agreed.' She waited for his reply. 'Owen?'

Owen leaned back in the chair and ran a hand through his hair. 'I've been trying to get in touch with George.'

'And?'

'He's on some sort of expedition in Peru, has been out of communication for ten days. He only accepted my call when I said it was urgent. He didn't even know about the missing vehicle and crew.'

Ann took a moment to allow the information to penetrate. 'So,' she said slowly, 'someone else at Key7 arranged it – Max Cavendish?' 'The only Max Cavendish I can find is at present in New York, and he knows nothing about this.'

'How can that be?'

'I don't know who's behind this, Ann, or why, but it must be someone very clever.'

CHAPTER 21

Immediately after Stephen set the alarm on his phone he zonked into an alcohol-fuelled sleep. As often happened, a couple of hours later he was wide awake. The moon had shifted in its orbit, was no longer visible, instead stars filled the view through the high, square window. He thought of Ann and wanted to tell her he loved her, and of Nathan. How often during the last two days had he wished he'd said no and gone home? Why did Lisa persuade Louise to take the job?

Stephen remembered Lisa as being very persuasive – and how, after a drink, he was susceptible to her manipulative ways. That's how Nathan arrived on the scene. A cloud drifted across the stars. Nathan was the only good thing to come from that relationship. Stephen covered his eyes with an arm. He'd make it up to him and to Ann.

*

The alarm on Stephen's phone reached an impatient crescendo before it penetrated the heavy slumber he had slipped into just before dawn. In a daze he fumbled beneath the coarse blanket before locating his phone and silencing the persistent tone.

Faint dawn filled the room and it took him a moment to figure out where he was. Another sound filtered through the rough wood door adding to his confusion. Hammering and urgent voices.

Reality hit like a splash of cold water and he hastily pulled on khaki trousers and ripped open the door.

Yash, face like thunder, stood in the kitchen. 'They've gone.'

Stephen, a little dazed, said, 'What?'

'Cavendish and that ... Italian.'

'Arturo?'

'Si signor.' Francesco appeared from behind Yash. 'I set them on the path to the next village an hour ago.'

Louise burst into the kitchen. 'They've gone, and—'

'I know,' Stephen cut in. 'And—' he gestured to the table where they had left the satellite phone. 'So has the phone.'

Louise, in a fluster said. 'But ... it's Ethan.'

*

93

Stephen stood inside the door of the house across the road where Cavendish, Arturo and Ethan were billeted, Yash and Louise at his shoulder.

'I can't wake him,' Louise whispered.

Stephen went over to the bed set against the wall. A little warmth still emanated from the stove in the corner. He stretched out a hand – hesitated – grasped and lifted the bed cover. 'Ethan?'

Ethan lay on his back, eyes open, lifeless.

Stephen touched the back of his hand to the pale, cool cheek of the veteran cameraman.

*

A breakfast of cold meat, cheese and bread lay almost untouched on the table in the house where Stephen had spent the night. He, Louise and Yash gazed at the basic fare with no appetite. Francesco, Nonna and Nonno hovered quietly in the kitchen before melting away to another part of the house.

Louise topped up mugs from a coffee pot kept warm on the stove.

'It must have been his heart,' Yash offered. 'He told us he had a heart condition.' He sipped at the strong brew. 'Didn't he say,' he insisted, 'that he had a heart condition?'

'Yes,' Louise snapped. 'But what are we going to do?' She turned to Stephen, 'What shall we do?'

Her insistent plea penetrated Stephen's thoughts. He set his coffee mug aside and, with it, his indecision. 'Wait here,' he told them. 'There's something I need to check.'

*

Stephen hesitated outside the door of the house where Cavendish and Arturo had slept, the only occupant now Ethan Quinn's lifeless body. He took a moment to steel his nerve. The first to concede he was more squeamish than the average man, this was no time to hesitate.

Inside, his attention went to the narrow bed against the wall. He pulled down the blanket to uncover Ethan's body which lay straight, arms by his side.

At a noise from behind, he swung around. 'God, Louise.' He ran a hand through his hair.

Louise glanced at the mound on the bed before aiming a questioning frown at Stephen, who said, 'You notice the patches on his face?'

94

'They look like broken veins.'

Stephen pulled up the blanket 'I don't believe Ethan had a heart attack. Help me look for Ethan's phone, or anything that might give a clue to what's going on, and then—' he fixed her with a look his father would have been proud of, 'you can tell me why Lisa really sent you here.'

Louise looked offended but then strode across the room and began rifling through Ethan's canvas shoulder bag which lay on a chair.

The cameraman had obviously emptied his pockets before getting into bed. A couple of foil strips, empty of tables, beta blockers and an anticoagulant; a handful of coins and his wallet lay on a stool by the bed. The wallet contained a photo of a lady Stephen presumed to be Ethan's wife, a couple of bank cards, some receipts and around fifty euros. Averting his gaze from the lifeless mound under the sheet, Stephen looked around the bed, eventually getting on hands and knees and reaching far beneath to retrieve a mobile phone.

As he stood, Louise said, 'There's the handheld camera he always carried, some lens wipes and a light meter. Nothing you wouldn't expect a cameraman to carry.'

Stephen slipped the phone he had retrieved from under the bed into a pocket. 'Let's have a look upstairs.'

A room off a narrow landing contained two beds, their covers rumpled. A table with a ewer and bowl stood against a wall. Stephen said, 'Francesco says this place hasn't been used for years. Nonna cleaned it specially. Most of the young people have moved further down the mountain or into the town.'

'No wonder,' Louise commented. 'No running water or proper lavatory. And there's nothing here to tell us what happened.' Louise's foot scraped something on the floor and she stooped to pick it up. 'Except, perhaps, this.'

*

Across the road at the house where Stephen had slept, he, Louise and Yash gathered around the kitchen table. On a bench along the back wall, Nonna chopped meat, mutton, Stephen guessed, on a thick board. He heard the splash as she added it to the cooking pot and smelled onions when she began preparing vegetables.

'Tell me, Louise,' Stephen began. 'Why was Lisa so eager for you to be on this jaunt?'

'It was my fault you almost died. I had to say how sorry I am.'

95

'I'm sure you are but that was nine years ago. Why now?'

She didn't reply and Stephen went on, 'Lisa is very good at manipulating an idea she's planted. What did she want you to do?'

Louise visibly shrank. 'She made me feel as if I should have known the cough medicine didn't mix with the medication you were on.'

'Louise, *I* didn't know, so how could you?' He leaned forward. 'What did Lisa ask you to do? You began to tell me about the Drama in Schools project, Andy Roberts' charity. You said something was wrong.'

'Lisa told me she believed something was wrong and she wanted me to warn you.'

'That she suspects someone is using the charity, and—'

'And that it might get you into trouble.'

'I've already said, I have nothing to do with the running of the charity. It's run by—'

'Yes, I know,' Louise almost shouted. 'It's run by trustees; and Lisa's boyfriend, Dean Henderson, is a trustee, so she should know.'

Yash interrupted, 'Okay, so this Dean Henderson might be defrauding your charity. What has it to do with us, this mini production for so-called publicity for a film that's yet to be made?'

Stephen placed Ethan's phone on the table. 'Can we get into the emails?'

Yash reached across, snatched up the phone and switched it on. '15% battery life. I know his password. His wife's name is Marian.' The screen pinged back to another request for the passcode. He tried again, spelling it out as he touched the screen.

'Try, o.n.' Stephen suggested. 'M.a.r.i.o.n.'

'Yes, here we go. Now, emails.' Yash scrolled back. 'A couple from George Deacon, Key7 Productions. Similar to mine – saying all preliminaries are complete, but—' Yash scowled. 'It says, the contracted cameraman has pulled out … count it as a personal favour … your expertise would be greatly appreciated by director Max Cavendish.'

Stephen sighed. 'My message asked if I'd do a favour for George with a couple of pieces to camera in costume to give a taste of what's expected. He said he'd like Max Cavendish to direct and all arrangements were in place.'

'Everyone knows George Deacon,' Yash confirmed. 'But I'd never heard of Max Cavendish until a few days ago.'

Stephen shrugged. 'I assumed George wanted to give him a break.'

96

'That explains how we were recruited,' Yash said. 'George Deacon. He's well respected, that's why we accepted.'

'Or,' Stephen said, 'someone used his name because they were fairly sure we wouldn't refuse. But you, Louise, weren't invited to join this expedition – Lisa persuaded you.'

Louise shrugged in bewilderment.

'To me,' Yash said, 'that means Lisa Brookes knows what this is about.'

CHAPTER 22

Nathan studied the night sky a while longer before he yanked the curtains closed. He hit a switch which operated bedside lamps either side the two single beds, sat on a hard chair and glanced through a *What's on in Birmingham* magazine. He heard Jessica emerge from the bathroom, bedclothes rustled, and the lamp beside her bed click off, plunging the room into half-light. Further rustling ceased and, sure she had settled, Nathan threw down the magazine and picked up his bag of toiletries. His legs brushed the end of the bed on his way to the bathroom and he resisted the urge to raise his eyes to the occupant.

A few minutes later, clad in T-shirt and underpants, Nathan left the bathroom and skirted Jessica's bed. He tossed jeans and sweatshirt onto a chair and slipped under the covers of the adjacent narrow bed. He lay still for a moment before reaching for the lamp switch. 'Goodnight.' He closed his eyes and tried to pretend Jessica was not lying less than half a metre away.

'Nathan?'

'What?'

'What shall we do tomorrow?'

'We should go home.'

'What about your mum?'

'Mum?' He sat up sharply.'

'I mean your mother, Lisa.'

'Oh.' Nathan relaxed and lay back on the pillow. 'Lisa,' he mused.

Jessica raised herself on an elbow. 'You think she's in danger.' It wasn't a question and Nathan didn't answer.

'And,' Jessica went on, 'I don't think you're planning to go home tomorrow.'

No good at the art of deception, Nathan grimaced, before saying, 'We can get a taxi to the service station where we left your dad's car.' Remembering her novice status as a driver, he added, 'Will you be okay driving home?'

'Not on my own.'

Even in the darkness, Nathan could sense her scowl.

After a moment, she said, 'You're not sending me home to face the music on my own.'

Nathan rolled onto his side, to face her. Her shape, a dark shadow. 'The people who have misused the charity know Lisa has details on a flash drive.'

'Then why doesn't she hand it over to the police?'

'She's frightened. And ...'

'What?'

'She believes the information on that stick will show that she's been taking money too. Or at least she's been paid for helping her boyfriend.'

'If she has, then ... perhaps you should go home—'

'And forget her?'

'There's nothing you can do, Nathan. You don't know where she is. Let's go home.'

Nathan let his arm dangle over the side of the bed and after a moment felt Jessica's warm hand in his.

*

Nathan woke at first light. A muffled noise followed by the sound of rushing water as the lavatory flushed drew his attention to the bathroom. A few minutes later Jessica appeared dressed in jeans and a jumper. Her hair was wet and, after stuffing yesterday's underwear into a carrier bag, she found a hairdryer in the top drawer of a chest.

Nathan collected clean pants and T-shirt and gave Jessica an embarrassed smile as he squeezed past her to get to the bathroom.

By the time Nathan re-emerged Jessica had dried and fluffed her mid-length dark hair, put on a little make-up and was sitting on the bed, her coat and carrier bag beside her. 'You're ready to go.'

She grinned at him. 'Can we have breakfast first?'

'Sure,' Nathan told her. 'Then we'll get a taxi to the service station, or all the way home, if you like. I can pay for someone to pick up your car.'

'You're a liar, Nathan Bryce.'

'What? I have enough money,' he assured her.

'You've no intention of coming home with me. You've got some plan to find your mother.'

Nathan conjured up an innocent expression but knew he had blushed.

99

'Get dressed,' she told him. 'Then take me for breakfast and tell me what you have in mind. And for the record, I'm perfectly capable of driving home alone, I'd just rather not.'

*

In the twenty-four hour café along the road, Nathan and Jessica sat each side of a scrubbed wooden table.

'This is good.' Nathan cut a piece of toast and loaded it with scrambled egg.

'You missed a proper breakfast at the pub,' Jessica said.

Nathan swallowed. 'I'm sorry about that. Can I come again when all this is over?'

It was said light-heartedly and she laughed, but suddenly both were serious.

'What are you going to do, Nathan?'

He pushed his plate away and, from the carrier bag propped against the table, pulled out the *What's On* magazine he'd taken from the hotel and placed it open on the table.

Jessica offered a quizzical look.

Nathan tapped the page. 'The FitzGilbert rubies are on display at this museum in Birmingham.

Little frown lines between Jessica's brows deepened.

'You wouldn't remember … well, I don't remember much but these—' Nathan again indicated the picture of the jewellery, 'belonged to my mum and dad. They sold them to the museum and used the money to set up the Drama in Schools Charity in Andy's name.'

'They're beautiful.'

'They're worth far more than the museum paid, but Mum and Dad said … well, Mum said that she'd never wear them again.'

'Why? Did your dad buy them for her?'

'No.' Nathan laughed. He was suddenly serious. 'Dad didn't buy them. My great-grandfather won them from a titled family. My dad tried to return them, but Lady FitzGilbert gave them to him and Mum as a wedding present.'

'Lady. Ooh. Posh. But that was a bit unkind, to sell them when they were a wedding present.'

'A lot happened before they decided to sell. I'm not sure of everything, except that Uncle Andy was killed and he enjoyed taking drama into schools.'

'And that's what the charity does?'

100

'Yeah,' Nathan said sadly.

Jessica put a hand on Nathan's arm. 'How does this help you find Lisa?'

Nathan folded the magazine and slipped it into the bag. He leaned across the table and in a harsh whisper, said, 'This jewellery is like a magnet.'

CHAPTER 23

In the Italian stone-built village house, Stephen rested his elbows on the table.

Yash stood. 'Ethan had a heart attack; there's nothing we can do for him.'

Stephen looked at Louise, who averted her gaze. 'I'm not sure,' she said. 'It didn't look right. You noticed, didn't you, Stephen? The way he was lying and the covers unruffled as if they had been straightened. Even the pillow didn't look as if it had been slept on.'

Stephen said, 'Let's say we have doubts. But I guess we can be certain Cavendish took the satellite phone, and I confess that for the first couple of hours last night anyone could have come in here, I wouldn't have known. Louise found this—'

Yash picked the tiny screw from the palm of Stephen's hand. 'Looks like it's from the plate that holds the battery in. I told you the solar panel would put some charge in it.'

'Do you think they've called the rescue services?' Louise asked.

Sceptical looks from the two men answered her question.

Her shoulders slumped for a moment before she lifted her chin and said, 'Then we'd better get ready for a hike down the mountain. Is there someone in the village who will guide us?'

Stephen got to his feet. 'I'll ask Francesco.'

'Si, signor.' The boy was already hovering at the door. 'I will take you.'

*

Stephen tightened the laces of his army boots and slipped on his padded anorak which he judged would be sufficient now, at lower altitude and more moderate temperatures. He was about to leave the khaki blouse over a chair in the kitchen but Nonna swept it into her arms. Stephen looked to Francesco for translation of her words.

'She wishes to keep the jacket.'

'That's fine. She's very welcome.'

'And,' Francesco went on, 'she has prepared food for us.' He stuffed a couple of loaves wrapped in muslin into a saggy canvas rucksack, together with cheese, cold meat and a bottle of wine. 'The wine is watered, signor. We must cross a stream a few kilometres away, the water is usually clear and good to drink but just in case—' He crossed to the sink, operated the pump and filled a leather flask.

'I'll carry that,' Stephen offered. He slipped the leather strap over his head and shoulder so the flask rested comfortably on his hip.

Nonna spoke, her words accompanied with an assortment of gestures and, again, Francesco translated. 'Nonna and the other women of the village will take care of your friend. They will take him to the old church, light candles, say prayers.'

Francesco had spoken on a subject Stephen found difficult to address, and as if reading his mind, the boy said, 'It is cold in the crypt, signor. Your friend will be okay until you can make arrangements.'

Stephen said, 'Thank you, Francesco,' before turning to Nonna. He stooped to kiss her softly wrinkled cheek. 'Thank you, Nonna. Grazie.'

Nonna responded by gripping his face between calloused hands and kissing him soundly on both cheeks.

Outside, Stephen and Francesco met Yash and Louise. Yash, with a small knapsack; Louise, a leather flask similar to the one Stephen carried.

'How long will it take to get to the next village?' Yash asked.

'At least two days,' said Francesco. 'If we can cross the stream. But with the weather recently—' he shrugged. 'Sometimes rain and melting snow from above ... we may have to go the long way round.'

Warm sunshine on their backs encouraged a smart pace along the narrow path worn from the village down the mountain, single file not conducive to conversation.   Mid-morning, the wind turned cool and ever-thickening clouds drifted from the peaks behind the hikers. The ground became uneven, the group stepping from rock to rock, awkward shapes throwing them easily off balance, with angular gaps between boulders waiting to twist an ankle or trap a foot. A background roar became deafening and, in the lead, Francesco halted. He pointed ahead and raised his voice above the sound of crashing water. 'Normally, we ford just here.'

The four of them gazed at the torrent.

Stephen leaned towards Francesco. 'Where can we cross?'

'We need to go upstream. Take care, fresh boulders have been washed down.'

103

As if Francesco's words were a signal, there was a cry from behind. Stephen swung around. Yash lay at an awkward angle, his leg, from the knee downward, wedged between the rocks.

Stephen took a couple of long strides back over the boulders.

Yash issued a string of expletives. 'Don't touch me,' the young electrician instructed. 'Give me a minute. My boot is stuck in a crevice.'

Louise caught up, she, Stephen and Francesco exchanging anxious glances. Stephen sat on the rocks and, having given Yash time to catch his breath, reached down and curled his fingers around the toe of the boot.

Obviously understanding Stephen's intention, Yash braced – yelled, 'Stop!'

Stephen immediately sat back. 'Okay, Yash, relax.'

'Relax?'

'Let me try,' Louise suggested. 'My hands are smaller.' Her efforts met with the same response. She straightened. 'Jeez, Yash, how did you manage to get jammed in there?'

'It was easy. One second I'm bounding along, then, wham, I've got my foot in a hole. Fuck me—' Yash writhed in pain. 'This is something a girl would do.'

Stephen saw Louise bristle.

She snapped, 'Don't feel obliged to accept help from a girl.'

Stephen ignored the wordplay and said to her, 'Can you get your fingers down there to untie the laces?'

Louise lowered her voice, at once serious. 'If we get his boot off, his ankle is going to swell, it may well be broken.'

Equally softly, Stephen said, 'Well, we can't leave him here. Have we got anything we can bind it with?'

Francesco's shadow fell over them. He unwound the scarf looped loosely round his neck and offered it to them.

Louise shrugged. 'So we get him out and bind his ankle. I doubt he'll be able to walk even if we get his boot back on.'

'Let's get him free, first,' Stephen said, 'then assess the situation.'

'Who put you in charge?' Louise snapped.

Stephen suppressed a sigh. He'd never come across such a contrary woman. Well, yes, he had, and was tempted to ask if she'd been taking lessons from Lisa. After a moment, he added, 'Then *you* make the decisions.'

'Great,' she retorted. 'Why should I take responsibility?'

Patience wearing thin, he corrected, '*We*—' his glance also encompassed Yash and Francesco, 'will make a decision.'

'Hey,' Yash called. 'Remember me?'

'Okay, Louise,' Stephen said. 'Untie the laces.' Stephen stood behind Yash and hooked his hands under the electrician's arms and round his chest. To Yash he said, 'When Louise gives the word try to hitch backwards; I'll help.'

*

Stephen, Louise and Francesco stood in the shelter of an overhanging rock. Stephen glanced at Yash who lay propped on an elbow, his face a mask of pain. His ankle, bound with Francesco's scarf, had already swelled to twice its normal size, and it was clear his knee had twisted when he fell.

'I can't walk,' Yash admitted.

'I will go back to the village,' Francesco offered. 'The men are no longer young but they will make a stretcher.'

Stephen said, 'We can't assume Cavendish or Arturo will send help. We're miles away from the original location and any rescue could take days.'

'One of us needs to go on,' Louise suggested, 'and we need Francesco to show the way.' She gave a resigned grin. 'I guess you've taken the last of your medication so you need to get down the mountain more urgently.'

Stephen said, 'Don't let that influence you. I'm sure a couple of days won't make much difference.'

'We can make Yash comfortable here,' Louise insisted. 'I'll go back to the village. I can get back with help before nightfall. You and Francesco carry on down the mountain. I don't want to be responsible for you being ill again.'

Francesco broke out the bread and cheese from his rucksack and handed it around. 'The path back to my village is easy to follow. I will write a note for my grandfather. I'll collect wood for a fire; it will be cold later.'

*

Having ensured Yash had some protection from the elements beneath the overhanging rock, Stephen watched Louise start on her way back. 'She should be at the village in a few hours.'

105

Francesco set out kindling and a few dry twigs he had found. 'There is very little wood for burning to be found here, but these branches from those bushes should keep a fire going for a while.' He stacked them within reach of Yash before shaking a box of matches at the injured man. 'Light it when you begin to feel cold, but not too soon, eh.'

Stephen put a hand on Yash's shoulder. 'We'll get someone back for you and Louise as quickly as possible.'

Yash grabbed his arm. 'Watch out if you run into that bastard Cavendish ... he's dangerous.'

Stephen thought of Ethan and said, 'Yes, I know.'

CHAPTER 24

Ann sat on the bed in her hotel room, head in her hands. 'Oh, Stephen, where are you?' On a deep sigh she lay back and put her feet on the bed. Someone very clever, Owen had said. 'Clever,' Ann murmured. *Why should some computer whizz-kid want to get all those people together?* Denied sleep, she stood, dressed and slipped a cardigan around her shoulders. Eager to escape a multitude of raging thoughts, she dropped her key card and phone in her bag and took the stairs to the ground floor. From the lobby she could see a few late-night drinkers lingering at the bar but was drawn to the front entrance. A walk in the night air might clear her head.

'Can't you sleep either?'

'Hello Owen. Too much happening,' Ann explained. 'I mean *as well* as Stephen. Our son is on a mission to find his birth mother. He knows who she is – everyone knows who she is, it's public knowledge, but they lost touch. He's seventeen and I'm trying to convince myself he's old enough to look after himself.'

Looking less formal than when addressing the relatives of the missing earlier, Owen leaned on a railing outside the hotel and smiled. 'Some seventeen year olds are older than others, if you get my drift.'

'He's a sensible lad, but I can't help but worry. And now I can't get in touch with Stephen's father.'

Owen glanced skyward. 'The weather is clearing and I've had confirmation a helicopter will fly over the area of the landslide at first light. They'll decide which way is safe for the rescue party to take and then widen the aerial search. I've sent the information to all concerned parties.'

'Oh.' Ann was prompted to rummage in her bag. Her phone showed two unread messages. One from Owen and one from Peter. She pulled her cardigan close around her, the night cooler than she expected. 'I'll read your message in my room.' She made to leave but turned back. 'When I know Stephen and the others are safe, we'll track down the mad bastard who set this up.'

In her room Ann scanned the message from Owen before reading Peter's message. A man of few words, it read simply, 'Any news?'

She gave a brief rundown of the next day's proposed events in her reply, adding, 'Have you heard any more from Nathan?' And finishing, 'You okay?'

It was too late to expect a response, so Ann settled in bed and tried to sleep.

*

Ann woke before dawn, more anxious now rescue plans were underway. It had seemed unreal before, but now ... She dressed, went downstairs and joined other relatives for breakfast. She found an unoccupied table in an alcove, ordered coffee and stirred it mechanically. Before long, Owen called them for an update.

*

'The helicopter sent back pictures of the area around the landslide,' Ann reported to Peter; an image of the scar in the landscape burned into her brain. 'The chalet they were using looks hardly damaged, but it's now about three miles further down the mountain. The good news is the road above is still intact, so if they weren't caught in the slide they could have reversed out of danger. There's no sign of the Land Rover, but as there's no shelter from the storm that was raging that night, the rescue team are working on the theory they moved higher up the mountain. Their guide, Arturo, would know of any huts, what we would call a bothy, for use by hikers and climbers, so they're widening the search.'

Ann's mobile emitted only an echoing silence.

'That's good news, isn't it? Can you hear me, Peter?'

'Yes, Ann. That's good news. Keep me informed.'

'Of course I will. Have you heard from Nathan?'

'Not since yesterday, so I assume he's making his way back. He knows he can call if he needs to be picked up.'

'Right.' Ann felt somehow deflated and suspected something else was worrying Peter. 'Is everything okay at home?'

'Kathy's staying for a few days. I think that's the other phone. I'll call you when Nathan's back. You take care.'

'Yes ...'

Peter hung up.

Still puzzled, Ann was relieved Peter hadn't asked about the satellite phone. That was the bad news. If Stephen and the others had escaped the landslide, why hadn't they used the phone? It would be so easy to home in on a signal.

*

108

'There could be any number of reasons,' Owen suggested after he had picked up the worrying point of the phone in the morning briefing. 'It could have been damaged. Maybe the battery ran down and with the weather it wouldn't recharge. Or the solar panel was damaged.'

After the meeting Owen ushered Ann aside. 'There is every possibility that the phone was damaged, but there is no sign of the Land Rover and it's equally likely that …'

'That the Land Rover was swept away in the landslide,' Ann finished.

Worry lines deepened around Owen's eyes and mouth. 'I'm sure you realise I have a delicate line to walk between being realistic and giving false hope.'

'I understand,' Ann said, before walking away. She joined the other relatives and with a smile said, 'I'm sure when the search is widened the helicopter will spot the Land Rover.'

They all nodded uncertainly.

CHAPTER 25

Nathan slung the rucksack containing their scant clothes and toiletries over his shoulder. 'We'll get a cab,' he told Jessica. 'I'll pay on my card. I'm done with trying to prove I can pay my own way.'

Jessica clutched his hand, almost dragged him along to a nearby taxi rank.

Nathan opened the rear door of the first vehicle and stood back. 'This is your last chance to say no. If you want to go home, I'll find an ATM and give you enough money to get back to your car. Or I can ring my grandad, and he'll ask someone to collect you.'

'Are you trying to get rid of me?'

'I've no idea what I'm getting into and I don't want you to get hurt.'

'I'd be more hurt if you tried to send me home,' her reply was indignant.

Nathan grinned and inclined his head.

Jessica got into the cab and slid across the back seat.

'The Jewellery Quarter, please,' Nathan told the driver. 'We'd like to go to the museum.'

The taxi driver glanced at them in the rear view mirror. 'Looking for an engagement ring?'

'No,' Jessica snapped but then shot a sideways glance at Nathan and giggled.

Nathan looked embarrassed and said, 'We just want to look.'

The driver grinned and pulled out into the road. After fifteen minutes negotiating city traffic he pulled up amid nineteenth-century red-brick industrial buildings. 'The museum is around the corner.'

Nathan said, 'Thank you,' and paid with his card.

He and Jessica walked past arched cream-coloured stone-mullioned windows, frames painted green, to an arched doorway, the door also green.

They hesitated in the entrance, Jessica eventually saying, 'What now?'

'Would you like to do a tour of the workshops?'

She shrugged. 'Why not?'

*

They emerged from the workshops with other tourists, continued into the shop and browsed the jewellery displayed in glass cabinets.

'What skill,' Jessica commented. 'They must still work the same way they did hundreds of years ago.' She gave Nathan a nudge.

'Yes.' Nathan paid attention. 'It was fascinating watching that man work.' He pulled her towards what had caught his attention. In an alcove was a display case where the glass was obviously thicker and designed with extra safety in mind. A small lingering crowd moved on. The view of the plaque, *FitzGilbert Rubies*, and display cabinet now unrestricted, he heard Jessica gasp.

'I remember Mum wearing them,' he told her. 'Just once. I was six or seven I suppose. When she moved they shot fire in all directions.'

'They're certainly impressive.'

Nathan looked around. He recognised the man they'd seen at a bench in the workshop. The man's sparse grey hair, ruffled, his spectacles pushed up onto his forehead.

'They—' the man nodded to the jewellery, 'were reassembled here, in Birmingham. Not this workshop,' he pointed out. 'We work mainly in silver.'

'Reassembled?' Nathan queried.

'Items were dismantled and smuggled out of Russia in the seventeenth century. We believe originally there were just a necklace and earrings. There was probably another row of stones on the foundation of the necklace. When the rubies and diamonds were gathered together in this country with a redesigned setting, the extra rubies were made into a bracelet, ring and brooch.'

'How did the FitzGilberts get them?' Nathan asked.

'Ah.' The man raised an eyebrow. 'That remains a mystery. But Lady Matilda FitzGilbert gave them as a wedding gift to Stephen Bryce.' The man looked at Nathan. 'You know, the actor? He and his wife let the museum have them for a nominal sum, the money to be used for charity, I believe.'

Nathan merely said, 'Yes.' He thought it best not to mention how his great-grandfather had acquired the jewellery from Nigel FitzGilbert, a fellow officer during the Second World War, in payment of a gambling debt, nor the rubies' troubled history since that time.

The silversmith nodded, smiled and turned to converse with a new group of tourists.

Nathan gazed around the shop, searching. Failing to find what he sought, he touched Jessica's elbow. 'Coffee and a snack?'

They settled at a table near the window in the museum café and opened a packet of sandwiches.

'You're always hungry,' Jessica said.

'That's what Mum says,' he grinned over the sandwich. A newspaper had been left on the table by a previous customer and he noticed an article. Feeling as if ripped in two, he laid down the tuna sandwich.

Jessica followed his line of vision. 'What does it say?'

Nathan read, 'There's no further news of Stephen Bryce and the missing film crew, but the search area is being widened.'

Jessica pulled the newspaper towards her and looked at the reproduced aerial shots.

Nathan stirred a latte at his elbow. 'I should be with Mum. Or at least at home with Grandad so she doesn't have to worry about me.'

Jessica placed a hand over his. 'We can go home if you like. Leave the police to sort out your moth— Lisa.'

Nathan clamped his jaw and fixed his gaze on the table. 'Yeah.' When sure he was in control, he repeated, 'Yes, let's go home.' He gathered the rucksack from under the table and they headed for the exit.

The fire of the FitzGilbert rubies working their magic, Nathan and Jessica halting before the fortified display cabinet for a last look.

'I knew you wouldn't be able to resist.'

Nathan whirled, knocking into Jessica with the rucksack. He took a moment to take in the hair, scraped back, and lack of make-up: Lisa. He inclined his head towards the ruby necklace, earrings, bracelet, ring and brooch. 'You too.'

Lisa pulled him towards the exit. At the door Nathan stopped, looked back. Jessica, scowling, hands on hips, still stood by the display case.

Nathan shook off Lisa's hand and strode back to Jessica. 'Coming?'

*

Outside the museum, Jessica slipped a hand through Nathan's arm. 'Where is she?'

Nathan looked up and down the street.

'She looked a mess,' Jessica said disparagingly.

Nathan fought off a desire to defend his mother and pointed further along the road where an old Vauxhall Astra was parked. 'Over there.'

They jogged to the vehicle. Nathan tossed the rucksack onto the back seat and held the door for Jessica, before slipping into the front seat beside Lisa.

Lisa scowled at Jessica in the rearview mirror and Nathan suspected she was about to object to her being there, but she rammed the car into gear and drove off.

'Where are we going?' Nathan asked. 'Was the dead man in the hotel Dean Henderson?'

Lisa ignored him but he persisted. 'The police are looking for you. I showed them the printout but they still need the memory stick.'

She continued to ignore him and concentrated on driving.

'Lisa, there are some really bad people who also want the information on the stick, or at least they don't want the police to get it.'

Lisa stamped on the brake and skidded to a halt. 'I know,' she yelled in his face.

Nathan pulled back.

The engine raced and the car shot out into traffic amid honking from vehicles behind.

Nathan heard Jessica's intake of breath and the pair remained silent whilst Lisa negotiated busy streets, eventually pulling round the back of a row of shops.

Lisa's outburst had shocked Nathan more than he cared to admit, his voice scarcely more than a whisper when he asked, 'Why have you brought us back to the charity office?'

Now more composed, Lisa said, 'Because the police are watching my place and Louise's flat, but I don't think they are here. Come inside.'

Nathan and Jessica meekly followed Lisa into the office by the metal stairs she and Nathan had taken before. Ellie, the office girl, had locked up and gone home as she had been bidden.

'The police must know about this place,' Nathan pointed out.

Lisa pulled off the hoodie she was wearing over a T-shirt and threw it on a chair before teasing out the band holding back her hair. She shook her head letting thick dark locks fluff around her face. 'This is a secondary office. No doubt they'll find it eventually, but right now I need to "put myself together",' she told the pair of youngsters. 'So while I do,

113

I'd like you to see what else is on this.' She pulled a flash drive from her jeans pocket and tossed it to Nathan.

Nathan caught the stick and, after watching his mother disappear into a back room, turned to face Jessica who had set the rucksack on the floor and was standing arms folded. Nathan shrugged an apology before settling at the desk. He fired up the computer, inserted the memory stick into the USB socket and after a moment rattled a few keys. Jessica came to stand behind him and he felt her warm breath on his neck. He had an urge to twist round and kiss her, and in other circumstances would have done so, but instead he said, 'There's nothing on this apart from the figures I already printed off.'

Lisa reappeared still wearing the hip hugging jeans but with a scoop-necked, silky top, her make-up immaculate. A handsome woman, with a pinched look around her mouth that spoilt her attraction. She also stood behind Nathan, and as if staking possession of her son, edged Jessica away. She looked over his shoulder. 'There should be more, a hidden or encrypted file.'

A few more keystrokes and Nathan said, 'There may be something else, but I can't get into it.'

'Of course you can,' Lisa snapped. 'Teenagers know all about computers.'

Nathan twisted around to look at Jessica who merely shrugged. He turned back to the screen. 'I know the basics but this is a professional set-up. I imagine my cousin Matthew could do it, or Mr Thompson, our IT tutor.'

'Well, we haven't got your IT tutor so please have another go.'

Nathan turned back to the screen and tried some other moves.

Lisa moved to the window, separated a couple of slats in a Venetian blind and peered through. 'Come on, Nathan, if there's information on there that could implicate me or your father perhaps it can be deleted.'

'How can it implicate my father?'

Again behind him, Lisa leaned forward and close to his ear, hissed, 'Because there are people who are obviously brighter than you, and probably far cleverer than your IT teacher or Matthew.' She returned to the window and looked out again. 'Matthew is Stephen's brother's boy isn't he?' she mused. 'Didn't they have a girl who's not quite right?'

'Lizzie was deprived of oxygen when she was born,' Nathan pointed out. 'She's a lovely girl.'

114

'Very well, Nathan, don't get shirty.' She let the slats in the blind flip back into shape. 'Close the programme, shut down the computer and give me the flash drive. If you can't crack the encryption you're not much use.'

Nathan clamped his jaw and did as he was bid before standing to face his mother. 'In that case I'll take this—' he held up the flash drive 'to the police.'

'No, Nathan, you can't do that.' Lisa made a grab for the stick.

He moved out of her reach.

'I'll be in trouble,' Lisa declared. 'Think, Nathan, your dad will be in trouble. We could go to prison.'

'Whatever is going on has nothing to do with my dad.' Nathan held out a hand to Jessica. 'Let's go.'

Jessica scooped up the rucksack, crossed the office and with Nathan headed towards the door.

A dark shape showed behind the frosted glass. The door flew open and slammed against the wall. Two men burst in, their bulk filling the room.

One man grabbed Lisa and held her arms. Jessica, also caught, grappled with the other man and barrelled into Nathan who crashed against a couple of filing cabinets. Nathan picked up a small metal statuette, an award presented to Andy and now kept at the charity's office. As Jessica struggled the man's back turned and Nathan caught him a blow on the side of the head with the trophy, fetching the man to his knees and taking Jessica with him.

The man groaned but maintained his grip on Jessica.

Nathan positioned himself for another blow. 'Let her go.'

The man across the room tightened his grip on Lisa. 'Put that down, son, or I'll break her arm.' Another tweak and Lisa shrieked.

Nathan took a step back.

'Put it down,' the man ordered. He adjusted his grip, an arm around Lisa's throat. 'Or I could as easily break her neck.'

Nathan laid the statuette on the desk and showed his empty hand.

The man on the floor regained his feet and, whilst maintaining a grip on Jessica with one hand, touched the other to broken skin on his scalp. He briefly examined blood from the wound before putting his weight behind a swinging backhander.

Stars burst behind Nathan's eyes. He crashed against the filing cabinets and slid to the floor amid swirling multi-coloured stars.

115

CHAPTER 26

Ann stood on the steps of the hotel, spring sunshine, pleasantly warm on her face. It was a relief to be away from an atmosphere of tension and worry.

Someone stood by her side and she turned eagerly, her 'Oh, Owen,' flat with disappointment. Foolish to expect Stephen to suddenly appear. 'A few days ago, Stephen and I were wandering alleyways, enjoying a holiday. Now I don't know if I'll see him again.'

Owen looked embarrassed. 'You were doing a good job keeping up their spirits.' He inclined his head to the others inside. 'I'm sorry if I put a damper on things. I was just trying to be realistic.' They walked around the corner to a small piazza, seats set around the edge.

Ann said. 'I didn't mean to be rude earlier. I'm sure you're doing your best.'

'I'm in an awkward position. Key7 Productions should send an expert PR person, but it's looking as if they aren't directly involved.'

'You mean someone is impersonating one of their representatives.'

'Yes. And there's another thing.'

'What other thing?' Ann asked, close to losing patience.

'A couple of police officers from the UK are arriving this afternoon.'

'I hope they're experts in cybercrime.' Ann ran her hands through her hair. 'I'm so tired.'

Owen's phone pinged, and after glancing at it, he said, 'News coming in. I'd better get back.'

Immediately alert, Ann hurried after, pausing momentarily as her own phone jingled. She greeted Stephen's agent. 'Hello, Lynn.'

'Ann, I've had a call from the police.'

'Yes, Owen Wyatt has just told me. I'm on my way to the hotel now, there may be some news.'

'Good news, I hope. I was about to suggest we update our statement, Ann, but—'

'I'll get back to you, Lynn, as soon as I can.' At the hotel entrance Ann took a breath and made an effort to appear calm and unruffled.

Press photographers gathered in the foyer turned to see who had entered; Ann, unsurprised when they returned their attention to Owen who began to address them. Grateful that she had successfully maintained a low profile throughout Stephen's career, she slipped into the dining room where other relatives of the missing were gathered.

Marion Quinn slipped a hand through her arm. 'Do you think they've found them?'

Ann merely patted Marion's hand and summoned a reassuring smile. She heard in the background Owen telling the press that whatever the news, the families of the missing would be the first to know.

'Come on,' she told Marion, 'let's get a seat.' They joined Louise's parents, Sarah and James, and Yash's partner, Adrian, in a corner of the dining room where the screen had been set up. Representatives of the rescue services and a couple of other people Ann hadn't seen before were already there.

Owen came in, closed the door on the press ruckus in the foyer and hurried over. 'Hello everyone. You know Angelo, head of rescue services who I believe has some news for us.'

Angelo stepped forward. 'The Land Rover has been spotted a good way from the site of the landslip and appears to be intact. It's not possible to land the helicopter there because of the terrain. There is no sign of the occupants so we must assume they are continuing on foot. Arturo is an experienced guide and he will lead the party to a higher altitude where, once above the area of the landslip, they can safely await rescue. By this afternoon we will have a team on the ground.'

Adrian, Yash's partner, raised his hand. 'Wouldn't it make sense for them to stay with the vehicle?'

'Certainly,' Angelo agreed. 'If the terrain is stable, but on the ground it would be difficult to judge.'

'How long will it take to find them,' Marion asked. 'Ethan has a heart condition.'

'I understand, signora,' Angelo said. 'We will know more later today. I'm sure they will have found shelter. There are shepherds' huts scattered across the mountain.' He gathered some papers and slipped them in a battered briefcase. 'Forgive me, I must return to my headquarters and direct operations.'

Owen stood, faced the captive audience and said, 'Angelo will contact me the minute he has any news. In the meantime, I know this sounds banal, but there are refreshments …'

117

Ann smiled at Marion intending to join her for refreshments when Owen called, 'Mrs Bryce.'

Ann whispered, 'I'll join you later,' to Marion and followed Owen to the corner of the room where a man and a woman were seated.

'Ann,' Owen said, 'this is Inspector Varma and Sergeant Carlton.'

The inspector stood, shook Ann's hand and invited her to sit. Sergeant Carlton nodded a greeting.

'Have you any idea,' Ann asked, 'who's behind the bogus emails?'

'We suspect they may be connected to another matter.'

Ann waited to be enlightened.

The inspector continued, 'You and your husband are on the board of a charity set up in the name of Andy Roberts. I believe Mr Roberts was a contemporary of your husband.'

'Yes. They were good friends. Andy was ...' Ann felt a rush of emotion as memories of events more than ten years ago surfaced. 'Andy was killed when I ... I was kidnapped and ...'

'Yes, thank you Mrs Bryce, we don't wish to drag up unpleasant memories. Can you confirm that you and your husband set up the Andy Roberts Charity and are still on the Board of Trustees?'

'Yes, we are.'

'We are looking into the possibility that substantial illegal funds are being passed through the charity's accounts.'

Bewildered, Ann waited for more information. When none was forthcoming she said, 'You mean ... like money laundering?'

'I mean exactly like money laundering.'

Again puzzled, Ann said, 'How can that be? Donations are made and then schools are invited to apply for funding towards music and drama projects. The sums involved are not immense but help with the productions of school plays and purchase of musical instruments.'

'No doubt a worthy cause,' Inspector Varma remarked.

'Going into schools was one of Andy's great joys; it seemed a fitting memorial.' Ann watched the inspector shuffle his papers and concerned about his line of questioning, added, 'There is an accountant and a solicitor also on the board. They act for a nominal fee and, of course, Dean does the administration. Stephen does some fundraising and we get an annual report but we have nothing to do with the day-to-day running.'

'I understand, Mrs Bryce, but we will need to do financial checks on everyone connected with the charity as well as have access to the charity's accounts.'

Ann scrutinised the inspector's face. His dark eyes reflected his seriousness.

'You seem reluctant, Mrs Bryce.'

'I'm sorry, I assumed you were here to track down who sent those emails. Someone is impersonating a senior executive of the film company and sent my husband and a film crew into a situation which is potentially life threatening.'

'There is a possibility someone wanted your husband out of the way for a short time, but no one could have predicted the sudden change in weather which was responsible for the landslide. I'm asking for your permission to access all relevant accounts, Mrs Bryce, but we can get a court order if you don't cooperate.'

Ann swallowed her anger and confusion. Nothing to be gained by losing her temper. 'Do whatever you need to, but please bear in mind that the guide employed by the film company – or by the person impersonating a senior executive of the film company – must have had access to up-to-date weather reports and should never have allowed anyone near that mountain.' Aware she was raising her voice, Ann glanced around to make sure no prying ears were nearby. Sitting back, she said, 'I'm as anxious as you to find out who is misusing Andy's charity, but you must forgive me if, at the moment, I'm more interested in the safety of Stephen and the others.'

'As we all are, Mrs Bryce.' Inspector Varma stood and with his sergeant left the room.

Ann sat for a while and, instead of joining the others, went into the foyer intending to take the lift to her room. Owen was giving the press an update on the rescue situation and to avoid them, she took the stairs to her room on the second floor.

She needed to speak to Peter but, at a knock at the door, she aborted the call. 'Sergeant,' was her surprised greeting to the woman at the door.

'Mrs Bryce, I wanted to let you know that we do understand your concerns regarding your husband and the others who are still missing.'

'Thank you.'

'You understand the inspector has to look at the whole picture, but I thought you'd like to know that—'

119

They were interrupted by the hotel internal phone. With, 'Excuse me a moment,' to the sergeant, Ann lifted the receiver and spoke to Owen. 'Yes, right away.' She returned to the door. 'I must go, Owen has some news.'

Sergeant Carlton stood back, Ann stepped through the door and pulled it closed behind her. She again took the stairs to the ground floor where Owen waited.

'Had a message from Angelo,' he said without preamble. 'I'll take you to Rescue Headquarters.'

'What is it? Have they found them? We should tell the others.'

Owen hustled her through the foyer and outside. 'I've a car over there.'

Ten minutes later, Owen parked outside the office of the local mountain rescue team. He and Ann went inside.

Powerful binoculars, mounted on a stand, were set at a window with an unobstructed view of the mountains. Angelo sat at a desk; behind him, another man and a woman attended computer screens, static emanating from a radio set.

Unable to contain herself, Ann said, 'What's happened?'

Angelo stood. 'Come into the back office, Mrs Bryce.'

Ann followed him to a smaller room, a desk scattered with papers and a pinboard behind, displaying photographs.

Angelo gestured for Ann and Owen to sit. 'I wanted to speak to you before passing certain information on.'

Consumed with dread Ann blurted, 'What, for heaven's sake? Please tell me.'

Angelo spread his hands on the desk. 'I have heard from the team on the ground—' He held up a hand to prevent Ann's further exclamation. 'They are above the site of the chalet and the place where the landslide originated and where the terrain seems to be quite stable. Low cloud has lifted and we can see more clearly where the Land Rover has been abandoned, which is quite some way further on.' Angelo pushed an enlarged photograph across the desk. 'Here,' he pointed, 'we see a shepherd's hut where we can assume they sheltered the first night when the storm was raging. We can't understand why, the next morning, they didn't wait there. Arturo would know a rescue operation would commence as soon as the weather cleared, or, if he was in any doubt, why he didn't lead them to this area.' He again tapped the photo. 'This is where my team is now and anyone familiar with the mountain knows it is a safe place to make a pickup by helicopter.'

Ann looked up from the photo, now more bewildered than ever. 'Then why aren't they there?'

'A question I ask myself,' Angelo agreed. 'You see this—' He dragged over another picture. 'It is a satellite photo of the same area, much enlarged.' He paused as if reluctant to go on, eventually saying, 'We have studied the picture and our conclusion is supported by what the team have seen on the ground.'

'Which is?'

'There have been minor landslides throughout the area but this—' He again pointed to the scar left when the major landslide took the road, chalet and tons of rock, halfway down the mountain. 'There is every appearance that the movement was artificially created.'

'I'm sorry, Angelo,' Ann said. 'I don't understand. Artificially created, sounds as if you believe it was started … deliberately.' She sat back in the straight-backed wooden chair, astounded at her own words.

'We believe that is exactly what happened. There is evidence of an explosion.'

CHAPTER 27

Reeling from the blow, Nathan crashed against the filing cabinets and slid to the floor. Rough hands hauled him to his feet. Shoved out the office door, along the corridor and on to the outside landing, Nathan's foot missed the first step and only a desperate grab for the railing saved a long, hard fall.

Bundled onto the back seat of a car, the journey was a blur. A sense of speed, of swaying around corners preceded more manhandling.

*

'Nathan, wake up. Open your eyes.' Jessica's insistent voice broke through.

Nathan did as he was bid. Dim light from a single bare bulb haloed Jessica's head. Struggling from his prone position, Nathan winced and put a hand to the back of his head.

'You cracked your head on the corner of a filing cabinet,' Jessica informed him. 'The skin's not broken, but there's a fair lump.'

'Yes,' Nathan agreed, fingering the spot carefully.

'You should see the other chap,' Jessica grinned.

Nathan's hand moved from the back of his head to his cheekbone.

Jessica's smile fled. 'You'll have a good shiner.'

'Where are we?'

'Lord knows. We were travelling for about forty minutes.'

Nathan felt in his pockets, but Jessica said, 'They took our phones.' She put her hands on his shoulders, examined his face, made sure he could focus properly before saying, 'They want the flash drive, the memory stick.'

Nathan's 'Yes,' was drawn out as he tried to recall events. 'I had it in my hand when those men came in. What did I do with it?'

'I bumped into you when he grabbed me, then you hit him with that trophy, so you must have dropped it, but they searched. They went through your pockets, the desk and even pulled out the filing cabinets. Lisa gave them the combination of the safe but, of course, it wasn't there.'

'Where is she?'

'She was bundled into another car.'

Nathan took stock of their surroundings. Cream painted brickwork, a metal riveted door, and high on the opposite wall, a narrow window of thick square panes covered by an iron grille. There was an old fashioned Formica-topped table with four chairs. A sink and draining board and, on an old chest of drawers, a kettle and half a dozen assorted mugs.

'I think we're in an old factory,' Jessica told him. 'Or maybe a disused warehouse.'

She helped Nathan stand, and ignoring a throbbing head, he examined the metal door. 'Looks like it used to be a strong room.'

'Yes, I noticed there's no handle on the door,' Jessica confirmed. 'And it fits into a lip all the way round.' She wandered over to the sink. 'It's been made into a serviceable kitchen.' She shivered. 'Even if it does feel damp.'

Nathan moved around the table and pulled out a chair.

'What is it,' Jessica leaned over.

Nathan lifted a laptop computer from the seat of the chair and placed it on the table. He opened the lid.

Jessica exclaimed her surprise and delight. 'Switch it on. We can get help.'

On an otherwise blank blue screen, a solitary icon blinked, demanding attention.

'Go on then,' Jessica said. 'Click it.'

As Nathan did so an eerie chuckle filled the room and Nathan felt Jessica's hand slip inside his own. 'Who is it, Nathan?' she whispered.

Nathan called out, 'What have you done with Lisa? Where is she?'

'Lisa is your mother. Why don't you call her so?' said the disembodied voice.

'That's between her and me. What do you want?'

'Well,' the voice went on, 'there are certain parties who would like the flash drive you so carelessly lost. Personally, I have other grievances.'

123

CHAPTER 28

'Why?' Ann asked no one in particular. 'Why would anyone want to do that?'

Angelo shook his head. 'Arturo is our best guide; I can't believe he would be involved.' Angelo stood. 'Forgive me: I have a meeting with the Italian authorities and your British police. In the meantime, I must ask you not to mention this to anyone until we have decided what our next move will be.'

*

Owen drove back to the hotel, Ann, in silent contemplation, beside him.

'I'll need to get the dining room closed off ready for when the Italian police arrive,' Owen told her as they drew into the car park at the rear of the hotel. 'For what it's worth,' he added. 'I don't believe you or your husband are involved in any fraudulent dealings … with the charity, I mean.'

Ann suddenly felt choked. How did he know about that?

Owen opened the car door to get out but Ann said, 'I'd like to be included in the talks with the police.'

With, 'I expect they'll want to speak to you anyway,' Owen closed the car door.

Ann exited the vehicle and headed for the back entrance of the hotel.

In her room Ann tried to ring Peter and then Nathan. Failing to reach either, she left a message for both. 'Nothing new here,' she lied. 'Hope to speak to you soon.'

Refreshed and changed, Ann stood on her balcony, warm sunshine on her face and arms. A cool breeze, a reminder it was still early spring.

The inevitable could be put off no longer and, collecting a cardigan, Ann took the lift to ground level and walked smartly to the dining room. An Italian uniformed police officer let her through the door and closed it behind. With Inspector Varma were a couple of other men, Italian, Ann guessed, in no doubt they were police.

'Ah, Mrs Bryce,' Inspector Varma greeted. 'These gentlemen are my counterparts in the Polizia.'

They nodded in Ann's general direction.

Varma led her to a nearby table and indicated for her to sit. 'I have some questions before we update the others.' He went on, 'If the landslide was a deliberate act, I need to know if it was intended to harm the whole film crew or an individual.'

'Yes.'

'Yes?'

'Yes. *I* would like to know if it was intended to harm the whole crew or an individual.'

Varma sighed. 'Enquiries are ongoing, Mrs Bryce, but at present your husband is the only person we can connect to anything vaguely ... illegal.'

Ann leaned forward. 'My husband is not connected with anything illegal, vague or otherwise.'

'But his girlfriend probably is.'

Ann sat back. 'Girlfriend!'

'Forgive me, Mrs Bryce, I should have said former girlfriend, the mother of his son.'

'Lisa? What has Lisa got herself into now?'

'We believe Miss Brookes is in possession of certain information that would be of value to our enquiries regarding the laundering of a great deal of money.'

Realisation prompted a spike of anxiety. 'My son, Nathan ... Lisa's son, went looking for her a couple of days ago.'

'We have already spoken to Nathan. Do you know where he is now?'

'I've been trying to contact him.' Information coming thick and fast made Ann's head reel. 'But if you've spoken to him ... don't you know where he is?'

'Nathan obtained printouts of various accounts we're interested in, but we need information held on a flash drive or memory stick which we believe is in the possession of Lisa Brookes. Nathan led us to understand he and the young lady he was with would be heading for home this morning.'

Ann fumbled for her phone. 'I'll ring Peter. I left a message earlier, but he hasn't got back to me.'

'We've spoken to Peter Bryce,' the inspector confirmed. 'Nathan isn't there.'

Ann's brain whirled. 'They travelled to Birmingham in Jessica's car. They must be on the way back.'

125

'The young lady's car, or, should I say, her father's car, is still parked at a service station outside the city.'

Having found her phone, Ann pressed the speed dial for Nathan but again reached the *unable to take your call right now* message.

'We tracked his phone to the vicinity of the Jewellery Quarter,' Varma told her, 'but it's now switched off.'

Whilst Ann struggled to digest this information her phone rang, making her jump. It was Peter. 'Where have you been?' she snapped. 'Is Nathan there?'

'Be calm, Ann, and listen.'

Ann took a breath. 'Okay, I'm listening.'

'Have you spoken to Inspector Varma?'

'Yes, he's here.'

'Then he will have explained what's happened. We're not sure where Nathan is, but they'll track him down. I'll let you know immediately if he turns up here. The inspector told me what's happening with Andy's charity and we'll sort it out, Ann, there's no need to worry.'

'Lisa is mixed up in it and she's involved Nathan.'

'Yes, I know, but there's nothing we can do right now. The police will find him then we'll get things straightened out. Any news of Stephen and the others?'

Ann felt unable to explain the new development and said merely, 'Nothing definite.'

She heard Peter sigh before saying, 'Be patient, there's bound to be news soon. In the meantime, there's something else I have to tell you. I'd decided not to say anything before but you ought to know.'

Believing her heart could sink no further, Ann's 'What?' was barely audible.

'Lizzie is in hospital. She had a seizure. It's not looking good.'

126

CHAPTER 29

From a curve in the path leading back to the village, Louise turned and waved to the others.

Leaving Yash as comfortable as possible, Stephen followed Francesco in a counterintuitive direction. It seemed an age before they found a safe crossing, and a scary leap from rock to rock over a gully of crashing water before they were again on the downward slope. The ground beneath the short wiry grass of the high pastures squelched beneath their boots, damp clothing steaming in midday sun.

After a couple of hours of steady walking, Francesco said, 'We rest here.'

'I'm okay,' Stephen said. 'I can keep going.'

'No, this is a good place to rest. We will soon reach the tree line and the forest is not a good place to stop. We will reach shelter by nightfall, then tomorrow it is only a few hours to the next village'

'Tell me, Francesco,' Stephen said. 'Do you believe Cavendish and Arturo came this way?' I can't help wondering where they're heading, and if they'll also need to spend the night somewhere.'

'They came this way,' Francesco confirmed. 'I'm sure Arturo was not party to what happened.' He gestured back up the mountain. 'He has connections to our village; he is a good man.'

'I'd like to believe that,' Stephen confessed.

'It is so,' Francesco said indignantly. 'Besides, this is the only way. They must go through the next village. They have phone lines and internet connection, so you will be able to contact your people.'

'How far ahead do you think they are?'

'Maybe two hours, but they will not reach the village before nightfall.' Francesco glanced at the sky which was once again filled with dark ragged clouds. 'There will be no moon; even Arturo will not travel at night.'

Stephen found a rock on which to perch, and they drank from the flask and ate the last of the bread and cheese. A feeling of unease, lurking since the inception of this fiasco, now swelled even more than when they had found Ethan. He met the boy's eyes and realised he, too, was aware of a predicament neither had foreseen.

Francesco voiced his fear. 'You think this man Cavendish does not want us to reach the village and get help for you and your friends.'

'This shelter you mentioned,' Stephen asked, 'what does it consist of?'

'It is a farmhouse, now deserted and mostly in ruin. But the wood stove still works and there is a well. People from our village use it when coming down from the mountain. I know what you are thinking, signor. But he is only one man. Arturo will help us overpower him.'

'We don't know if Arturo—'

'Arturo is a good man.'

Stephen eyed the boy with sympathy. It would be hard if Francesco's admiration of the mountain guide was destroyed. He thought of Nathan who, he imagined, would now be so disappointed in his dad and not without reason. Stephen pushed regret aside, more immediate matters to be dealt with before he could contemplate how to make amends for a lost holiday. 'Let's consider,' he said, 'if, for whatever reason, Arturo is not able to help and Cavendish needs to prevent us getting to the village and raising the alarm.'

'Then the farmhouse would be a good place to watch for our approach, it sits on a grassy slope and is exposed from all sides.'

'Is there any way we can avoid the farmhouse and get to the village first?'

'Not before nightfall. We need to go through the forest and it is not a good place to be at night; there are wolves.'

'That's all we need,' Stephen muttered.

'There is something else, signor … a rifle is kept in the old farmhouse. Mainly for rabbits,' added as if in mitigation.

Stephen screwed the cap on the flask. 'Would you be able to get back to your own village before nightfall?'

'Maybe, but …'

'Maybe you should.'

'And you go on alone? No signor, you do not know the way. I will come with you; your friends need help quickly.'

Stephen put a hand on the boy's shoulder. 'Okay Francesco, we should have thought this out before we started, but let's not jump to conclusions before we know what we'll find. Tell me when we get close to the farmhouse.' He slipped the strap of the flask over his head and shoulder and gestured to Francesco to lead the way.

128

The temperature dropped noticeably as they followed a narrow path into the forest. Trees, at first sparse and scrubby, multiplied and became tall and thin to cope with winter snow. 'Tell me about the village,' Stephen said. 'It must be difficult through the winter months.'

'Only around a dozen people live there all year. Sheep graze on the hills in the summer, and they bring them inside for the winter. I came up a couple of weeks ago with my uncle and two others to bring supplies. We stockpile at the farmhouse and then it must be backpacked the rest of the way. I don't know how long my grandfather and grandmother will be able to remain. It's rare that anyone attempts to reach them in the winter, but I stay with them throughout the summer then I return to school. But this year,' Francesco turned to Stephen and grinned, 'I go to college and learn to be an engineer. And when I get a job, my grandparents can come to live with me in the city.'

'That's an admirable ambition. My son, 'Stephen told him, 'is anxious to have a year off before going to university.'

'Is he to be an actor, like you?'

'Well, he'd like a course that includes drama as well as English and media studies. Where depends on his A level results.'

'Ah, I'm sure he's had the best education money can buy.'

Stephen took it as a statement with no hint of animosity or jealousy, but felt compelled to say, 'We all try to do the best for our children, but a lot depends on their own efforts. Nathan enjoys the literary side of things. His cousin, who goes to the same school, is into technology. Like chalk and cheese,' Stephen smiled. 'But they get on very well.'

'My father worked for a firm of civil engineers,' Francesco told him. 'He helped build some of the highest bridges and flyovers in the country, but there was an accident and he was killed when I was very young. It was difficult for my mother after that and she, well, Nonna, my grandmother, says, just gave up.'

'I'm sorry, Francesco.' Stephen watched the boy striding out, leading the way and silently promised that when he got home he'd make sure Francesco had every opportunity to realise his ambition.

They strode on for an hour, two, an angry sky syphoning daylight away through a network of coniferous branches, and Stephen wondered if they would indeed reach the farmhouse before nightfall.

The sky cleared and Stephen guessed most rain must have fallen higher up the mountain. He thought of Yash and hoped by now, with help, he would be on his way back to the village. Dusk filtered between thinning trees, a slight brightening ahead indicating they were reaching the boundary of the tree line.

Francesco slowed his pace, halted and beckoned Stephen to join him. Concealed behind the trunk of the last pine, they looked out onto an expansive grassy slope with steep rocky outcrops either side. Perhaps half a mile away, standing almost central, was the disused farmhouse, its outbuildings now in ruins.

Stephen squinted into late evening sunshine. 'No way to tell if anyone is already there. How far is the next village?' He asked Francesco.

'See across the valley?'

Stephen nodded, peering beyond the grassland and over a margin of deciduous trees marking the lower tree line to where the valley sides seemed to cross.'

'The village is just out of sight. As I said, more than half a day's journey, too far to reach before nightfall.'

'I don't doubt you, Francesco.'

The sun slowly sank, shadows creeping from the forest, extended across the grass and enveloped the house. A moment later a dim light appeared in a window.

'That answers our question,' Stephen pointed out.

Darkness thickened, a second wave of angry clouds filled the sky and a chill wind forced its way between the trees.

'Are you okay, Signor Bryce?'

'I'm fine,' Stephen answered automatically, but a tiredness had swept over him, the effect, no doubt, of a lengthy trek and two days without medication.

'It is my fault, signor. I assumed we would be able to spend the night here—' he gestured to the farmhouse, 'and did not come prepared to stay outdoors.'

'It's not your fault, Francesco. You've done all you can to help us.'

'My grandfather will not think so, he will say I should have known better.'

'We can all say that,' Stephen admitted. He sat on the ground and leaned against a tree.

'What happened, Signor Bryce? To make you ill?'

'About ten years ago, I drank some cough medicine without checking first and it reacted badly with some prescribed medication. I

130

was in a coma for twenty-one days, and now my body just doesn't work as well as it should.' Stephen found a wry smile for the boy. 'I should have known better. And please, call me Stephen.'

'You cannot stay out here all night. I will go to the farmhouse. Arturo will help us.'

'No.' Stephen put a hand out to stop him. 'Let's wait until it's really dark, then perhaps we can shelter in the outbuilding without being seen.' An idea occurred. 'Maybe we can start down to the other village before dawn, beat them to it. Warn the authorities. I hate to think of Cavendish getting away with murder.'

'We would need to reach the lower trees before he saw us or we would be sitting birds.'

'Ducks,' Stephen corrected. 'Sitting ducks.'

'Well, whatever the species,' Francesco grinned. 'I wouldn't want to be it.'

CHAPTER 30

Nathan looked around the room and spotted a camera in the corner of the ceiling. 'I don't know where the memory stick is,' he told the camera. 'I must have dropped it. And Lisa doesn't know either.'

Silence.

'Yes,' Jessica joined in. 'We can't help you, so you might as well let us go. We just want to go home.'

Silence.

'*He's* not the one who wants the stick,' Nathan told her. 'He said he has other grievances.'

'What grievances? We haven't done anything. We don't even know who he is. What does he want, Nathan? Who is he? Is it something to do with your mother?'

Nathan glanced up at the skylight over the sink unit but Jessica again demanded his attention.

'Why does he talk about your mother? Do you know who it is?'

Nathan ignored her. 'I wonder if we can get through the window.' He put a chair near the sink unit and climbed onto the draining board. 'You were right, this is a basement. There's a narrow footpath just below the window, between us and the river. Hand me a knife and I'll see if I can shift this catch. It looks as if it's been painted over a dozen times.'

Jessica rattled in the cutlery drawer for a while before passing him a stainless steel knife. 'Is this any good? It looks as if it wouldn't cut butter.'

'It doesn't need to be sharp as long as it's strong enough to chip the paint off.'

'And then what? It would be a squeeze to get through, even if there wasn't a grill.'

'Someone may hear us.' Nathan heard the scraping of a chair and twisted around to see Jessica drag a dining chair into the far corner of the room. She returned and found a sliver of soap in a dish between the taps.

'We don't want *him* watching what we are doing.' She climbed onto the chair and squashed the soap into the pencil sized lens of the camera. 'Maybe he'll come storming in to see what we're doing.'

'I expect he can hear us,' Nathan said, still scraping at paint on the window catch. 'But I think he's too much of a coward to come in here and explain what this is about.'

Jessica lowered her voice. 'Do you think you should antagonise him like that?'

When Nathan didn't answer, she went on, 'You know who it is.'

He stopped scraping. 'It sounds like someone I know, and he mentioned my mother, but I have no idea why he should do this.'

Jessica's face hardened. She folded her arms. 'I'm fed up with this. It started out two days ago as exciting, but since that man was killed at the hotel, and the police, and those, those ... thugs ... and my dad will be going spare.'

Nathan climbed down from the draining board. He reached out but didn't touch her, unsure what to do. 'I'm sorry. I didn't know it would turn out like this. I'll get you out of here, Jessica. I'll make sure you get home safely.'

'How?' she snapped at him. 'We can't get through the window. Even if you got it open no one is going to hear us ... except *him*—' she gestured at the camera. 'Nathan, if you have any idea who it might be, please tell me.'

Reluctantly, Nathan said, 'It sounds like one of the teachers from school.'

'Really?'

'Yes, really. A lecturer in IT. Which is more Matthew's scene than mine.'

'Matthew?'

'My cousin. He's a whizz at that sort of thing. I'd be typing up an essay or ideas for a play and Mr Thompson would tell me off for not paying attention.'

'And you think it's this Mr Thompson?'

'I said it sounded like him. If he got me on my own, he would go on about how pleased I should be to know who my mother is and how there are others who aren't so lucky. Lots of people know about my dad and Lisa because of who they are, so I just ignored him.'

'Whoever it is, he's certainly got a thing about you and your mother and, remember, he's connected to money laundering at your charity.'

'Lisa does fundraising for the charity, so that's a connection.'

Jessica's fear broke through the covering anger. 'All of which doesn't help us with the immediate problem of getting out of here.'

'People will miss us,' Nathan pointed out. 'My mum and your dad, they'll try our phones and when there's no answer …'

'They'll think we're ignoring them like we have been for the past couple of days.'

'When they're past being angry, they'll be worried,' Nathan pointed out.

'I don't want to wait until then.'

Nathan glanced up at the window before crossing the room and pushing on the door. 'The door is solid. Like you said, it was probably a strong room.'

When he turned back to Jessica, she had filled the kettle. He watched as she plugged it in, turned to face him, and leaning on the worktop, folded her arms. 'Let's have a coffee. It might help us think this through.'

Nathan gave a frustrated sigh and threw himself on the chair before the now lifeless laptop computer on the table. He switched it on and gazed at the screen – abruptly he sat up. 'It's on. Jessica, it's on. But it says there's no internet connection.' Nathan clicked the signal icon. A list of networks shot up the screen.

'Try the first one without a lock,' Jessica instructed.

'I am.'

'Is it connecting?'

'Yes, we're connected.'

'What are you waiting for? Get a message off to the police,' Jessica urged. 'Search Google Voice and ask for 999.'

'It's not as simple as that …' Before he could remonstrate, bolts grated, the iron door opened and two men burst into the room, filling it with their bulk. Nathan stood, stepped back from the computer and placed himself between the men and Jessica. One heavy reached across the table, closed the laptop and tossed it over to his associate. Nathan raised his hand to the burgeoning bruise on his cheekbone and took half a step backwards.

The other man smirked and said with false pleasantry, 'We've brought you some company.' With a cruel grip on Lisa's arm, he shoved her into the room. Nathan caught her, both almost knocked off their feet.

CHAPTER 31

'May I join you in one of those?'

Ann's deep introspection interrupted, she invited Sarah Austin to take the seat opposite at a table in the bar of the hotel. Ann gestured to the glass of brandy before her and said, 'I don't usually drink this early in the afternoon but—'

'I'll have one of those,' Louise's mother told the waiter.

Both women smiled tentatively until a further brandy was placed on the table and the waiter had retreated. Sarah leaned towards Ann. 'I need to get some things straight between us.'

All attention, Ann sat up. 'Yes, of course.'

'I've been thinking about what Louise told me about Lisa. I didn't realise when all this kicked off that she was ... well that—'

'That she was the mother of Stephen's son,' Ann finished for her. 'It was a very brief affair before he and I got together. I thought everyone knew.'

Sarah said. 'I did know but didn't realise she was the young woman who was sharing the flat with Louise. I've been trying to find a connection between the people who have been conned into this project and Lisa Brookes is the only thing in common I can come up with – at least between your husband and my daughter.'

It was something Ann had been considering. 'You've probably heard,' she said, 'that Stephen and I are caught up in some trouble about Andy Roberts' charity. Lisa has been fundraising for it recently and ...' Ann buried her head in her hands for a moment before lifting it and saying, 'Lisa can be a pain in the bum at times, and in the past she has done some foolish things, but I really don't think she'd be involved in putting people's lives at risk. Not intentionally anyway,' added in an undertone. 'And—' Ann had given it some thought, 'I imagine it would take someone with a great deal of technical knowledge to trick so many people into believing those fake email messages, as it would to use the charity account to launder large sums of money and leave hardly any trace.'

'And you, your husband and Lisa are involved with both.'

Ann winced and Sarah went on, 'I'm not accusing you, I'm merely pointing out connections.'

Ann took a sip of her brandy. 'You're not the only one: the police are suspicious, but I assure you, Sarah, I'm as much in the dark as you.' Ann shot a glance at the other families of the missing and wondered what they believed – Marion Quinn, Louise's father, and Yash's partner, Adrian.

Ann became aware of someone standing close and looked up to see Inspector Varma, his sergeant in close attendance.

Sarah picked up her glass, smiled and retreated to where the others were sitting.

Ann said, 'Hello, Inspector' and gestured for him to take the place Sarah had vacated. 'Any news of Nathan?'

Inspector Varma ignored the question and made himself comfortable before extending a hand to Sergeant Carlton who passed him a folder. 'I wonder, Mrs Bryce, if you are able to help us with any of these photos.' He dealt out six pictures as if they were playing cards.

'That's Dean Henderson,' Ann said, immediately picking out a head and shoulders full face photo. 'I met him three or four times at various events. He deals with finances for the Andy Roberts Fund.'

Varma returned the photo to the folder and gestured at the others still on the table.

Ann scanned them one by one before returning to a picture of a man caught striding across a busy road and glancing towards a traffic or CCTV camera. 'He looks vaguely familiar but I can't bring to mind where or when I've seen him.'

'Keep the photo,' Varma said. 'Think about it.'

'What about Dean? You must have spoken to him about the money.'

'No.' The inspector smiled grimly. 'Mr Henderson was found dead in a room at the Regency Hotel in Birmingham yesterday.'

Ann caught her breath. She recalled a man of around forty, dark wavy hair, maybe just a little too full of himself.   'Dead? How?'

'We're treating his death as suspicious. What can you tell me about him?'

Nonplussed, Ann stuttered, 'I … I don't think he's married … he has his own business consultancy but was willing to take on the administration of the charity from the office in Birmingham. The board would have run a check on him. No doubt there is a report at the head office.'

'Not a good enough check, as we believe Dean Henderson was actively involved in laundering money for a larger organisation, and it seems he either decided he wanted more than his share or maybe he wanted out. Whichever, it seems it didn't go down very well with his associates.'

'They killed him?' Ann's voice a mere whisper.

'He may have threatened to hand over records, and as we know he was working closely with Lisa Brookes, we're working on the theory that she now has that information.'

Ann tried to digest the information. Her head snapped up. 'And Nathan? He's not at home; I've checked with Peter.'

Inspector Varma again delved into his folder. 'These were taken this morning by the CCTV camera at the Jewellery Museum in Birmingham.'

Nathan with a dark-haired girl in jeans and a gold-coloured, blouson-style jacket. The time, at the corner of the photo, read 11.06. Ann glanced at her watch. 'Just over four hours ago. So where is he now?'

'Jessica's car is still parked in motorway services just outside the city.'

'What were they doing at the Jewellery Museum?'

'We are hoping you might be able to tell us.'

Ann examined the photo more closely. 'That's Lisa in a hoodie. They're speaking to Lisa … and … in that display cabinet it looks like … the FitzGilbert jewellery.' She sat back. 'I heard they were to be put on display. Those rubies have had a fascination through four generations of the Bryce family.'

'They also hold a fascination for highly organised criminals who then use a well-meaning charity to launder their payoff.' Inspector Varma leaned forward. 'Or would have done if your Mr Henderson hadn't had an attack of conscience, and your stepson hadn't decided to visit his mother. Five minutes after the museum CCTV camera showed your son with his girlfriend and Lisa Brookes leaving, all power in the area failed and the museum evacuated. Ten minutes later, when the lights came on, this is what was found.' He slapped on the table yet another photo of the inside of the Jewellery Museum. This time, it showed the display cabinet with a hole neatly cut into the reinforced Perspex.

Ann pushed the photo away with trembling fingers. 'Nathan is in trouble.' She reconsidered, and said, 'Nathan, Jessica and Lisa are in trouble, but they are not involved with this.'

137

'Jessica and Nathan should have gone home this morning, Mrs Bryce, and now they could be in the greatest danger. Whether Lisa Brookes is innocent remains to be seen. Are you sure there is no more you can tell me.'

Ann shook her head. 'No, but perhaps you can tell me what you are doing to find them – and please don't say, "we're doing everything we can."'

'That's exactly what I was going to say, but specifically, I can tell you that there are several people and properties we are watching closely. As soon as I hear anything I will let you know,' Varma collected the photos, beckoned to his sergeant and left.

Ann sat motionless, mind churning.

'Are you okay, Ann? What did the policeman say? Has he any news?'

Ann looked up into Sarah's worried face.

'Has something happened?' Sarah went on. 'Have they found Louise and the others?'

'No, Sarah, he didn't have any news about Louise, Stephen and the others but … my son. He's in trouble and I ought to go home.' Ann stood and whirled round. 'Bloody hell, Stephen. None of this would have happened if you'd told Cavendish to get lost, that you'd already promised to take your son on holiday.' She felt a firm hold on her elbow and was propelled out of the dining room and into the garden.

'Calm down, Ann,' Sarah soothed. 'You'll stir up the press and get them thinking there's more going on than there actually is. I'm sure we all feel the same way. I know Ethan's wife does: she said he was thinking of retiring before he was asked to join this crew.'

Ann took a couple of calming breaths. 'Yes, indeed. Whoever is behind it must be very clever, or at least have someone working for them who's a computer genius.'

They strolled in the garden. 'Who would believe only a few days ago the weather was so dreadful,' Sarah mused.

Ann wondered if she should mention that the catastrophe may not have been altogether a result of the weather but knew another update was due soon. Best leave it to the authorities. 'Sarah, it's unlikely the rescue team will find Stephen, Louise and the others today, there's too much ground to cover. I'm worried about my son, and I'd like to go home.'

'Of course, I'm sure your husband will understand.'

138

'I'm not sure how long it will take to make sure my son is safe, but as soon as I know, I'll come back.'

Sarah glanced back at the hotel. 'The press are still gathered in the lobby. They'll want to know why you're not here. I can tell them you're not feeling well.'

'No, don't do that. If they ask where I am, just say you don't know but assume I must have been delayed. They'll suspect something is wrong anyway, and I'd rather not be caught in a blatant lie.'

CHAPTER 32

Dark clouds covered a three-quarter moon and cast deep shadow from the depth of the forest across open ground to encompass the ruined farmhouse. A faint light twinkled, presumably, according to Francesco, from the only habitable room.

Stephen fastened up his anorak. 'I didn't realise it could get so cold in this part of the world.'

'You forget the altitude,' Francesco told him. 'The temperature will drop below freezing. We need to get to shelter. Only last week, I and a couple of other men from our village brought supplies, some are stored at the back of the building. The only window is at the front. If we stick to the fringe of the wood we could reach the back of the building without being seen.'

Stephen glanced skyward again. Neither moon nor stars penetrated thick clouds. 'Best go now,' he suggested. 'Before it gets so dark we can't see our way.'

'Si. Over there—' Frankie waved vaguely to the left, 'over there the ground drops away to steep cliffs.'

Away from the path, uneven ground and clumped underbrush made walking difficult. Twilight faded into pitch black and Stephen stumbled yet again; a herd of elephants crashing through the jungle came to mind. With the occupied room at the front of the old farmhouse, and their approach from the rear, Stephen risked using the light from his phone. It exaggerated the darkness beyond the beam, until he feared they'd lost their bearings.

'Wait,' Francesco ordered. 'We must be far enough along. We need to cut across the open ground.'

Stephen doused the light. 'It occurs to me that if Cavendish suspects we are following, they'll keep a lookout from the back of the building.'

Stephen sensed Francesco shrug and point into the darkness. 'It should be that way.'

Stephen followed the sound of the youth's boots stirring meadow grass which in a few weeks would be long and lush. The chill air felt damp and the going, though now much easier, still uneven.

Francesco outpaced him; Stephen halted to listen. With no point of reference the direction was unclear. 'Francesco,' he called softly, searching the darkness.

The youth appeared before him. 'Switch on the torch for a few seconds.'

Stephen did so.

'We've turned too soon.' Francesco took hold of Stephen's sleeve and struck off, blind, at an angle.

Stephen felt some comfort at being in physical contact – stepping into darkness like stepping off the edge of the world.

The smell of wood smoke warned they were close and another brief flash from the torch revealed the outline of a partially ruined building. At the rear, the roof overhung and gave shelter from rain which now rattled on the slates. Knowing only a wall, albeit of substantial stone, separated them from Cavendish and Arturo they made an effort to move silently.

Francesco found an oil lamp, and by its dim yellow glo they arranged bales of last year's hay. 'Are you okay, Signor Stephen?' Francesco whispered. 'I can start a fire, I'm sure it will not be seen.'

'That would be welcome and I suppose they—' Stephen jerked a thumb at the back wall. 'Won't notice the smoke.'

Hay bales formed a protective square, spacious enough for Francesco to build a small fire from twigs and other detritus. They sat on a layer of straw and leaned against the wall. Stephen felt Francesco's weight as, in sleep, the boy leaned against him. Plans and revised plans for the next day rattled round Stephen's head keeping him from similar rest. He held out his hands to scant warmth from the fire, the smell of steaming damp hay rank in his nostrils. Was Ann sleeping? Did she believe he and the others lay beneath a thousand tons of earth? If only he could tell her. Taking care not to disturb Francesco, Stephen found his phone. The battery at 11 per cent, the icon showed red. He pressed the call button for Ann – calling. Calling! The phone to his ear he listened above his beating heart for the dialling tone. Silence.

Stephen's throat constricted as disappointment overwhelmed him.

Battery at 9 per cent – should he try again?

A rustling from outside their shelter. Stephen pocketed his phone; the movement disturbed Francesco and Stephen put a hand over the boy's mouth.

141

Francesco quickly understood. Stephen removed his hand; both listened, ears on stalks. Rainwater dripped from broken guttering, more rustling. A grunt and sigh – the unmistakable sound of a man peeing behind the ruined walls.

Francesco sprang to his feet, Stephen too slow to catch the boy's elbow and restrain him.

'Arturo,' Francesco called.

Stephen stayed in the shadows. With his limited understanding of the language, he deciphered the exclamation as, 'Frankie, what are you doing here? Did those film people send you?'

'One of them, the old man, is dead, one is injured and Stephen has no medication left.'

Stephen sensed a hesitation before Arturo said, 'There was no need for you to come. It is only a few more hours to the next village. I will send help.'

Francesco swung around to Stephen. 'You see, Signor Stephen, I told you Arturo had gone for help.' Turning back to the guide, Francesco continued, 'You and Signor Cavendish left without saying anything, the others, they thought—'

'What did they think?' This from another man who appeared from the other side of the building. Silhouetted in pre-dawn light, Max Cavendish cradled a rifle. 'Did you think we had something to hide? Come inside and I'll explain.'

Stephen noticed Arturo glance sharply at Cavendish, before he moved towards the front of the farmhouse, Francesco happily followed. Cavendish gestured for Stephen to join them. Feeling he had no option, Stephen strode over the hay bales and, avoiding the drips from broken guttering, made his way round the side of the building and through the front door. Francesco was eagerly warming his hands over a wood burning stove, whilst Arturo hacked slices from a loaf of bread and put them on a plate with some pancetta.

'Come in, Signor Bryce,' invited Arturo. 'Have something to eat.'

'Yes,' Max Cavendish, said from immediately behind Stephen. 'Relax, get warm and have something to eat. We, however,' he addressed Arturo, 'must be on our way.'

Stephen's sense of unease increased as he noticed what looked like the satellite phone on the table.

Francesco also saw the case that had contained the phone; he looked to Cavendish and Arturo in turn. 'You said it was broken.' The lad grinned. 'If it's mended, we can——' he took a step towards the table.

'Leave it!' Cavendish ordered, raising the rifle.

Francesco looked towards Stephen, who held out a restraining hand, indicating he should stay put.

Stephen strode over to the table, looked down at the phone and said casually, 'Was it ever broken? Why go off taking the only means we have of contacting help? Who are you, Max Cavendish? Why do you want to leave me and the rest of the crew stranded in the mountains?'

'Shut up, Bryce.'

Stephen persisted. 'Why did Ethan Quinn have to die?

'Your cameraman was ill,' Arturo ventured. 'We could do nothing for him.'

'Except put a pillow over his face.'

Arturo's gaze shot to Cavendish and Stephen suspected it was the first Arturo knew about how Ethan had died.

'Did Ethan discover the satellite phone was never broken?' Stephen opened the case on the table and studied the contents. His mind raced, in no doubt Cavendish had his own agenda and was unlikely to allow him access to the handset which fitted snugly in a foam recess in the case. He figured maybe Arturo was an unwilling accomplice and he'd stand a better chance if he could get the Italian guide on his side.

'How did you get involved, Arturo? You know this is wrong. Help us now.'

'I am sorry about the old man.'

'Why did you leave, Arturo?' Francesco appealed. 'You are from our village.'

'Tell the boy,' Cavendish ordered.

Arturo looked pained.

'Arturo likes to gamble,' Cavendish informed them. 'He owes people money.'

'And what about you, Max?' Stephen tried a friendlier tone. 'What's in it for you?'

Max shrugged. 'We all have our price, and it increased considerably when we were all nearly buried in that landslip. I've been able to negotiate a pretty good deal for Arturo and myself.'

Stephen glanced again at the phone. 'Negotiations having taken place over the phone, I assume.'

143

'Shut up, and get away from the table.'

'Who's paying you to keep us out of the way,' Stephen insisted. 'You must know who.'

Cavendish ignored the question and again raising the rifle said, 'Please step away from the table.'

With a final glance at the phone, Stephen took a reluctant step back.

Cavendish shot a look at Arturo and inclined his head at the case containing the phone. 'We can't afford any delays, and we can't have these two following us.'

Arturo fastened the case and was about to tuck it under his arm when Francesco flung himself against the guide and wrestling with him, panted, 'Leave the phone. We won't call for help until this evening.'

Cavendish stepped forward, swung the rifle butt and struck the boy on the back of the head, fetching him to his knees.

Stephen grabbed the rifle, tried to wrench it from Cavendish. Cavendish jerked the gun back, caught the trigger and an explosion threw Stephen back to crash against the table.

Arturo stepped forward. 'What have you done? Wasn't it enough to kill the cameraman?'

'The old man saw the phone,' Cavendish growled. 'He knew it was working. He heard me talking.'

'This is not what I signed up for. After the landslide, I agreed to delay any rescue but I didn't know it would lead to this.'

'You're being well paid, Arturo, and now it's as much in your interests as mine to keep these two out of the way until we can collect our due and get a plane ticket to somewhere there's no extradition agreement.'

Francesco, obviously stunned, staggered to his feet and scrambled for the door. Cavendish raised the rifle, aimed at the boy.

Stephen levered himself from the table and again made a grab for the gun. 'Run, Frankie.'

The gunstock smashed into Stephen's midriff. Winded and overcome with a black sickness he fell to his knees.

144

CHAPTER 33

Even as Ann stepped from the taxi outside the gates of Holly Cottage she felt her heart fragment; but Stephen would want her to find out what was happening to his son, to be there when he was found. Framed by evergreen shrubs, early dusk softened the red brick cottage, warm light showing from downstairs windows.

Ann allowed the double electric gates to open just enough to let her through before pressing the remote to close them. The action would have alerted anyone in the house, and the front door beneath the porch canopy opened, Peter already on the threshold.

She let him hug her and for a brief moment and wallowed in the warmth of his arms. Stepping back, she patted him on the chest. 'Tell me about Lizzie and all you know about Nathan.'

'Stephen?' Peter queried.

Ann shrugged. 'They're widening the search. But there was something very wrong with the email messages asking him and the others in the crew to meet Max Cavendish.'

Peter led her to his own section of the house where Kathy waited in his sitting room.

Peter's long-time companion rose and after exchanging a warm greeting with Ann, said, 'I imagine you've not eaten; I'll make sandwiches.' Kathy allowed a hand to lay briefly on Peter's arm as she left the room.

'It seems,' Ann continued, 'neither Stephen nor anyone in the crew had previously met Max Cavendish. It was because Stephen believed George Deacon asked him as a special favour that he agreed.'

Peter frowned in concentration before saying, 'The immediate question is, do we know if they escaped the landslide?'

'Those in the first vehicle believe the others were far enough behind not to have been caught, and they have a mountain guide with them who, the man in charge of rescue services believes, would have led them away from the site to more stable ground.'

'As I see it,' Peter said, 'that is the most important question, and the identity of the man Cavendish can be dealt with later.'

Ann understood his logic. Locate them, get them home. Was it that simple? She summoned up a nod of agreement before saying, 'Lizzie?'

Peter's eyes clouded. 'She's not come round. Jules and Fiona are taking turns to be with her.'

'Does Matthew know?'

'He's hiking with school in the Scottish hills, but they'll give him the message when they get back tomorrow.' Peter covered his face. 'I should have rung for an ambulance sooner but she's had seizures before and recovered within a few minutes.'

'You couldn't know this time was more serious.'

'That's what I told him.' Kathy bustled in with a plate of sandwiches, left them on a side table and said, 'I'll have mine in the kitchen, we can catch up later.'

Ann mouthed her thanks, grateful for Kathy's consideration. She turned to Peter. 'I didn't have any breakfast.'

Peter poured tea and they ate in silence until Ann put down a half-eaten sandwich and said, 'The two police officers I spoke to about Nathan were on the plane with me. I tried to have a word with the inspector but lost track of them at the airport.'

'What did they tell you?'

'Nathan and Jessica went to the Jewellery Museum where the FitzGilbert rubies were on show. Nathan has heard us speak about them over the years and must have wanted to see them. The inspector showed me photos from the CCTV. Lisa was there. The CCTV blanked for about ten minutes and when it came back the jewellery was gone.'

'Blasted jewellery,' Peter muttered, covering his eyes. He lowered his hand and sat back.

'I know what you're thinking, Peter,' Ann said, 'but she is his mother.'

'It could have been arranged for him to see Lisa at any time. He didn't have to get mixed up in whatever shenanigans she's involved in.'

Ann put a hand on his shoulder. 'That aside, I need to know what I can do to help find him. I wish James was here to drive me to Birmingham.'

'I'm sure the police are doing everything they can, and you'd be in the way.'

146

'Maybe so, but I feel I need to be closer.' She sighed before saying, 'Can we see Lizzie? Just for a moment before I decide what to do.'

CHAPTER 34

Nathan caught Lisa as she was propelled into the basement strong room. The momentum knocked them into Jessica. By the time they regained their balance, the door had slammed, the men and the laptop on the other side.

'Are you okay,' Nathan asked. 'Did they hurt you?'

Lisa shook herself free of the two youngsters. 'What did you do with it?' Her hair in disarray, she frowned from under her fringe.

'What?'

'The damn memory thingy. What did you do with it?'

'I don't know what happened to it. I'm fed up telling everyone,' Nathan yelled back at her.

'Well, you had better think,' she snapped.

'Stop it.' Jessica smashed down a mug.

All three gazed at the broken crockery until Lisa huffed and turned her back.

Nathan and Jessica bent as one to pick up the pieces, almost clashing heads. Nathan dropped a couple of larger shards into the sink, and as Jessica stood, he noticed tears had welled. As he reached out to touch her face, a light flashed across the high, narrow window, a moment later thunder rumbled. Jessica gripped his arm. 'We must find a way to get out.'

Lisa, obviously making an effort to control her temper, said, 'You have no idea who you are dealing with. The only way is to give them what they want.'

'I can't.' Nathan's voice, almost a whisper. 'And if I did, would they really let us go? They killed your boyfriend, Dean, right there in the hotel room.'

Lisa's lower lip began to tremble. 'Yes, I know.'

Nathan's attitude softened. He put an arm around his mother's shoulder, felt her trembling as he led her to a chair at the table. He drew up another couple of chairs, turned to Jessica and said, 'Best put our heads together and see if we can figure out what's happening.'

Jessica, arms folded, raised an eyebrow almost imperceptibly, towards the camera high on the opposite wall, then briefly touched her ear. Nathan understood. The lens obscured by soap, where was the microphone?

Rain lashed the window. All three at the table, Nathan leaned towards his mother and kept his voice low. 'Did you know Dean was laundering money?'

Lisa said stubbornly, 'He was being paid for doing extra bookkeeping.'

'You mean you enjoy expensive presents and didn't care where he got the money, even if it was from Uncle Andy's charity.'

Lisa's face, a picture of innocent indignation. 'It wasn't until later he told me what it entailed. He wanted it to stop but they wouldn't let him.'

'They?'

'Some sort of organised crime gang who don't like anyone interfering with their plans. Dean told me they blackmailed him into allowing their own computer expert to take control of the transactions. Somehow, they transfer huge amounts of money leaving hardly any trace. Dean kept the details on the flash drive, and I thought giving it back would get us out of their control, but they killed Dean, and they'll kill me if I don't get it.' She leaned forward. 'You had it when we were in the charity office.'

'That man hit me. It must have been knocked out of my hand.'

Lisa reached across the table, Nathan pulled back before she could touch his bruised cheek. She withdrew her hand, saying, 'They searched. They turned the office upside down. They moved the desk, tipped over the filing cabinets, even had the carpet up.'

'I had the memory stick in my hand when those men burst into the office, and I remember grabbing a statuette and hitting the one who held Jessica, so I must have dropped the stick when the men knocked into us and we fell against the filing cabinets.'

'They searched.'

'Then I don't know.' Nathan's voice rose, before he again whispered, 'It doesn't matter now, we can't get it anyway.'

Jessica joined the conversation. 'Forget about the memory stick, let's just find a way out and let the police deal with it.'

Nathan was about to agree but something niggled, he needed to know. 'This computer expert, did you see him?'

Lisa shrugged. 'How would I know? What does a computer expert look like? That horrible man wouldn't stop asking me questions.

149

They put me in here to find out where the stick is.' Lisa sat upright. 'There was a man working on a laptop at the back of the room upstairs. He had very thin fair hair, his scalp shone pink beneath but he wasn't old. He kept glancing up and staring at me. I wondered if he might be a fan: I get some creepy ones.'

A picture formed in Nathan's head.

'So what do we do?' Jessica's voice broke through his reverie.

'Well,' Nathan responded. 'If they've realised I don't know where the stick is and we're no further use, then—'

'They'll kill us,' Lisa wailed. 'Maybe we could wait behind the door and when they come we could—'

'What could we do?' Jessica challenged. 'Did you see the size of that man?'

'We can't just sit here.' Nathan stood and realised he was paddling in a centimetre of water. He moved his chair, climbed onto the draining board and peered through the high, narrow window. 'The river has burst the bank at this side, water's splashing up against the building.' He jumped down and looked in the cupboard beneath the sink which was fastened directly to the wall with no backboard. Water was indeed forcing its way through a broken pipe and crumbling mortar before trickling down the wall.

An exclamation from Lisa confirmed the pool of water had seeped across the cement floor and reached her. She tiptoed in flimsy shoes to a corner of the room.

Nathan again climbed up to the window and hacked at the catch with the kitchen knife. 'I'll never get this open and if I did there are bars on the other side and water rushing past.

Lisa stood on tiptoe, winding one leg around the other. 'Nathan, do something.'

'If you don't want to get your feet wet, stand on a chair,' Nathan shot back.

Bolts again grated on the other side of the door, all eyes on the opening gap.

This time, a man was propelled into the room. He fell full length across the floor. The door clanged shut, the workings of a lock clunked. In the shocked silence, no one moved until the man eased himself to his knees. He shoved spectacles, awry across his face, into place on his nose. Thin strands of fair hair stuck to his forehead.

150

Nathan jumped down from the worktop, trainers squelching in water.

The man struggled to his feet, the knees and lower leg of his trousers wet.

Nathan, dumbstruck, it was left to Jessica to ask, 'And who are you?'

Finding his tongue, Nathan said, 'Mr Thompson is an IT teacher at Edgehill.'

'Ah.' Thompson shoved his spectacles further on to his nose. 'Yes, I have been teaching at Edgehill.'

'What are you doing here?' Nathan demanded.

'I tried to help you, Bryce, but you weren't quick enough.'

'What do you mean? Do you know these criminals who are holding us?'

'I left you the laptop, you could have contacted the police.'

'Those men barged in here before—'

'Like I said, you weren't quick enough.'

'And now they've chucked you in here with us. Mr Thompson, what's your connection with this? Have you been helping them steal money?'

Thompson threw up his hands. 'It's much more of an art than simply stealing.'

CHAPTER 35

A chill mountain mist curled through the open door of the ruined farmhouse. Stephen hauled himself to his feet and put a hand across his ribs as the pain from the rifle blow registered.

The room was empty. Cavendish and Arturo gone.

Where was Francesco? How badly injured? Obviously dazed from the blow to his head, would he make his way down the mountain to the next village for help? Stephen thought not. He would hide and wait to see what happened.

Stephen went outside, called, 'Francesco.' He checked the ruined part of the farmhouse, the hay bale den where they'd spent the night. He looked towards the wooded area higher up the steep meadow now shrouded in mist. A good hiding place.

Stephen struck off up the slope, in what he hoped was the right direction. The farmhouse, lost in mist, behind, trees, shrouded, ahead, he succumbed to the sensation of being trapped inside a globe.

Dark shapes materialised to his left – must be the trees. *What had Francesco said the previous day? To the left the ground dropped away to steep cliffs.* He cursed the curtain of mist – he was disorientated. A hand in his pocket, he fingered the empty blister pack that had contained his medication and tried to clear his mind. Last night they were heading in the other direction, towards the farmhouse – left was now his right.

'Francesco,' Stephen called again. 'Cavendish has gone. Fran— ' the ground beneath his feet crumbled.

*

It took time for Stephen to realise the noise of a thousand bees was in his head. The ground on which he lay was hard and rocky. Pain seared through his shoulder and back. He raised himself on an elbow and tried to focus. Looking up, he saw he must have slithered down a steep bank of scree. He tentatively put a hand to his temple, blood on his fingers, more on a nearby rock.

He looked down and immediately recoiled from the edge of the rocky ledge. Hundreds of feet below stretched a valley, looking green and picturesque in spring sunshine.

Stephen muttered, 'Shit,' before carefully getting to his feet, setting off a further cascade of gravel. 'Well done, Bryce, you've made a bad situation even worse.'

CHAPTER 36

'Stealing is stealing no matter how you do it,' Nathan retorted.

Thompson looked around the room and at the metal door which closed against a raised lip. He shrugged. 'Academic now. I seem to have upset my masters and I guess I won't get paid, so I'll have to be content with a certain sense of satisfaction.'

'What do you mean? How come you're here?' Nathan tried to piece together fragments of information. 'You knew about me and my family before you came to Edgehill. You spoke about my mother and encouraged me to keep up with IT classes when you knew I wasn't really interested.'

'One never knows when a bit of technical knowledge will come in handy, though I admit your talents lie in other directions.'

Jessica stepped forward. 'Are you really a teacher at Nathan's school?'

'Unlike this young man, IT and modern technology are my life, so coming up with references and a personal history wasn't difficult.'

Nathan paddled about in the few centimetres of dirty water now collected in the room. 'You've been hacking into the charity's computer and shifting money about; you must be working for someone else.'

'Big business, Nathan, and lucrative; for your friend Dean as well, Miss Brookes.' Thompson shrugged philosophically, 'Or it was, until they discovered he'd had a change of heart, and I, another agenda.'

'What other agenda? Something to do with me,' Nathan said, 'and my ...' as always he hesitated to say mother.

'You fucked up my relationship with my mother, so I decided to fuck up yours.' He let his gaze rest for a moment on each of them. 'You all look as if you've stuck a finger in an electric socket.'

'You're mad,' Lisa commented. She tiptoed through the water, climbed on a chair and sat on the worktop. 'I don't know you.'

'But you were there, as were Ann Bryce and your friend Andy Roberts.' Thompson snorted a laugh. 'Ironic we chose to use accounts belong to a charity set up to remember him.'

'Andy was killed when ...' Lisa's eyes widened, she shuffled back on the countertop and fixed her gaze on her hands.

154

Thompson pushed the table to butt up to the worktop and used the chair to step out of the water. To Nathan, he said, 'Being only five or six years old at the time, I don't expect you to remember. 'He jerked his chin in Lisa's direction. 'But she does.'

Heads turned as something thumped and crashed against the window set high in the wall. A tree branch visible for a moment was swept away by a wave of water. The trickle from the broken pipe under the sink now gushed sending ripples across the concrete floor.

CHAPTER 37

Ann pressed fingertips into her eyes. 'Poor Lizzie.'

Peter nodded. 'Our lovely girl never really had much of a chance.'

Both sipped coffee in the ensuing silence.

An alert sounded. Peter glanced at his phone. 'Who's this at the gate?' He showed Ann the screen.

The driver of a car parked outside the gates held an open identification wallet to the camera.

'It's Inspector Varma. There must be news.' Ann pressed a button to open the gate and beat Peter to the door. She stepped onto the drive and, curbing her anxiety, said, 'Inspector, please come in.' She led him to Peter's sitting room.

The two men shook hands, and without any further preamble, Varma said to Ann, 'Did you think any further about the man in the photo I left with you?'

'No, I'm sorry, I forgot. It's still in my bag, I'll go to get—'

'Don't bother Mrs Bryce, I have a better shot.' He handed over another picture which Ann examined.

'He seems familiar. I should know him, but from where or when …' She put a hand to her mouth as, from dim memory, recognition crept, piece by piece.

'Well?' Varma prompted.

'About ten years ago, there was some trouble.'

'I've seen the Friedman file.'

'Then you'll know there was a young man, Leo Montague, who wasn't apprehended at the time. He's obviously older, prematurely losing his hair by the look of it. He was, what I suppose you'd call, a computer wizard.'

Peter looked over her shoulder at the photo. 'I know him.'

'I don't think you saw him, Peter,' Ann said.

'I didn't see young Leo Montague at the time, but I saw that man—' he indicated the photo 'at Edgehill School when I went to pick up Nathan and Matthew. The boys pointed him out as their new IT teacher. I can't remember his name.'

'I'll get someone on it,' Varma confirmed. He took out his phone, turned his back and after a short conversation returned his attention to Ann. 'Tell me all you know about this man.'

CHAPTER 38

Jessica scrambled onto a chair and joined Lisa sitting on the worktop,

Water swirling around his ankles brought Nathan an horrific memory and he fought back rising panic.

'Nathan.' Jessica reached forward to touch his arm. 'That door looks watertight.'

Nathan saw a Norfolk backwater thick with tangled weed, heard Ann scream, 'Nathan, run.' He ran along the muddy bank of a fast-flowing river, reached a plank bridge over an inlet, grass on the bank wet, he slipped between tall rushes. Ice cold water stole his breath, closed over his head...

'Nathan,' Jessica persisted, 'we can't stay here, we must find a way out.'

'Nathan, do something,' Lisa screeched. 'I saved you from drowning.'

'Yes ... you did.' He cast around the room, empty of all but a table and chairs. 'Can you see anything I might use to prise open the door?'

'You'll not get that open,' Thompson added sardonically. 'This used to be a secure storage room.'

'Very helpful,' Nathan muttered.

'They won't leave us here? Will they?' Lisa pleaded. 'You.' She prodded Thompson's shoulder. 'They'll come back, won't they? They won't leave us to drown.'

'Shut up,' Jessica snapped. 'No one's going to drown.'

Water now around his knees, Nathan also climbed onto the table. 'You're in this as well, Mr Thompson. Even if we don't all drown, it's going to get uncomfortable. I know you've got it in for Lisa and me, and maybe for my mum—'

'Ann.' Lisa interjected. 'Your step-mother's name is Ann.'

'For my *mum*,' Nathan reiterated. 'I don't know why, and right now, I don't care, but *you* got us into this, so you can damn well start thinking of a way to get us out.'

Leo Thompson calmly scratched his head, ruffling sparse hair. 'Research is the key,' he declared, as if that would solve their problems. 'Research. Find the weakness and exploit it.'

'What weakness?' Nathan demanded. 'What do you mean?'

'There's always a weakness,' Thompson told him. 'I found their weaknesses before I sent the emails.'

'What emails? Emails to who?'

'Ethan Quinn is nearing retirement. It cost him an arm and a leg for his daughter's wedding last year. He even dipped into his pension fund. Extra money for a straight forward two-day shoot would come in handy.

'Yash Patel and his boyfriend want to buy a house. You, Lisa, did my job for me by continually taunting Louise about her buying Stephen Bryce the cough medicine that put him in a coma for however long it was all those years ago, and this was an opportunity for her to apologise.'

'What?' Lisa sat forward. 'And how would you know what I said?'

'Your boyfriend, Dean what's-his-name, was useful for other things as well as creative accounting.'

'All I said,' Lisa's voice rose, 'was that it was an opportunity for her to apologise.'

'And I gave her that opportunity.' Thompson turned to Nathan. 'Your father, of course, was merely doing a favour for George Deacon. His weakness is that he's too conscientious and doesn't like to disappoint people. If he's asked to do a job, he'll do it, even if it means disappointing his son.'

'That's not true,' Nathan hissed. 'He would have been back in plenty of time if it wasn't for the landslide.'

Thompson ignored him and went on, 'To the other crew members, it was just another job; they accepted instructions from what they believed to be a legitimate source. I wanted Stephen Bryce out of the way for a couple of days. Unfortunately, as you said, Nathan, I got the timing wrong, and if it wasn't for the landslide, your dad would have been back on time, you wouldn't have been disappointed and no matter how hard I tried to plant the seed of you setting off to find your mother, you would have gone off on holiday and none of this would have happened.'

159

With a glance through the narrow window at the rising water, Nathan said, 'Now your plans have backfired, Mr whatever your name is, get thinking of a way out.'

Thompson sat on the table, pulled up his knees and locked his hands around them. 'I don't think there is a way out,' he said, apparently unconcerned. 'Unless someone can withdraw the six bolts on the other side of that door. It was lucky I remembered about the jewellery and that it was worth far more than I owed, and a bonus that you were at the museum at the same time. As well as persuading you to hand over the flash drive, I pointed out that you would make a good bargaining tool should the police get too close. Well, it may not have been my idea, but the people I deal with don't have much regard for whoever gets in their way.'

'What I don't get,' Nathan asked, 'is what it is to you whether I look for Lisa.'

'She's your mother.'

Nathan was on the verge of saying that Ann had been far more of a mother to him than Lisa ever was, but a glance at Lisa, stripped of her arrogance and so obviously afraid, made him stop. Instead he said, 'So?'

'Ten years ago I helped Ann Bryce at no small risk to myself and then, because of her and Stephen Bryce, I lost a mother and a father I'd never known. I guess they never explained it to you.'

Lisa jumped in, 'I knew it would be your father's fault.'

'How can you say that?' Nathan retaliated. 'This man is a gangster, a swindler, a hacker, a thief, maybe even a murderer, and if he's expecting his gangster friends to come and rescue him, he's going to be disappointed.' He turned on Leo. 'You are stuck here as much as we are.'

CHAPTER 39

Ann felt Inspector Varma's scrutiny as he sat passively in Peter's sitting room at Holly Cottage. She paced the room and exchanged a meaningful glance with Peter who, after a resigned sigh, said, 'I thought we'd done with all that, Inspector. You must have a file on everything that happened.'

'People died,' Ann said. 'Including Stephen's best friend, Andy Roberts.'

'And it's the Andy Roberts' charity that has been targeted,' Varma emphasised. 'There's always more to learn than what is in a file, Mrs Bryce. Anything you can tell me about this Leo Thompson may help find your son.'

Ann sat in an armchair opposite the inspector. 'Hank—' she baulked at saying the name. 'Hank Freidman and Robert Marshall had previously been convicted of drug offences and holding Stephen and Lisa against their will and when they got out of prison he … in his words, he, Freidman, made it his mission "to make us pay."'

'About ten years ago Stephen had had an allergic reaction to some medication; he was in an induced coma and on life support.' Ann stood, and again paced to and fro. 'You know about the FitzGilbert rubies, Inspector?'

Inspector Varma nodded.

'Then you know Freidman had found a buyer for the jewellery. Despite a man, Mike Haywood, being assigned to protect us, Freidman abducted Nathan and me and was taking us to a place on the Norfolk Broads. Nathan was only six. Mike and I tried to get him away but it was wet and muddy, Nathan slipped down the river bank.' Ann sat on the edge of the armchair. 'I believed Nathan had drowned. I was insane with fury and refused to help Friedman get the jewellery. That was the first time I saw Leo: he was sitting in front of a computer screen. Friedman said he could hack into the hospital system and threatened to … switch off Stephen's life support.' Ann threw up her arms. 'I don't know if that's even possible … but thought I'd already lost Nathan and couldn't take that chance.' Ann felt the crushing pain she had endeavoured to put behind her. After a deep steadying breath she said, 'I can't remember how Lisa and Andy became involved, but I learned later she had pulled Nathan out of the water.' Ann brushed away welling tears. 'But you want to know about the young man I knew as Leo Montague. He was in his early twenties, wore wire-framed glasses with round lenses which he was continually pushing higher on his nose. I suppose you'd call him a computer whizz-kid.' Ann sifted through muddled memories. 'As time went on, it became obvious Leo hadn't realised what he was involved in. People were getting hurt. He helped us get away.' She blinked back renewed tears. 'But not before Stephen's friend Andy was shot and killed.'

'As I understand,' Inspector Varma consulted the file, 'Leo Montague had left the scene before police arrived.'

'Yes,' Ann confirmed. 'And we never saw him again.'

'But that wasn't the end of it, was it, Mrs Bryce? The officer in charge at the time was also shot and killed.'

Her 'Yes' barely audible. 'I'm sure you have all the details.'

Varma's gaze remained steady – challenging Ann to elaborate.

Ann shot another glance at Peter who gave the briefest of nods to encourage her to go on. 'A few weeks later, Stephen was well enough to attend a charity dinner. We had decided that I should wear the FitzGilbert rubies one last time before they went to a museum. The police wondered if it might flush out the man who had employed Hank Freidman. The buyer who, it seemed, would go to any lengths to get them.'

'Who turned out to be Sebastian FitzGilbert,' Varma filled in.

'When Lady Matilda FitzGilbert gave us the jewellery as a wedding present, she said it would prevent her remaining and very distant relations from getting their hands on it. As it turned out, Sebastian had already obtained a good many valuables from various sources, legal and illegal.'

'According to the file, your husband's former agent—' Varma checked his papers, 'Jane Randall, lured your husband to a meeting with Sebastian FitzGilbert at your former home, Elliston House. According to records, your husband and Miss Randall had a good working relationship but she refused to say how or why she'd been *persuaded* to become involved.'

Ann explained, 'Twenty-odd years previously, Jane had a child which she gave up for adoption. Jane was told her son was in considerable

162

trouble with the police, and if she helped FitzGilbert, she'd be given enough money to get herself, her son and her son's father, who she'd recently become reacquainted with, out of the country.'

'And she told you this?'

'No. She told Stephen at that *meeting* when he confronted her.' Ann leaned forward. 'Come on, Inspector, it's suddenly very clear to me.'

'Clear?'

'I wrote to Jane. I should have written sooner but it took some time for me … for all of us, to come to terms with what had happened. We used to be friends, and I wanted Jane to know that I understood the lengths a mother would go to for her son. Unfortunately, Jane had become terminally ill and died shortly after. Her son is Leo Montague.'

'You know this for certain?'

'She told Stephen. Jane and Leo had only just found each other and I can see, if he was looking for someone to blame for her death, it would be us.'

Ann waited for Inspector Varma's reaction, her apprehension vindicated when he said, severely, 'There's no record of this being reported at the time.'

'No.'

'We'll need to speak to your husband when he gets back, have his explanation of why he didn't tell the investigation at the time.'

'I sincerely hope he'll be back very soon, but surely all you need to know is that Leo Montague and Leo Thompson are the same person and he has the skill and motive for getting at us as a family.'

'Mrs Bryce, there's more at stake here than your family.'

'At the moment I'm only interested in my family: getting Nathan and Stephen back … and of course Jessica who has unwittingly become involved.'

'Okay, Mrs Bryce. We know there is an organised gang needing to launder enormous amounts of money. They employ Leo Montague/Thompson to use his computer skills. Leo knows Lisa Brookes is Nathan's birth mother and Lisa's boyfriend is the accountant for the Andy Roberts' charity. Things are falling into place. Excuse me whilst I update my team.' Inspector Varma stood and made to leave the room but hesitated and turned back. 'Your husband also witnessed the shooting of Ian Beresford, the officer in charge of the case at the time.'

'I believe so.'

'I wonder if there's anything else he omitted to tell us.'

163

Ann didn't answer.

Varma found his phone and a few moments later fragments of conversation filtered from outside the sitting room.

Ann put a hand on Peter's shoulder and he covered it with his own. There was nothing to say.

CHAPTER 40

Stephen's attempt to climb the cliff set off yet another avalanche, an accumulation of gravel threatening to force him from the ledge. A glance down made him giddy. He wiped a hand across his cold, clammy brow. 'Shit.'

A few more pebbles rattled from above.

'Stay there. There'll be rope at the farm.'

'Francesco? Frankie?'

'Stay there.'

'I'm not going anywhere, Frankie.' Stephen almost wept. 'I'm not going anywhere.'

*

With an elbow over the cliff edge, Stephen hauled himself onto the grass.

Hands pulled at his jacket, dragged him to safety, and shook his shoulder. 'Signor Stephen. You okay? Please, Signor Stephen.'

The rope around his chest loosened and Stephen took a painful breath. He rolled onto his back and looked into a clear blue sky. Was this the same fog-bound meadow he'd stumbled across – how many hours ago?

He was shaken again. The voice, insistent. 'Please, Stephen,' it sobbed.

Stephen reached up, hooked an arm around the boy's neck and pulled him close. 'I'm okay, Francesco.'

'I thought you were … dead.'

Stephen winced as Francesco hugged him.

'You are hurt.'

'Just a bit battered.' Stephen focused on the boy. 'What about you?'

Francesco put a hand to the back of his head. 'I have a bump the size of an egg, and I must have stumbled around for a while. It's a wonder I didn't fall down the cliff also.'

Stephen managed a short laugh. 'A good thing you didn't. There's not enough room for two on that ledge. Help me up.'

*

Stephen leaned on the doorframe of the farmhouse. 'They have a good start, and will probably be long gone before we get help.'

165

Francesco pushed past and moved into the room. He opened the door of a pot-bellied stove and shoved on a couple of split logs. 'I'll make something to eat.' He paused in his search for food to look at Stephen. 'Please don't think I don't care about catching that man, but we haven't eaten since yesterday. You need to rest and, besides, I can't help being hungry.'

Stephen held his ribs and joined the search. 'Nathan is always hungry.'

'I'm sure your son will be waiting for you – when you get home. And your wife, she will be worried.'

'I tried to ring Ann last night; I believed, for a moment, it connected.'

'Do you think anyone picked up the call?'

'I don't know, Frankie.'

Francesco continued, 'We always leave food here. When we have eaten, then we must go. I don't want to be on the mountain when it gets dark.'

Stephen straightened from looking in a cupboard, and winced.

'Signor Stephen, are you okay?

'Fine as long as I don't breathe too deeply.'

'Look what I've found.' Francesco unwrapped a muslin cloth exposing a slab of pancetta and began cutting thick slices.

*

Stephen looked through a half-shuttered window. 'How far is it to the next village?'

'Just over half-a-day's walk. If we start now, we can reach the outskirts before it gets too dark. We have a truck for bringing supplies for the home village as far as here, then it's backpacked the rest of the way up the mountain. I stay with my grandparents and the others return to their jobs.'

Stephen couldn't remember when he'd taken the last of his medication. His limbs felt heavy and he was sweating.

'We should start now.' Francesco told him.

Stephen felt in his pockets. 'Do you know what happened to my phone?'

'Perhaps you lost it when you fell. Are you ready to go?' Francesco hitched a rucksack across his shoulders. 'Signor Stephen?'

'What?'

'We must go.'

166

'Go?'

'I think, signor, you are not well.'

'I'm fine Frankie. Let's go.' Stephen stumbled, grabbed a chair, saving himself from a fall.

Francesco put a hand under Stephen's arm. 'Please sit.'

Stephen felt for the seat of the chair and gratefully let it take his weight. 'Damn. I wasn't expecting this to happen so quickly.'

'What is wrong?'

Stephen pulled the empty blister pack from his pocket and slapped it on the table.

CHAPTER 41

Lost in thought Ann didn't hear Inspector Varma return to Peter's sitting room.

'You'll be getting a call from the search and rescue authorities in Italy.'

Ann paid immediate attention.

'Last evening,' Varma told her, 'they picked up a brief signal from your husband's phone.'

Hope rose. 'Can they trace it? Do they know where he is? What about the others?'

'They have a rough location, but in an area that is nowhere near where they would expect, but I understand a search is underway.'

Ann found it difficult to speak so nodded her understanding before asking in a whisper, 'And Nathan?'

'We picked up an associate of the person we believe to be the boss man on an unrelated issue, and to help himself, he gave us some information. It seems your Mr Montague or Thompson was working on his own as far as planning moves against your family, and it has worked to our advantage. His employers are none too pleased about their funds being used for his private purposes. He appears to be in as much trouble as your son.'

'Leo Montague deserves all the trouble he gets. What about Nathan? Do you know where he is?'

'We're working on it. Gummy Gibson,' Varma sniggered, 'is not a man to cross lightly, so information is not easily forthcoming.'

'Gummy what?' Ann asked.

'Forgive me, Mrs Bryce. In his youth, Gibson was hit in the mouth with a baseball bat. The name stuck even though he now has the best set of teeth money can buy. And it's not a name his subordinates use, at least not to his face. But—' the inspector returned to the subject at hand. 'We believe your son, together with the girl and Lisa Brookes are still in the area. We know Gibson owns a number of canal-side developments, so that's where we're concentrating our efforts.'

'I should be there,'

'There's nothing you can do, Mrs Bryce.'

Ann's phone jingled, she snatched it up. 'Yes? ... I understand. Thank you.' She returned her attention to the inspector. 'That was Italian search and rescue. They have a helicopter ready to go.'

'In that case,' Inspector Varma said, 'I'll leave you to make appropriate arrangements and assure you I'll be in touch the minute there's any news about your son.'

As the house surveillance system showed the inspector's car leaving, another vehicle entered through the gates.

Ann hurried to welcome her nephew, Matthew, who'd obviously cut short his holiday.

'I've been to the hospital,' he told her. 'Lizzie is just the same.'

She led him into Peter's sitting room where he exchanged an embrace with his grandfather.

Ann and Peter quickly brought Matthew up to date with the situation with Nathan and with his Uncle Stephen. Ann paced the length of the room, turned and said, 'I should be there, but where? Where do I go?'

'It's my fault,' Matthew declared. 'I knew he was going to look for Lisa; I should have stopped him.'

Ann put a hand on his arm. 'He was determined to go, Matthew. You couldn't have prevented it.'

Peter said, 'I'm in touch with Brian Foster, Jessica's father. He's obviously anxious for news. I could pick him up and travel to Birmingham to be nearer Nathan, though I'd like to be on hand should there be any news about Lizzie. She was in my care when she had the seizure and I feel responsible.'

'No.' Matthew reassured his grandad. 'You're not to blame. She's had these fits before.'

Ann covered her face with her hands. 'My head's in a whirl. I don't know what to do.'

'I do,' Matthew declared. 'None of us can split ourselves into three,' he turned to Peter, 'I don't think you should drive into the city.'

Peter looked affronted. 'I've been driving many more years than you, young man.'

'No offence, Grandad,' Matthew said, 'but when was the last time you drove in London? Traffic is bound to be as bad in Birmingham, and you're not used to it anymore.'

Ann cringed as Peter's expression darkened. Nearing eighty, he was fit for his age, but she couldn't recall when he'd last driven any distance.

Matthew persisted, 'I'll collect Jessica's dad and be there when they find Nathan. And you, Aunty Ann, should get the next flight to Italy.'

Ann and Peter gazed at each other and then at Matthew.

Ann said. 'You should be on hand for your mum and dad, Matthew. I don't care who actually gave birth to Nathan, he's my son. I'll collect Jessica's father and Peter—'

'Now, *you're* giving me orders,' Peter bellowed.

'You've given plenty of orders in your time, Peter. Please listen to me. Will you go to Italy?'

'But Aunty Ann,' Matthew interrupted, 'you don't like driving.'

Ann couldn't help regretting James wasn't around to drive her, but taking a deep breath, she said, 'There are a lot of things I don't like, Matthew, but it doesn't mean I can't do them. Stephen would want me to be near Nathan. We'll keep in close touch so we'll know immediately if there's any news. So no more arguments.'

'Let me go with you, Aunty Ann. I'd like to see Lizzie again first, but please let me go with you,' Matthew insisted. 'I'll drive.'

'Will you get a taxi to the airport, Peter?' Ann asked.

When Peter nodded, Ann said, 'Okay, Matthew, you come with me, but clear it with your mum and dad first.'

170

CHAPTER 42

Seepage into the storage room increased to a flood and water now lapped the table. Leo Thompson carefully stepped from the table to stand, with a squelch of wet shoes, on the worktop. Lisa inched away from him and shot Nathan a *do something* look.

Jessica drew back her feet, leaned towards Nathan and whispered, 'Perhaps we should have another go at the window. Maybe I can squeeze through the bars and get some help.' She elbowed him. 'Nathan, we must do something.'

'He's scared,' Lisa threw at them. 'since he fell in the river. Did I tell you, I pulled him out and saved his life?'

'And you've tried to buy my love with it ever since.' Shocked by his own words, Nathan rested his head upon his drawn-up knees and hid his face. For years he'd had nightmares – sliding down the bank, breath snatched away, cold water closing over his head.

Jessica squeezed his arm. 'We're all scared, but we can't just sit here.'

Nathan slowly raised his head. 'Weakness. Mr Thompson—' Nathan despised himself for calling the man responsible for their predicament by name, but manners prevailed. '*He* said he looked for weaknesses. The wall beneath here—' he rapped on the worktop, 'where the outlet for the sink is, is where water is coming in between the bricks. My dad told me that when he was trapped in the cellar at Elliston House, he was able to chip away at crumbled mortar.'

'Elliston House?' Jessica queried.

'Where we used to live, but it was built on medieval foundations and the bricks and mortar in question were over five hundred years old.'

'Yeah, well,' Jessica sighed, 'if you're thinking of chipping away at those bricks you need to get below the water line, and making the hole bigger will only let in more water.'

'Very useful,' was Lisa's sarcastic comment which attracted frowns from Jessica and Nathan.

Nathan's gaze shifted to Leo who seemed to be hiding a smirk, and snapped, 'Are you still expecting your bosses to come to your rescue?'

171

'My skills are unique and of value. They need me.'

'So we wait until someone dashes in to rescue you and we—'
Nathan gestured to the others, 'sit here and let them.'

Leo shifted position and glanced at the door before saying, 'If
you tell me where that memory stick is, they may let us all out.' He
cocked an eye at the camera in the corner of the ceiling.

Nathan followed his line of vision. 'Then they'll have to watch
us drown because I don't know where it is.'

'That's not clever, Nathan.' Lisa kicked out, caught Jessica's
heels.

'Hey, careful. You'll have me off here and in the water.'

'That's what will happen anyway if you don't do something.'
Lisa hitched herself more securely on the worktop.

Nathan was reminded of the reason he'd neglected to keep in
touch with her. It took all his self-control not to say as much – it would
serve no purpose. Instead, he said to Leo, 'You were there when my mum
and that other man, what was his name … Mike Heywood, were locked
in a room in the building on the Norfolk Broads. I remember her saying
a man boasted he could switch off my dad's life support remotely.'

'A bluff,' Leo laughed. 'It was meant to frighten her.'

'She was told the man was a computer genius. It was you.'

'Did she also tell you I helped her get away?'

'Yes. But before then, when they were locked in that room –
how did they get out?'

Leo looked to the ceiling. 'There was a hatch into the roof space.
They broke through the ceiling into another room, but don't get excited,
there are several storeys above here and no hatch.'

Nathan retrieved the kitchen knife he'd used to chip at
paintwork on the window catch and standing on the worktop jabbed it at
the ceiling. Flakes of plaster drifted down.

CHAPTER 43

Ann handed her overnight case to Matthew who stowed it in the boot of his little Peugeot beside his own holdall.

Matthew nipped around the car and into the driving seat.

Ann settled into the front passenger seat and with a sidelong look at her nephew, said, 'I *can* drive, you know.'

'I know, but there's nothing I can do for Lizzie, and I'm sure the police will track down Nathan and we'll be back home tomorrow.'

Nice try, Ann thought. She smiled as though reassured, but remained unconvinced.

Matthew set up the onboard satnav and they set off.

An hour into the journey, Ann's phone rang. 'That's great, Peter. Use my room at the hotel. Speak to Owen Wyatt he's liaising with the rescue team. I know you'll keep me informed, and I'll let you know immediately … Okay, take care.' She slipped the phone back into her bag. 'Grandad Peter's about to board.'

A while later, Ann said, 'I told Brian Foster I'd ring when we're almost there.'

Matthew glanced at the satnav. 'About twenty minutes,' he informed her.

Ann fended off another call from her son, Chris. 'You're in no way responsible,' Ann told him. 'Neither is Richard. Nathan has to take responsibility for his own actions. I'll let you know as soon as I have any information … and about Stephen.'

Ann recognised the village of Crich, a local beauty spot with the added attraction of the Tramway Museum.

'There,' she pointed to a sign hanging over the door of a stone building, a couple of benches and tables set outside.

Matthew pulled up just beyond. 'Have you ever spoken to Mr Foster? Does he still think Nathan stole his car?'

'I hope not,' Ann muttered as she alighted from the vehicle.

'Mrs Bryce?'

Ann swung round to meet a man emerging from a side gate. 'Brian Foster?'

The man gave a brief nod.

'Please call me Ann, Mr Foster.'

'The name's Brian,' he said gruffly. 'I'll get my stuff.'

'We've been on the road a good while; may Matthew and I nip to the loo before we set off again?'

Brian showed them the back entrance into the kitchen. Through an open door, Ann saw a cosy pub with a polished dark wood bar, traditional beer pumps, and beyond, tables with upholstered seating. An ingrained beery smell drifted through.

'I've had to get a relief manager in for a couple of days,' Brian told her as they headed back towards the car. He nodded towards Matthew. 'He's a bit young for a chauffeur, and I expected a Rolls at least.'

Disinclined to explain their regular chauffeur was on holiday, Ann said, 'Matthew is my nephew. I'm not—' she gave it some thought, 'an enthusiastic driver, and Matthew volunteered.'

'My car is somewhere in Birmingham, so I appreciate the lift. I'm not keen on city driving either.'

Settled in the car, Ann said, 'I hope Nathan didn't encourage Jessica to take your car.'

'I doubt she'd need much encouragement. Apparently she was looking for me to ask, but she must have known I wouldn't let her borrow it; certainly not to go on some damn silly jaunt that would get her into so much trouble.'

'Nathan had a disappointment at home and it must have sparked off a ... need for him to speak to his birth mother. If he'd said he wanted to see her, we could have arranged it but he ... well, *I* thought ... judged he was old enough to make up his own mind.'

'He seemed like a sensible lad, Mrs Bryce ... Ann.'

'Yes, he usually is. It's his not-so-sensible mother who has a habit of getting everyone else into trouble.'

'When he stayed here, he said he considered you his mother and it wasn't because of anything you had done ... that ... well, you know what I mean.'

Ann felt tears burn and swallowed hard before saying, 'Thank you.'

After a while, Brian said, 'I haven't heard much about your husband recently. Is he safe now?'

'I don't know. His father, Peter, is on a plane to Italy right now.'

'Let's hope we can get this present problem sorted and you can join him.'

'I hope so.'

Miles rolled by and the peaks and dry stone walls of Derbyshire were replaced by a more urban landscape. Ann said, 'Do you know where your car is?'

Brian rummaged in a pocket. 'The police gave me details. Here—' he handed Ann a folded paper and she relayed the location of the service station where Nathan and Jessica had left his car to Matthew.

Matthew glanced at the screen of the satnav and said, 'It's a few miles further on, just off the motorway.'

Ann handed Brian a sheet of printed information. 'We've booked into this hotel. I told them we might need another room so if you've not made your own arrangements ... I'll pay for it.'

'No need for that,' Brian bristled.

'I know, but I feel responsible, and if there's an excess parking charge you must let me know. Nathan usually gets a holiday job: I'll make sure he repays it.'

Brian snorted his amusement. 'I was thinking Jessica owes me a few hours work in the pub.'

They both smiled, obviously feeling a little more comfortable in each other's company.

Matthew turned off the motorway into a service station car park.

'That looks like my car over there.'

'I'm intending to go to the police station first,' Ann said. 'Maybe there will be some news.'

With 'I'll see you there' Brian slammed the car door and strode across the car park.

CHAPTER 44

Nathan jabbed at the ceiling. Beneath plaster the knife hit a hard substance.

'Told you,' Leo said. 'It's solid concrete.'

Nathan threw the knife into the water. 'Then why are you looking so smug? You're trapped in here the same as us and are just as likely to drown.' Nathan slid from the worktop into waist-deep water; it was cold, and for a moment, it took his breath. He splashed across to Leo, 'Or are you?' Nathan glanced up. 'Is there another camera? Are they still watching? Are they expecting that at the last moment I'll tell you where the memory stick is?' Nathan pulled the front of Leo's jacket, jerking him off the table and into the water. 'Because I'm not. They're going to watch you drown.'

Taken off balance Leo lost his footing and slipped beneath the water, Nathan, still grasping a handful of clothing held him down.

Nathan felt a tug on his arm.

'Let him go. Nathan!' Jessica screamed.

Leo's arms and legs flailed.

Suddenly aware – Nathan let go.

Leo seemed unable to gain his feet, thrashing under the water.

Nathan reached down, again grabbed the man's lapels and pulled him up.

Leo surfaced, coughing and spluttering. 'You little bastard. You could have killed me.'

Nathan stepped back – shocked by his own actions.

Waist deep in murky water, Leo took a couple of shaky breaths – he patted the pockets of his jacket, delved into an inside pocket, then reached under the water and pulled out the linings of the pockets in his trousers. 'You bloody, little fool, you've made me lose it.'

'Your mind?' Nathan snapped. 'You lost that before you started this ridiculous enterprise.'

'The key.' Leo began wafting his hands in the water as if trying to clear the murk. 'I've lost the key.'

Nathan wondered if he'd heard correctly.

It was Jessica's turn to grab Leo's lapels. A head taller, Leo gasped as she pulled him down to her level. 'What key?'

176

'They gave me the key. Help me find it.'

Nathan joined in. 'Who gave you what key?'

Leo glanced towards the camera in the ceiling. 'I've had enough. I'm getting out. Help me find the key.'

*

Ann waited in the corridor of the police station. She ignored a row of chairs against the wall and instead paced to a door with a plaque displaying *DCI Varma* in yellowed italic script and back to double swing doors at the other end. She was joined by Brian Foster who inclined his head towards the DCI's door and said, 'I asked at the desk, he's on his way.'

Ann nodded her understanding, and to avoid a collision both sat on the tubular metal, plastic-seated, chairs.

A moment later, the double doors swung open and Varma, clutching a folder, strode along the corridor. He ushered Ann and Brian into his office and, taking the seat behind the desk, invited them to sit opposite.

'We've picked up a couple of gang members,' the inspector told them, 'and from their information we have been able to narrow the search for Nathan and Jessica to some canal-side properties. It's been made more difficult by the combination of heavy rain and a breach in the old canal wall.

'Mrs Bryce, we were puzzled why the Andy Roberts' charity was targeted to launder money. A charity is subject to a good deal of scrutiny and any unlawful activity would soon be discovered. It seems Leo Thompson or Montague chose it specifically because of the connection to you through Nathan's mother, Lisa Brookes.' Varma opened the file on his desk and said, 'Perhaps you'd like to go over the details of events we were discussing this morning.'

Ann glanced at Brian who sat patiently on the chair beside her. He deserved to know what his daughter had inadvertently become involved in. 'It was over ten years ago; Leo was working for a man named Hank Freidman, who already held a grudge against Stephen. He and Leo kidnapped Nathan, who was just a little boy, and me in an effort to obtain the FitzGilbert rubies.

'Jane Randall, who was Stephen's agent, was Leo's mother. He was adopted as a baby and she'd only recently tracked him down. Hank Freidman coerced her into working for him.' Ann explained. 'He told her that her son Leo was in trouble but promised them enough money for her

177

and Leo to start over if she helped him to steal the FitzGilbert rubies. To cut a long story short, Leo helped us get away. He escaped arrest and disappeared, and I suppose he expected that because he helped us, we, Stephen and I, would help his mother, Jane, but she'd become more deeply involved and, eventually, she was arrested and given a prison sentence. Sadly, she became ill and died a few years ago.'

Brian shifted in his chair. 'And now this Leo chap is holding Nathan and my daughter?'

'Not exactly.' Varma again shuffled some papers. 'It's looking like Leo used gangland cash to fund his activities against the Bryce family.'

Ann said, 'Would those activities include sending fake emails to Stephen and the others to get them on that so-called … shoot? I imagine it wouldn't be difficult for someone of Leo's talent.'

'I think that's a fairly safe bet,' Varma confirmed. 'What's left of the computers seized from the Roberts' charity offices are with forensics right now. They were smashed to pieces but I'm sure the information can be lifted even if they've tried to wipe them. All of which will take time so having the memory stick would make things quicker and easier.'

'Forgive me,' Brian interrupted, 'but that's not helping to find my daughter.'

'There are hundreds of canal-side properties: teams are there right now and we're trying to narrow down the target area.' Inspector Varma collected his papers into the folder. 'The best thing you can do is return to your hotel and I'll be in touch immediately if there's any news.'

*

On the steps of the police station, Brian zipped up his coat and turned to Ann. 'I can't stand by and do nothing.'

'Neither can I. There's a book shop over there. I'm going to buy a map of the canal.'

'There's a satnav in the car,' Matthew piped up. 'And maps on my phone.'

Ann and Brian exchanged a glance. Ann said, 'I'll buy a map anyway and we'll use both.'

Ten minutes later, the three of them sat around a table in a nearby coffee shop. 'The man in the shop told me this map is what the canal boaters use.' The large scale map opened into a long strip, a blue line showing the route of the canal. 'It shows the location of all the marinas,

178

water points, sewage disposal stations and other useful infrastructure. Supermarkets, laundrettes and the like.'

'How is that supposed to help?' Brian asked.

'I'm not sure,' Ann admitted. 'But there are places where there's nothing marked and other stretches that show abandoned warehouses – where canal boats used to unload. If I tell you where, Matthew, will you look on your phone for more information?'

Matthew laid his phone on the table. 'I got chatting to one of the cadets whilst you were with the inspector, and she gave me the name of the apartments where they are doing house-to-house enquiries.'

'Let's try somewhere the police aren't looking,' Brian suggested.

Ann ran a finger along the blue line representing the route of a canal out of town. 'There's an out-of-town shopping centre, then a marina, then a gap before it goes into the countryside. Oh, this is useless. There are more canals here than in Venice, and this chap could own properties anywhere.'

Matthew scrolled through his phone, yet again. 'Why don't we go to the area of those apartments where the police are and—'

'And what?' Brian queried.

Ann said, 'The police must have some information that has led them there.'

After more scrolling, Matthew said, 'I've got the postcode.'

Brian drained his mug of coffee and plonked it on the table. 'Let's do *something*, I can't just sit here.'

*

Following Matthew's instructions, Ann drove through city suburbs, occasionally mumbling, 'I hate city streets. Where are all these people going?'

'Just concentrate,' Brian called from the back seat. 'Watch that taxi!'

'Next left,' Matthew instructed. 'Then follow the road around to the right.'

Surprised to find an area of parkland, Ann said, 'This is pleasant.'

'Those flats look expensive,' Brian commented.

'Canal-side apartments, Brian,' Ann corrected. 'And I guess they're much sought after.'

'There are a couple of police cars down there,' Matthew pointed out.

'Let's go and have a word.' Brian was out of the car almost before Ann had drawn to a halt.

Leaving the car at the kerbside, Ann caught up with Brian who was speaking to an officer who had exited the main entrance to the apartment building.

Brian said, 'They've been to every flat here and are moving on. Do we follow?'

Ann shrugged and turned to ask Matthew but saw he had wandered over to the grassy area further along and was jogging back towards them.

'Aunty Ann, there's a towpath and some picnic tables over there'

'Just like Nathan, you're always hungry but this is no time—'

'Behind those trees there's a lock and it looks as if a river runs alongside the canal.'

'All very attractive,' Brian chipped in, 'but—'

'There are some buildings on the other side, I just thought …'

'They are old factory or warehouse buildings,' the police officer told them. 'They're on our search list, but there has been above average rainfall and there's a danger of flooding: the buildings aren't safe. We have to wait for a specialist team, and they've been called to an incident elsewhere.' As if reading their minds the officer said, 'We'll get to them as quickly as possible, but in the meantime it's best if you keep out of the way. We'll see if anyone in the next block has seen anything.' The officer joined half a dozen others who piled into the two police vehicles.

Ann's phone rang – it was Peter.

180

CHAPTER 45

Peter stepped from the taxi to be greeted by Owen Wyatt waiting on the steps of the hotel.

'Hello, Mr Bryce. We've just had a briefing from search and rescue, so if you'd like to come into the meeting room, I'll bring you up to date.'

*

Thirty minutes later, Peter threw his holdall onto the bed in Ann's hotel room, drew out his mobile and rang her number. She answered immediately. 'Ann, rescue services picked up a brief phone signal last evening but in an unexpected area. A team has been sent out. I'll let you know as soon as I hear anything. Any news of Nathan?'

'Police believe he and Jessica are being held together, possibly with Lisa. They're searching properties and doing house-to-house enquiries in case anyone has seen anything. Are they hopeful?' She went on without pause.

Peter knew she was referring to Stephen and the Italian rescue services. 'They'll know more when they get out there. What will you do now?'

'Matthew is calling, must go. I'll ring later.'

'Ann, don't do anything—'

She was gone. He tossed the phone to join the hold-all on the bed. Despite recent bad weather in the area, it was now much warmer than he had anticipated, so he nipped to the bathroom to freshen up and change his shirt before returning to the hotel meeting room.

Someone called his name and he turned to face an attractive woman in her fifties, he guessed.

'I'm Sarah Austin,' she told him. 'Owen pointed you out as Stephen's father. My daughter, Louise, was the production assistant for this shoot and is still missing.'

He took the offered hand. 'I'm Peter. Have I missed anything?'

'You know about the phone call?'

'Yes.'

'Assuming they all stayed together, Louise and the others will be with Stephen. I know Owen said we should wait here, but I'd like to go to the rescue headquarters ... to be nearer.'

Peter glanced around the room. Owen was speaking to other relatives; he watched him usher them outside to the patio where a continual supply of coffee and snacks was available.

To Sarah, he said, 'Give me ten minutes to organise a hire car.'

*

Sarah settled into the passenger seat of a Fiat 500 and handed Peter a scrap of paper. 'This is the address, it's just out of town.'

'Right,' said Peter, scratching his head. 'My Italian is limited but let me see if I can programme the satnav.'

Peter drew up outside the perimeter gates of a square building situated inside a fenced-off area. A helipad was marked out on an expanse of tarmac. 'Looks as if an aerial search is already underway.'

As they watched, a team of five individuals, orange suited and helmeted, piled into an all-terrain vehicle. Gates hauled open, the vehicle rolled along the road and towards foothills which led to the mountain range beyond.

Peter drummed his fingers on the steering wheel for a moment before exchanging a glance with Sarah.

She nodded briefly. He put the vehicle into drive and followed the Land Rover.

The road became a track, the Land Rover, easily negotiating the rough terrain, was soon out of sight, and it was some time later, high in the foothills, Peter and Sarah entered the outskirts of a village. Dirt roads separated roughly built houses, the settlement sparsely populated.

'There's the Land Rover,' Peter pointed to the remains of a small piazza, obviously at one time the hub of village life.

At a sound from above, they stepped from the car and gazed into the sky. A helicopter swooped down from the hills and hovered for a moment before it settled behind a row of houses. Peter and Sarah followed the rescue team and villagers gathering on the meadow where the aircraft had landed.

Sarah gripped Peter's arm. 'There's someone strapped to a stretcher.'

Wishing it were Ann by his side, Peter gently prised her fingers from his arm. 'I'll find someone to speak to.'

*

182

Peter introduced himself to the person appearing to be in charge.

Angelo Russo, said, 'You shouldn't be here, Mr Bryce. I'll be in contact with Owen immediately we have definite information.' Angelo, glanced across to the helicopter where a body was being lifted into the Land Rover and obviously taking pity on Peter and Sarah, said, 'It is Arturo Morretti.'

'The guide?' Sarah said.

'Si.'

'Who's that?' Peter asked as a youth was accompanied from a building nearby and, with a blanket around his shoulders, was ushered into the rescue Land Rover.

'A boy from a village high in the mountains. Please return to rescue headquarters, Mr Bryce, where I'll give you all the information we have.'

Peter took Sarah's arm. 'Let's get back.'

*

An hour later Peter and Sarah sat facing Angelo and Owen Wyatt at Rescue Headquarters. The youth they had seen at the village sat to one side.

Angelo said, 'I should be briefing Owen in order for him to pass on all the information we have to the relatives of the missing, but as you're here, I can confirm, Mrs Austin, that we believe your daughter Louise, and lighting man, Yash Patel, should be safely at a village high in the mountains. The helicopter is on its way right now.'

Sarah's rigid posture relaxed, a muscle twitched her cheek as she fought tears.'

Peter laid a hand briefly over hers and swallowed the million questions rattling around his head.

Owen rose. 'I must tell the others. I'll take you back to the hotel, Sarah.' He put a hand under her elbow, helped her to her feet and led her from the room.

Peter watched them leave before fixing an icy gaze at Angelo. His effort to convince himself he was ready for anything, in danger of failing.

'Francesco?' Angelo prompted.

Peter looked towards the boy and was reminded of his own grandsons. He managed a smile of encouragement for the lad.

'You are Signor Stephen's father?'

'Yes, Francesco.'

183

'Stephen is a nice man.'

'Yes.' A moment's silence hung before Peter said, 'Do you know where he is? Is he okay?'

'I wanted him to come with me, but he had run out of his medication, he didn't feel well—'

'There's an armed team with medics on the way,' Angelo told Peter, 'and I must get to the control room.' He turned to Francesco. 'You'd better let the medics check you over.'

'Just a second,' Peter called. 'What's this about an armed team?'

'Ah,' Angelo hesitated.

'Please,' Francesco interjected. 'Please, I would like to tell Signor Bryce all I know.'

'Come on,' Peter said gently. 'There's a coffee shop around the corner; let me buy you something to eat.'

Ten minutes later, comfortably ensconced at the rear of the coffee shop, Francesco took a bite from a slice of traditional Italian pizza.

Peter sipped a strong coffee, and waited until the boy sat back, wiped his mouth with a paper napkin and said, 'Grazie.'

'You're very welcome, Francesco. I know how hungry young men get.'

Francesco grinned. 'Like Nathan?'

'Yes, exactly like Nathan and his cousin, Matthew. They must be around your age.'

'Signor Stephen told me about Nathan. How they should have been going on a special holiday. Stephen is sorry to cause you all so much worry.'

'Yes,' Peter murmured. 'We are all worried.'

After a period of silence Peter's patience was rewarded when Francesco went on, 'Arturo brought them to our village. Four men and a woman. He said there had been a landslide, they were unable to get down the mountain and had been walking for two days. Stephen was dressed as a soldier and Nonna – my grandmother – believed he was one of the escaped prisoners of war who took refuge in the village when she was a girl.'

'That's what the film will be about,' Peter said. 'They were filming a taster, a preview.'

'Stephen tried to explain, but Nonna … well, it was better to let her believe he had come back, as the soldier promised all those years ago.

184

'I go to the village when I can, to help Nonna and Nonno, but there are only old people still in the village, so there are plenty of empty houses. Arturo, the one they call Cavendish and an older man, I think they called him Ethan, bedded down in the big house. The woman, Louise, she stayed with the widow Romano and the other man … err—'

'That would be Yash,' Peter helped out.

'Si, Yash, he was in another room. Stephen stayed with us.' Francesco paused to take a swig of cola. 'We believed Arturo intended to lead them to the next village further down the mountain the following day in the hope of getting a phone signal and asking for help.'

'The satellite phone must have been lost in the landslide,' Peter concluded.

'The next day we found—'

'What did you find?' Peter prompted.

'Arturo and the Cavendish man had left before dawn and the other one, Ethan, he was … he had died during the night.'

Peter wondered if he had heard correctly but didn't interrupt as Francesco went on. 'The others, they decided perhaps Arturo and Cavendish would not send help and that they must make their own way down the mountain. The streams are running high, the way is not used often and is unclear and they would need to spend the night safely, so I show them the way.'

'That was good, Francesco,' Peter encouraged. 'But what happened?'

'The young man, Yash, slipped on rocks, his leg twisted. It was nearer to go back to my village than to go on. They discussed who should go back and who would continue and decided as Stephen had no more medication his need was greatest, he and I would go on. We caught up with Cavendish and Arturo at the old farmhouse and hid overnight but next morning, they found us. I believed Arturo was a good man, Signor Bryce but he and Cavendish they … tried to kill us before setting off again towards the lower village. I heard them say arrangements had been made to pick them up. They had no intention of sending help back to us and the others. I told Stephen we could follow, get to the village and send help. It would mean letting Cavendish and Arturo get there first and make their escape but maybe the police would find them.'

'That was your plan, but Arturo is dead. What happened? Where is Stephen?'

CHAPTER 46

Ann and Brian followed Matthew across the expanse of grass towards the canal. 'Who would believe it would be so pleasant close to the city centre?'

'We're more into the suburbs,' Brian noted. 'Where's the lad leading us?'

'We need to cross the lock gates,' Matthew called back to them. He balanced across the gates that held back the dark and murky waters of the canal.

The deep lock, providing access to the river at a lower level, was empty. Water trickled through gaps in the planks, aquatic plants clung to bricks lining the sides. Beyond, the river churned and boiled. Ann gripped the handrail and carefully followed along the crossbeam, stepping over the narrow gap at the V where the gates met in the middle.

Brian followed, joining the others on a circular brick area surrounding the winding mechanism that operated the paddles in the gates.

'What do you think?' Matthew asked, pointing across a rough, grassy area towards some old warehouse buildings surrounded by a rusty wire fence, trees and river beyond.

'I think, Matthew,' Ann said, 'that it looks derelict and we should wait until the police search team arrives.'

'We can at least have a look.' Matthew set off across the rough ground and slipped through a gap in the wire fence.

Ann and Brian followed, catching up with the boy as he used a stick to try to prise open a rusted metal door.

The stick broke with a crack. Matthew tossed it aside and stooped to peer through a barred basement window. 'It's boarded up on the inside.' He moved to other windows, some looked into empty rooms, others with disintegrating boxes scattered around. He shinned up a rusting drainpipe and with one foot on a sill looked into rooms on the first floor. He eased down the pipe and dropped the last metre to the ground.

'Nothing.' He trotted around the side wall, red brickwork crumbling in places.

Brian pointed out, 'The river has broken its bank, look, through those trees.'

Ann stood her ground. 'I can hear water splashing.'

Brian, now someway in front, said, 'The river narrows and is crashing over the weir.' He turned back. 'What's the matter?'

'Nathan doesn't like water. I mean he swims for his school but he won't go near a river, especially when it's ... like this.'

'No one in their right mind would go near the bank.' Brian glanced around. 'Where's your other lad gone?'

'Matthew,' Ann called, 'come away from there.'

Balanced on a low rampart alongside the disused warehouse, Matthew clung to a drainpipe with one hand and, leaning out over the river, was peering around the corner where barred windows looked directly over the water.

Ann hesitated, shoes sinking into soggy ground, before again shouting, 'Matthew! Get down.'

'I can reach the bars on the window,' Matthew called back. 'If I can get a foothold, I'll be able to see inside.'

'Matthew, don't.' Ann turned to Brian. 'Tell him to come back.'

'This is the sort of place they could be held.' Brian climbed onto the wall beside Matthew. 'If I hang on to your sleeve, can you lean out a little further?'

'No,' Ann almost cried. Ten years ago she'd believed she'd lost Nathan to the treacherous flood waters of the Norfolk Broads. She was already wondering how she'd tell Julian and Fiona if Matthew should fall into the river.

Ann gnawed her knuckles, torn between urging them on and wishing them to return to safe ground.

A foot on a crumbling sill, Matthew held on to the bars of the window above. 'Just an empty room,' he called.   'There's   a basement window but the river is gushing over the sill.'

'Leave it, Matthew,' Ann called over the roar of the river. 'I'll ring Inspector Varma, find out how long it will be before they can search.'

Ann strained to hear Matthew shout over the noise of the river. 'I can reach.'

Brian had inched around the corner to take up Matthew's previous position; Matthew was now a window further on and spreadeagled against the wall, one foot planted on the sill that was awash. Ann couldn't see how he was holding on, but he reached down, bending double to look through the narrow barred window.

CHAPTER 47

'What sort of key?' Nathan demanded. 'There's no keyhole.

'It's like a fob for a car key,' Leo said. 'It operates the bolts remotely. It was specially fitted.'

Limited visibility beneath the water hindered Nathan's search. He swept his hands across the floor, trying to locate the key. Bursting to the surface he gasped for breath.

'Wait.' Jessica, water almost to her shoulders, instructed. 'Stop splashing about. Let the water settle.' Her voice trembled – cold beginning to strike. 'Check your pockets properly,' she told Leo.

'It was here.' Leo searched the inside pocket of his jacket. He turned the lining inside out, while Jessica and Nathan patted and prodded the rest of his clothing.

Nathan pushed him away. 'To say you're a technical genius, you are the most stupid man I've—'

'There's someone outside.' Lisa, kneeling on the worktops banged the flat of her hand on the thick glass. 'I saw someone outside.'

Nathan heaved himself up to kneel beside her and craned his neck. 'It's the river bashing against the window.'

'No, I saw someone.'

'I've found it.' Jessica cried in triumph.

Nathan twisted around to see Jessica, wet hair plastered to her head, holding aloft what looked like a small square remote control. Forgetting the cold, Nathan slipped into the water, he and Jessica exchanging a glance of hope as she pressed one of the two integral buttons.

Nothing.

She tried the second, then pressed them each repeatedly. 'It must be waterlogged. We need to dry the battery.' She endeavoured to slide the casing apart.

'Let me try.' Nathan first tried the 'lock' and then 'unlock' buttons, just to be sure, before pulling the gadget apart. A collective weight of despair descended as he showed the others the empty space where a tiny battery should fit.

Leo's eyes widened, disbelief writ plainly on his face.

'Your so-called friends intend you to die with us.' Nathan fought despair. Did he escape drowning as a child to succumb as a teenager? He glanced across to where Lisa sat on the worktop under the window, knees pulled up to her chin. Expressionless, she shivered, gazing ahead, trancelike.

Leo was also sitting in water that had now reached several centimetres above the worktop. It hit Nathan that he would get very little help from that direction.

A current of water swept against him, it swirled and lapped the walls. He looked towards Jessica, who'd also noticed.

Indicating for Jessica to stay put, he tucked the two halves of the key case into the pocket of his jeans before filling his lungs with air and diving under the sink unit to the site of the initial leak into the room. Mortar between the bricks, where water had first seeped through, was now displaced, the bricks loose.

He surfaced, sucked in air. 'There's ... a ... way.'

Jessica grabbed handfuls of his jacket, hope written, desperately, in her eyes.

'But,' he warned, 'it's dangerous. It might be better to wait here.'

'It's dangerous staying here.'

'Water finds its own level,' Nathan pointed out. 'It will only rise to the height of the river.'

'The river is still rising,' Jessica told him. 'It's above the level of the windowsill.

Nathan glanced towards the window.

'Besides,' Jessica went on, 'we'll all be dead from hypothermia before then.'

CHAPTER 48

'Francesco,' Peter persisted. 'What happened to Arturo?'

'It was late morning by the time we, Stephen and I, had prepared for the journey. We decided to give Arturo and Cavendish time to get well ahead but still allow time for us to get to the village before dark. Stephen was not strong...'

'Give me a minute.' Stephen waited for his head to clear. 'Okay, let's go.'

Francesco set a good pace, Stephen determined to keep up.

The sun broke through high clouds, and at a lower altitude, the temperature soon rose. There was no distinct path, but Francesco's direction didn't falter. Stephen followed, concentrating on the boy's heels as they stepped through fresh spring meadow grass.

An hour seemed an age and the distance between Stephen's army footwear and the heels of Francesco's boots extended with every stride. Sweat trickled into Stephen's eyes and soaked into his khaki shirt, the cause, he was aware, more than a brisk walk on a warm spring day.

He increased his concentration. One foot in front of the other. One foot in front— the ground rotated. Grass where the sky should be.

With Francesco's hand guiding his own, Stephen sipped tepid water from the flask.

'A couple of miles further there is scrubland and bushes which will give us shade,' Francesco told him. 'We can rest there.'

Stephen forced himself to stand. It had been a shock to discover how quickly his condition deteriorated without regular medication.

'Stay here.' Francesco said, when they reached a shady spot. 'I will go on.' He left the flask with Stephen...

*

'I walked until mid-afternoon,' Francesco told Peter. 'When I came to the empty buildings on the outskirts of the village I knew there was not far to go.' Francesco put his head in his hands. 'I should have carried on into the village, but I heard a commotion and went to look...'

*

Francesco stepped from the path towards one of the empty houses lining the road into the once busy town.

'No one is coming.'

Francesco recognised Arturo's voice and ducked below a glassless window in the ground floor of the empty stucco building.

Cavendish said, 'Arrangements have been made to pick us up, I just need to tell him where and when.'

'When did you last have contact with *him*?'

'It's this damn satellite phone, maybe it *is* damaged.'

'You said I would be paid when I led your party far enough away to make rescue difficult. I did not bargain for you murdering that old man.'

'He had a bad heart.'

'Kneeling on his chest with your hands around his throat didn't help.'

'Shut up, Arturo. He saw the phone was working and heard us discussing our next move.'

'When will I get my money? I need to pay some people. People who won't wait. Nothing has gone right since we started. That explosion was supposed to just block the road, not bring down the whole mountainside. We could all have been killed.'

'It's not my fault the whole area was unstable.'

'I could have told you—'

'Well, it's too late now and if that bastard has left us in the shit, I'll—' Cavendish slammed the phone's handset into the casing.

After a few moments Cavendish retrieved the handset. 'I'm fed up with trying to deal with the monkey; it's time I spoke to the organ grinder.'

It took a while to wade through a sea of minions but eventually, Cavendish allowed Arturo to lean in to the speaker and hear a voice say, 'Hello, Max, what's the problem? You've done good work for me in the past, but you should know better than to contact me directly.'

'Your man promised to get us out, Mr Gibson. Where's the transport?'

'None of my doing, Maxy. It seems a protégé of mine has rather taken advantage of my good nature.'

'Protégé?'

'A young man I believed had good prospects with the firm. A computer wizard, he could move money around leaving hardly a trace. The thing is, Maxy, Leo moved it to the wrong places. I can't allow anyone to use money meant for the organisation for their own purposes so I've had to … sort of … let him go.'

191

'But you can still send transport to pick us up?'

'Not my problem, Maxy. Seems Leo has a vendetta with this actor fellow and his family. Nothing to do with me, though he did put us on to a few gems that weren't as secure as they might have been. Still, it's not good for the image to be taken advantage of. Oh, and don't bother trying this number again, it's time it was changed.'

Francesco peeped over the windowsill. Max Cavendish, looking shell-shocked, let the phone handset dangle. 'Looks like we're on our own.'

'I need the money,' Arturo pleaded. 'My family ...'

'Let's go into the village, find some transport and get out of here. There'll be time enough to settle up with—'

Both men looked towards the window.

'Get him,' Cavendish ordered.

Francesco bolted.

Arturo nipped out of a side door, barged into Francesco and with his superior weight knocked him to the ground before dragging him inside. 'I'm not going to hurt you, Frankie, but we need you to stay here for a while.'

Cavendish pushed Arturo aside. 'We can't afford to have anyone raise the alarm.'

'I'll tie him up, leave him in the back room.'...

*

'Cavendish had a gun,' Francesco told Peter. 'There was a scuffle. The gun fired, Arturo fell and I ran. Arturo is ... was not a bad man,' Francesco mumbled into his hands.

'Arturo was a gambler, up to his eyes in debt,' Peter explained. 'He feared for his family.' He gave Francesco time to recover a little before saying, 'We know who's behind this. A man we, my family, had dealings with years ago. A clever young man who's used his talents for the wrong purpose. Ann, Stephen's wife, believed she had given him a chance to change, but then his mother, who was once a friend of Ann and Stephen's, died and ... she was ill and I honestly don't believe we've done anything to warrant the bitterness he obviously feels towards us, not after—' Peter found it difficult to articulate the cruelties of Leo and his former associates ten years ago and returning to the present said, 'Leo not only successfully deceived Stephen and other crew members that the emails setting up a couple of days' work came from a genuine source but has somehow manipulated my grandson Nathan into chasing after his

192

birth mother whose boyfriend is … was mixed up with a money laundering scam which Leo was operating for an organised crime gang. Now Nathan and his girlfriend are missing and Ann ripped apart, not knowing where to be.'

'Stephen told me he is sorry to have disappointed Nathan. He spoke of Ann and how he misses them both. This man Leo, the same man who set things up with Cavendish, you think he has done something to them?

'From what you say, and what the inspector has found out, Leo used gangland money and now they've thrown him to the wolves. It's anyone's guess what he'll do.'

They were interrupted. 'The teams are ready to leave,' Angelo told them. 'A helicopter is on its way to your village, Francesco, to pick up Louise Austin and Yash Patel and a couple vehicles ready to search for Stephen Bryce.'

Francesco stood, almost knocking over the chair. 'I will go with them. Vehicles can only get so far, then it will be on foot.'

Peter also got to his feet but was met with, 'No, Mr Bryce.' Angelo was firm. 'Francesco can show us the way but there is no more room and we don't know what we'll find.'

CHAPTER 49

Nathan glanced towards Lisa who was sitting on the worktop, arms wrapped around her knees, every muscle trembling.

Jessica followed his line of vision. 'We must do something soon, for all of us.'

'As soon as I pull the bricks away, water will flood in. It's a strong current but if I can grab the bars over the window—'

'Do it,' Jessica implored. 'Maybe you can climb up and fetch help or at least attract someone's attention. I'll help. I can hang onto you from this side for as long as I can hold my breath.'

'Okay,' Nathan agreed and inclining his head towards Lisa, said, 'I'll tell her.' He hitched onto the worktop beside his mother. 'I'll try to get help.'

Suddenly alert, Lisa said, 'You can't leave me.'

'I'll fetch help.'

'I'll come with you.'

'No. I need to get out into the river. It's dangerous.'

Leo Thompson leaned across. 'What are you doing?'

Nathan ignored him and continued to Lisa, 'Water will rush in but won't get any higher than here—' He indicated about half a metre from the ceiling. 'It shouldn't get any higher as long as the river doesn't rise any further.'

Lisa glanced at water crashing against the window before gazing at her son. 'I know I've never been much of a mother to you, even at a distance, but … I do love you.' She touched his face.

Nathan gripped her wrists. It crossed his mind to say *You've never shown it* but, with tears stinging his eyes, gave her a tight smile and slipped off the counter and into the water. He picked up the knife they'd used earlier and, taking a deep breath, sank below the water. Under the sink unit, around the waste pipe, he jabbed at the cement between the bricks where water was already seeping through. He pushed his fingers into the crack and dislodged a brick, the surge of water knocked him back, other bricks tumbling inwards. He pushed up, broke surface, choked and gasped for breath, river water bubbling up from the hole in the wall.

Jessica had taken off her gold coloured jacket and told Nathan to take his off, helping drag the wet garment from his shoulders. She tied

194

a sleeve of each coat together, then tucked one of the other sleeves into Nathan's belt.

'What are you doing?'

'Tie it round your belt.'

He pulled the sleeve through and into a knot.

'When you get through the hole the force of the water will drag you downstream. You need to push up above the windowsill and get a grip on the bars.'

Nathan nodded. 'Once I've got my feet on the sill I should be able to climb up.'

Jessica gave the knot in the sleeve wrapped around his belt a final pull to ensure it was tight. She wrapped the furthest sleeve around her hand a couple of times.

Nathan said. 'As soon as I've got a firm hold outside, don't forget to let go or you'll be dragged out as well. Take a couple of deep breaths, and on three, we go. One, two—' they sank, fighting the incoming water. Immediately on reaching the hole, Nathan felt the current change. It had been forcing him back but now it grabbed him, sucked him into the river and, like a steam hammer, punched him downstream.

The makeshift rope stretched, held, jolted him to a halt, the surge of water tossing him around as if in a washing machine.

Something bumped against him, was gone, left him wondering which way was up.

*

Jessica felt the tether pull taut, almost wrenched from her hands. It jerked around as Nathan kicked and struggled. She braced against the wall, loose bricks moved. Seconds ticked by and Jessica's lungs begged for air.

A splash from above, something hit Jessica, knocked the remaining breath from her lungs, she breathed in water, let go of the lifeline and thrashed her way to the surface. She coughed, sucked in air and coughed again. Gasping she hauled herself on to the counter.

*

Nathan felt the lifeline give way. The current threw him into the wall of the building – a glimpse of a window sill, bars set into the concrete. Grab – now. Hang on. His body streamed horizontal in the current, like a flag in the wind.

Cold fingers, curled around an iron bar, began to slip. Nathan tried to adjust his hold – let go and he'd be swept down river to where water crashed over the weir.

195

CHAPTER 50

At the edge of the lower village, the main road dwindled to a rough path as if the settlement had run out of the energy needed to continue expansion. Francesco directed the driver of the rescue vehicle along the path and into an expanse of meadow grass, the four-by-four vehicle leaving a trail of flattened grass.

Further along, the ground became uneven and the vehicle bumped over a dozen miles of bushes and scrubland.

'There.' Francesco pointed. 'I left Stephen just beyond those bushes.' He slipped from the vehicle and jogged ahead, waved them on, then stood and looked bewildered. He cast around left and right, moved further into the bushes and stubbly trees.

A couple of the team joined Francesco as he stooped to pick up a leather water bottle. 'I left it with Stephen.'

'Spread out,' the leader instructed.

CHAPTER 51

A hand reached down and gripped Nathan's wrist.

'I gotcha, Nath. Hang on.'

The support allowed Nathan to adjust his grip on the bars, get a knee on the sill and haul himself out of the water.

'Stand on the sill,' the voice insisted. 'Reach for the bars on the window above.'

Nathan mechanically did as he was told. When standing on the basement sill and holding on to the bars of the above window, he chanced a glance to his left. His lips moved but couldn't utter the name.

'It's two windows across to the bank. Just one foot at a time, Nathan. Move one foot, then the other.'

Nathan felt his knees tremble. Fingers frozen around the bars on the ground floor window. He couldn't move.

'Where's Jessica?' someone further along called.

Jessica! Nathan moved his left foot along the sill, left hand to the next bar. Inch by inch, to the second window, where he'd seen Brian Foster clinging to the bars. Brian was now standing on the grass by the end of the building.

As he moved sideways step by step, Matthew kept up his encouragement. 'Nearly there, Nathan.'

Matthew dropped to the ground followed by Nathan whose legs collapsed beneath him.

Dear faces floated before him. Ann's voice, arms, warm lips on his forehead – then, 'Where are the others?'

Another voice, 'Where's Jessica?'

Nathan pulled himself from Ann's arms, sat up and began picking at the soaked material of his jeans' pockets. He dragged out half the casing for the key. 'Go round the front,' he gasped. 'Door. Basement.'

'What's this?' Brian yelled.

'It's an electronic key.' Nathan struggled to his feet the easier to work the other half of the casing from his pocket. 'It needs a battery – quickly … water rising.'

Matthew grabbed the pieces and took off towards the front of the building, Brian Foster on his heels.

Nathan followed, heavy footed, trailed by Ann.

Sound from distant sirens drifted from over the canal and a glimpse of officers crossing the lock gates registered vaguely as Nathan caught up with Brian and Matthew at the main door which was padlocked.

'There's a secure room in the basement,' Nathan told them.

A policeman pushed past and inserted a crowbar behind the bolts holding the padlock and prised it off.

Nathan ran across an expanse of warehouse flooring, wet trainers slapping and leaving a trail of footprints, to a series of doors on the far side. One led to a stone staircase, another row of doors set along a corridor below. The first room was empty, the second door opened on to a computer room, desks, equipment smashed to pieces among a tangle of wires. Further along the corridor, water had trickled from minute gaps under a metal security door.

'Get it open,' Nathan appealed to anyone and everyone. 'Water has come in from the river and is this high—' He indicated his head height.'

Several police officers had followed, and these moved aside to allow access to a man in plain clothes who Nathan recognised as Inspector Varma.

'I know,' the inspector said, 'that the river runs alongside the building but how come the room is flooded?'

'Because I had to make a bloody hole in the wall to get out,' Nathan snapped. 'But it was coming in before. There were gaps in the brickwork under the sink, cement must have been washing away for years. They left us here to drown or die of hypothermia. Please, get the door open.'

The officer with the crowbar had already inserted it behind the metal lip against which the door closed, but Matthew called, 'Don't damage the door,' above the general hubbub. 'We need a battery for this.' He held up the remote fob. 'Unless you know the override code, there's no other way of opening it.' He pulled out the hem of his T-shirt and dabbed at the inside of the casing of the electronic key.

Ann rummaged in her bag and found the remote for the gates at Holly Cottage.

Nathan snatched it from his mum, but fingers cold and trembling failed to open the casing. A police officer took it from him, prised it apart, took out the tiny button battery and handed it to Matthew. 'Try this.'

Matthew pressed in the battery, snapped the casing shut and pressed the 'open' icon – mechanism grated – the sound of multiple bolts sliding back. Three officers threw their weight against the door.

'It's the p-pressure of w-water on the other side,' Nathan told them, through chattering teeth.

The officer with the crowbar again slotted it behind the metal lip. The lip bent, twisted. Water dribbled through a crack.

Nathan tried to contain panic. 'Go on. Quickly. Keep trying.'

'Okay, son, we've got it,' Varma told him.

Water at last gushed from the room – Nathan first to squeeze through the gap into subsiding river water. Jessica, sitting on the worktop, hugged her knees and gazed at him as if in disbelief. Slowly, she unwound and slipped from the counter into the water and into his arms.

People filed into the room behind Nathan. Brian Foster forced his way through the uniformed officers and Jessica slipped from Nathan's arms and into her father's.

Water still bubbled from under the sink but now flowed through the damaged door and would, no doubt, spread across the whole of the basement.

'Where is she?' Nathan asked no one in particular.

Jessica turned from her father. 'She's gone.'

Nathan shrugged his bewilderment.

'She ... Lisa ...' Jessica, teeth chattering, put a hand on Nathan's arm. 'She ... pushed me out of the way when I was holding on to you and ... disappeared.'

Before Nathan could digest this information, Inspector Varma had joined them.

'Get these two out of here,' he instructed. 'Get them checked out and find them some dry clothes.'

As Nathan was led away, he heard Varma continuing to give orders. 'Get as much evidence as you can from here and the computer room next door before the water ruins everything.'

Ann paced the grassy area between the canal and lock gates, and the warehouse on the bank of the river. Police, parked on the other side of the canal, were obliged to troop in single file over the lock gates. The occupants of a narrowboat, waiting to enter the lock, were directed by officers aboard a police launch to moor further down the canal. Divers on board the launch prepared to conduct a search.

Paramedics carrying equipment followed the police across the lock gates. Ann, waiting by the main warehouse door, watched a foil sheet being thrown around Nathan's shoulders as he emerged with Matthew. Then came Brian, his arm around Jessica who also accepted a foil sheet.

Initial relief expended, feeling alone and surplus to requirements, Ann trailed them back across the lock gates. Ambulance doors closed on Nathan accompanied by Matthew; Brian and Jessica escorted into a second vehicle.

An ambulance door was flung open and Matthew stepped down. 'Aunty Ann.'

She was there in a moment. 'How is he?'

'He wants to speak to you.' Matthew helped her mount the step and closed the door giving them privacy.

Ann met Nathan's outstretched hand with her own before they closed in a hug, pleased to note some colour was returning to his face now his wet clothes had been discarded and replaced by a fleece tracksuit.

'He's fine,' the paramedic declared.

The ambulance door opened again and Inspector Varma stepped inside. 'We'll get you checked at the hospital, and then I'll need a full statement at the station.'

'Yeah, sure,' Nathan told him. 'But I'd like to speak to my mum.'

'Five minutes.'

Nathan waited for the inspector to close the door.   'What are you doing here, Mum? I thought you were with Dad. Have they found him?'

'I'm waiting for a call from Grandad. He's gone to Italy whilst I came with Matthew and Jessica's dad. We didn't know where you were or what was happening.'

'I'm sorry. I shouldn't have … but Lisa was here and I don't know where she is now. I think she might have gone in the river.'

'The police have divers out. They'll find her.'

'And there's the man I thought was my teacher but he's not—' he stifled a sob. 'They left us to die.'

Ann squeezed his trembling hands, brushed his fair, curly hair now wet and straggly, from his forehead. His arms tight around her waist, she held him. 'But you're safe now, darling. You're safe.'

Nathan pushed his mum to arm's length. 'They will find Dad, won't they?'

'Yes, they'll find him.'

Ann felt a return squeeze of her hand before Nathan swallowed hard, and said, 'I'm okay now. You go – find him.'

Ann's heart split in twain.

*

Ann made her way to the second ambulance. The doors were open, Brian sitting beside his daughter. Ann climbed inside.

Before Ann could speak Jessica had taken her by both hands and said, 'It's not Nathan's fault, I shouldn't have taken Dad's car.'

She judged the girl's hazel eyes to be full of genuine concern. 'Don't worry about that now, we're just pleased you are both safe.'

'What about Nathan's mother— I mean Lisa?'

'We don't know, Jessica, they're still looking.' Ann glanced at Brian, still by his daughter's side. She found it difficult to say, 'I have to go. I've had a message to say that the Italian search and rescue team is close to finding Stephen and the others.'

Ann tried to think ahead but Matthew put his head inside and interrupted. 'Aunty Ann, I've had a call from Mum. I should go home.'

'Yes, Matthew, of course you should.' Mind awhirl, Ann put a hand to her temple.

Brian came to her rescue. 'I need to go to the police station with Jessica. I'll bring Nathan back with us, at least as far as my place.'

'Thank you, Brian.' She turned to Matthew. 'Will you be okay driving home alone?'

'Of course I will.' He sounded slightly offended, but added, 'What about you?'

The confidence of youth, she thought, before saying, 'I'll check to see if there are any direct flights from Birmingham.'

*

Fifteen minutes later, Ann gave Nathan a final hug as he and Jessica, with Brian in attendance, were taken to a local hospital to be checked before going on to the police station.

'I'll drop you near the airport,' Matthew told her.

'I'll get a taxi. You go home, give my love to your mum and dad, and I hope Lizzie—' she choked back a sob. 'Just go, Matthew, and please be careful.'

CHAPTER 52

By mid-afternoon, a direct flight to Pescara circled the airport, and within an hour a car arrived at the Hotel Vittoria in Sulmona.

Ann saw reporters gathering outside the hotel and inwardly groaned. Owen Wyatt hardly gave her time to exit the taxi before hustling her to a second car. 'We've got positions for most of the crew.'

'Most?' Ann queried. 'Are they safe?'

'There's a chopper on its way to a village high in the mountains. We know Louise and Yash are there.'

'So where is Stephen? And Ethan?'

'A boy from the village turned up at the rescue station. He came with Stephen as far as the foothills before the lack of medication must have kicked in and he had to leave him a dozen miles back.'

A stab of apprehension took Ann's breath. 'We were warned that one day transfusions or even a bone marrow transplant would be called for.' But that, until now, had been merely a cloud hovering on a distant horizon.'

'There's a medic with the team and the hospital is on standby,' Owen told her.

Unable to speak, Ann nodded her appreciation.

As they reached the rescue station Ann's phone rang. 'Matthew, how is Lizzie? … I see … yes ... We're almost there. I'll let you know.'

*

Stephen lay on sparse, rough grass in the foothills and drifted to the surface of consciousness. He sat up, waited for the ground to cease spinning and fought to piece together the events of the last few days. How could a crew, supposedly merely doing a job, end up in such a plethora of trouble? Just a couple of days' work, he'd told Ann. He shaded his eyes from spring sunshine and remembered how cold it was higher in the mountains, how many days ago? He wasn't sure.

Francesco? Stephen looked around. 'Francesco,' he called before remembering the boy had gone on ahead to get help – how long ago? He remembered Louise and Yash. And what would he say to Ethan's family?

Ann and Nathan – he had a lot to make up and goaded by that thought, forced himself to his feet. He took a few steps the way he'd seen

202

Francesco leave, every step taking him closer to home – or further away. There was no distinct path, his vision blurred, he struggled to lift his feet over the rough ground—

When Stephen raised his head, fingers of shadow were extending from the mountains, now shrouded in mist, and creeping towards him. Late afternoon would soon be overtaken by twilight. He laid a hand on the leather flask by his side and was about to take a swig of water when a movement caught his attention. 'Francesco?' A moment later Stephen gazed into a face he didn't at first recognise. Max Cavendish stood over him. Unshaven, eyes in hollow sockets, betraying his desperation, a ghost of the promising young director he purported to be a few days ago.

'Max, what are you doing here? I thought you'd be long gone.

'So I should be.'

'Where's Francesco?'

'That lad's a pain in the arse,' Cavendish rasped. 'He got Arturo killed and he'll have the polizia out here soon, so I need to make preparations.'

Arturo – killed – polizia, the only words registering. 'Francesco?'

'The little rat was too quick for me, which has forced a rethink. I've been let down by our paymaster and you, Stephen Bryce, will make amends.'

Stephen gathered his wits. The penny dropped. 'Hah. You've been taken for a ride as much as the rest of us.'

'Shut up.'

Stephen fell back under the weight of a thump to his shoulder. 'Who is it, Max? Who's clever enough to con us?' He choked on a laugh. 'And has no qualms about leaving you in the shit.'

Cavendish waved a handgun under Stephen's nose. 'There are people who will pay to get you back in one piece.' He tried to haul Stephen to his feet. 'Get up. What's wrong with you?'

Stephen tried to clear his mind, weigh up what his life was worth. If he didn't get some treatment soon – not a great deal.

Cavendish grabbed the shoulder of Stephen's jacket and dragged him into the cover of some scraggly bushes.

'What's happened to your paymaster, Max? Has he left you to carry the can? The only thing for you to do is give up, help find whoever set this up. Don't let him get away with it.'

203

'It's too late for me, Stephen.'

For the first time Stephen was reminded of the young director who had started out with them, how many days ago? 'And possibly for me,' Stephen muttered.

Max Cavendish slapped a hand on Stephen's shoulder. 'I can't afford to drag an invalid along with me, but—' he jerked his head towards a young man heading towards them 'Francesco thinks a lot of you and wouldn't like to see you hurt – or vice versa – so you had better co-operate.'

In Stephen's fevered mind, it was Nathan who approached. He shook his head to clear his thoughts. Perhaps a change of tack was called for. 'If you're thinking of a hostage, Max, I'll be easier to handle. You might even get a decent ransom, enough to get you out of here.'

'It's tempting, but I can't afford to hang around, and I'll wager you'd be prepared to pay to keep that lad safe.'

In the distance Stephen saw a Land Rover rolling over the rough ground. It halted some way off and four orange overalled figures exited the vehicle and spread out. He heard Francesco call, 'Signor Stephen.'

'Call him over,' Cavendish hissed.

Stephen covered his face with his hands and mumbled, 'I don't think so.'

The cold, hard muzzle of a gun rested against his neck, a rough voice insisted, 'Call him.'

Stephen's silence earned him a blow which caused him to fall forward from the cover of the bushes.

The movement attracted Francesco's attention.

Stephen staggered to his feet. 'Get back.' Something thumped, hard, into Stephen's back, he fell forward and hit the ground.

204

CHAPTER 53

Inspector Varma took a seat behind his desk and indicated for Nathan to sit opposite. 'How are you feeling now?'

'I'm okay. But no one will tell me about Lisa, my mother. Have they found her?'

'You don't live with your mother.'

'No. I've not seen her for years. She never bothered about me and I wish I hadn't—' Nathan swallowed hard and gazed at the floor before saying, 'Jessica would like to go home.'

'You can both go home shortly, but it's important we establish what happened.' The inspector rubbed his forehead. 'Now, tell me what happened when you went back to the charity office.'

'We plugged in the memory stick, but I couldn't get into the files.'

'Do you have any idea of what was in those files?'

'I suppose it was details of transactions through the charity. Lisa said she wanted to make sure there was nothing incriminating her or my father. But my father has nothing to do with running the charity. Dean Henderson was in charge of administration.'

'Well, Mr Henderson won't be giving us any information, so we'll come back to him later. Tell me about the memory stick.'

'Lisa was annoyed because I couldn't open the files. I told her we should take it to the police.'

'And what did she have to say about that?'

Nathan decided it was best not to mention her reluctance and went on, 'We were about to leave when two men burst in. One of them grabbed Lisa and the other caught hold of Jessica. Jessica struggled, they knocked into me and fell to the floor. I picked up something from the desk.' Nathan raised his hand. 'And hit him.' He mimed the action.

'And the flash drive?'

Nathan looked at his open hand. 'I must have dropped it.'

'It would be very helpful in tracking down the real villains, the ones who don't get their hands dirty, if we could get hold of that memory stick. The office had already been searched before we got there and events indicate it wasn't found. So—' Inspector Varma rubbed fists into his eyes before again fixing Nathan with a bloodshot gaze. 'Think. What could have happened to the stick?'

Nathan's first thought was that the inspector looked as if the last few days had been as rough for him as they had for himself – well, almost. He frowned in concentration. 'I was knocked backward against the filing cabinets. It could have gone behind or beneath. A couple of the drawers shot open a fraction so I suppose it could even have fallen inside.'

'Most of the drawers had been emptied, but we're getting a search team to look again.'

'Mr Varma, do you think they've found Lisa?'

'I've left a message for us to be informed immediately there's any news. But let's move on to the man who was masquerading as a teacher at your school.'

Nathan shifted in his chair. The walls of the small office were closing in. He wanted to see Jessica, and wondered if his mum Ann had any further news of his father. And what about Lizzie? He straightened his shoulders and sat back in the chair. 'What about him?'

'We've run checks on the references he provided and at first glance they look genuine enough. It took a while for our tech guys to find cracks, and from there we found similar deceptions in the messages your father and other members of the missing film crew received.'

Nathan lifted his head in anticipation. Did the inspector have any news of the crew? *Of my dad? Dare I ask?*

'Tell me what you know about him.'

For a moment Nathan believed it was his dad the inspector wanted to hear about but dragged his mind back to Mr-Thompson-not-Mr-Thompson. 'I didn't like him. He was brilliant with technical things but not good at explaining. I couldn't always follow the jargon like Matthew could. That's my cousin who was here earlier,' Nathan explained. 'And I couldn't understand why he made a point of speaking to me about my mother, his mother and, well, mothers in general.'

Varma muttered, 'Not only a technical wizard but a subtle manipulator of feelings.'

Nathan felt foolish and stared at the floor.

'Don't feel too bad, son, he's deceived many more.'

'He believes we, my family – Mum, Dad, Lisa and me – were responsible for the death of his mother. I can just remember her. She worked for my dad's agent.'

206

Varma flicked open a file and read. 'Jane Randall. Convicted as an accessory to the kidnap of you and Ann Bryce ten years ago. Died of ovarian cancer whilst still in prison six years ago.' Varma closed the file and pushed it aside. 'And your Mr Thompson is her son, real name Leo Montague. He must have been planning this elaborate scheme for years. He's been making a good living as Gibson's blue eyed hi-tech man, making untraceable transactions though "innocent" accounts to launder crime money. We don't know whether Dean Henderson was being paid to allow access to the charity's account or if he was taking money to keep quiet. He must have told Lisa, who went along with it for a while, but when she had suspicions the police were getting close, she wanted out. And no one walks away from working for Adam Gummy Gibson.'

'So they killed Mr Henderson,' Nathan said, lamely.

'So it appears,' the inspector confirmed. 'Leo Montague used money he'd skimmed off from the laundered transactions to finance his elaborate plan. We know the guide was paid to lead the film crew away from any prospective rescue party, as was the man impersonating Max Cavendish, the director.' Varma rubbed a hand over his face. 'As soon as the gang guessed that Montague was using their money for his own purposes, he was thrown to the wolves, or more accurately, into the leaky strong room along with you and Jessica, and now no money is filtering through to his accomplices, they're left to their own devices to escape capture and arrest.' Varma leaned across the desk. 'I'll be candid, Nathan, we've not yet tracked down the top man and he wants that memory stick.'

'Are you saying Jessica and I are still in danger?'

'You're safe here and we're keeping an eye on Jessica and her father.'

'But?'

'We need that stick.'

'I told you, I don't—'

'Yes, I know, but I'd like you to go back to the office with me, you might remember something.'

Nathan sighed in exasperation, 'If it will help get me out of here.'

*

A uniformed policeman lifted a yellow and black tape stretched across the back door of the charity office, allowing Varma and Nathan to enter.

'Forensics have finished so don't worry about prints,' Varma told Nathan. 'Show me where you were standing and what happened.'

207

Nathan took position. 'I was standing here, holding the memory stick. Those men came in, grabbed Jessica. She struggled and they knocked into me, I fell back against the cabinets.' Nathan leaned back, his right arm flung back from the shoulder.

'So if it shot from your hand it would fly over the filing cabinet and may have gone down the back, but—' Varma called to the officer at the door. 'Give me a hand.'

'The forensic team has been through here, sir.'

'I know, but humour me.'

The two men dragged out one of the filing cabinets, scraping it across the floorboards.

'They had all the drawers out as well, sir.' the policeman said.

Varma shone a pencil torch left and right along a gap in the floorboards then beneath the skirting board. He shoved the cabinet further – damage to the rolled hem of its metal sides scored the wooden boards adding to evidence it had been moved previously.

With a resigned sigh, Varma said, 'I had to see for myself.'

'May I go now?' Nathan asked.

'What?'

'I'd really like to go home.'

'Yes, of course. No!' Varma snapped. 'Sorry, Nathan, I'd rather you stay here, in town, where we can keep an eye on you, at least until—'

'What's that?' Nathan pointed to the groove in the floorboards. He judged that Varma was about to tell him that it was exactly that, so stooped to run a finger along the crease. Nathan did as he'd seen Ann do when struggling to pick up a tiny fragment of something. He wet his finger and pressed it over the object in question. It stuck to the end of his finger. 'Look.' He showed Inspector Varma. 'It's a little metal loop that could be from the end of a memory stick.'

Varma looked carefully. 'So it is.' He pulled a small polythene bag from a pocket and held it open allowing Nathan to let the tiny item drop into it.'

'I bet the stick was caught under the cabinet,' Nathan grinned. 'And when it was dragged out it broke.'

Varma beckoned to the uniformed officer at the door. 'Help me.'

A man each side, they tipped the cabinet, the drawers slid out and stepping quickly out of the way the men let the cabinet crash to the floor under its own weight.

Nathan was first to crouch at the base. He ran a hand around the base. 'Ouch.' Sharp metal cut his fingers, but a moment later he prised from inside the damaged hemmed edge of the cabinet's side panel, a twisted flash drive.

Nathan dropped the memory stick into the evidence bag leaving a smudge of blood on the plastic bag.

'Here.' Inspector Varma handed Nathan a white handkerchief. 'I'll get this back to the office, then we'll see if there's any news and arrange to get you back home.'

*

At the police station Nathan rinsed his fingers under cold water, dried his hands and pulled fabric plasters over paper cuts on his middle and fourth fingers before a constable escorted him to the inspector's office.

'Ah, come in Nathan.'

'Is there any news about—' the inspector's demeanour made Nathan hesitate before continuing, 'About Lisa, my ... mother?'

CHAPTER 54

At Stephen's warning, Francesco halted, heard a shot, saw Stephen fall, then again rushed forward and fell to his knees beside Stephen. A hand grasped his shoulder. A gun touched his temple.

'Got you this time, you little rat.' With a hand grasping Francesco's collar, he called to the rest of the rescue team, 'Let's have you over here.'

With glances to and from each other, the team walked slowly to where Cavendish held Francesco.

'Hold it, there.' Cavendish waved the gun. 'Throw your phones and radios in the back of the Land Rover and move away.'

The team hesitated, Francesco felt the gun barrel press hard against him and Cavendish's harsh, 'Do it.'

Francesco laid a hand on Stephen's prostrate form. Was he breathing? Tears stung. A buzzing in his head overrode the sound of negotiations between Max Cavendish and the leader of the rescue team.

Hauled to his feet, Francesco's legs buckled as he was dragged away and forced into the front passenger seat of the Land Rover. He gagged at the sight of blood on his hands and twisted in the seat to see orange overalled figures converge around the body of his friend.

Cavendish drove erratically this way and that with no obvious direction. The vehicle bumped and bounced over outcrops of rock, swaying from side to side.

'What are you doing?' Francesco yelled in his native tongue. 'You'll have us in the gully.' He leaned across, grabbed the steering wheel.

Cavendish shot out a hand, catching the boy in the face with his fist. He wrenched at the wheel, too far, the vehicle lurched, the bonnet dipped over the edge of a steep gully, front wheels pounding air. His foot on the accelerator, the rear wheels gripped and shot the Land Rover over the edge.

Under the force of Cavendish's blow, Francesco fell against the door of the Land Rover. He fumbled with the handle, the door swung open and he was flung out of the vehicle. It seemed an age before the hard earth slammed into his back, forcing breath from his body.

Francesco groaned and gingerly levered himself into a sitting position. There was no sign of the Land Rover.

'Are you hurt?' An urgent query from an orange clad team member filtered through Francesco's ringing head.

'No.' He eased his aching back and flexed a shoulder. 'I don't think so.'

'Stay here.'

Francesco watched three of the rescue team clamber down the steep slope to the Land Rover, its nose buried in a clump of trees, wisps of steam and smoke spiralling from under the bonnet.

Turning away from the scene, Francesco got to his feet and staggered to where Stephen lay, two medics in attendance.

On his knees, Francesco appealed, 'How is he? Is he dead?'

'Out of the way.' Another team member returned from the hijacked Land Rover with a number of phones and some radio equipment. He conferred with the man attending to Stephen, before calling for an air ambulance.

'We'll get him to hospital. What about you? Are you hurt?'

Francesco held out his grazed hands. 'Not really.' He glanced over his shoulder towards the rim of the gully where the Land Rover went over the edge.

'He was ejected from the vehicle,' the man in orange told him. 'He must have been thrown into that gully.'

Francesco nodded and moved back to allow other members of the team access to Stephen. They brought with them more equipment from the wrecked vehicle, and Francesco watched as they prepared a stretcher and oxygen equipment: Stephen's face, waxen; breathing, shallow.

Nothing to do but wait, Francesco sank to the ground beside the stretcher, searched under the red blanket and grasped Stephen's hand. Did his eyelids flicker?

It seemed an age until the whump-whump from the blades of a helicopter beat overhead.

Francesco watched overalled figures disembark; they worked unhurriedly, each knowing what to do. He trailed them to the aircraft as they loaded the stretcher. The man in charge leaned down, 'We can't take everyone. There's another team on its way by road.'

Tears gathered, Francesco's breathing deepened – the emotional band attaching him to his friend stretched and would snap at any moment.

Instead of retreating with the others left behind, he looked into the eyes of the team leader standing inside the open door of the helicopter who, apparently after a moment's thought, reached out a hand. 'Come on.'

Francesco grasped the hand and was hauled on board.

*

'That was Matthew,' Ann told Peter. 'He's home safely and is just off to the hospital to see Lizzie. He'll get back to us later.'

Peter nodded, rose from one of the utilitarian chairs at rescue headquarters, paced the length of the room and returned to sit for a few more minutes.

Ann took her turn to circle the small waiting room before saying, 'Do you think they'll let us know when they've reached them?'

'I suppose it might be a couple of hours or more before they get back.'

The room swayed, Ann staggered.

Peter at her elbow in a moment said, 'When did you last eat?'

'I'm not sure.'

'Come on. I took Francesco to a place round the corner earlier – they do a marvellous pizza,'

'I really don't want ...'

'You have your phone; they'll let us know immediately if there's any news.'

'All I ever do is wait to hear from other people. I'm waiting to hear from Nathan.'

*

'I can't eat any more.' Ann pushed away her plate.

Peter beckoned the waiter and asked for the remnants of the meal to be boxed. Carrying the paper bag, he and Ann wandered to the end of the street before heading back to rescue headquarters.

Ann grabbed Peter's arm. 'Listen.'

'Helicopter,' they chorused, and broke into a run.

At the gates of the rescue centre they stood back to allow two limousines to enter. Ann glimpsed the worried faces of Louise's parents, Marion Quinn and Yash's partner, Adrian, among others in the vehicles.

Ann and Peter rushed through the car park to the waiting area by the side of the large operations room which looked out onto the helipad where, at a safe distance, Angelo Russo the head of rescue services and other personnel gathered ready to receive its passengers. The aircraft settled, its downdraught causing them to shield their faces and turn away,

212

but even before the rotor blades had stilled, they were assisting the discharge of its occupants. A young man was helped down and into a wheelchair, his right leg encased in an inflatable splint.

Adrian rushed forward to greet Yash, accompanying him to the first aid station and then, presumably, to hospital. Next, Louise was helped out and led into the waiting room where she fell into the arms of her parents.

Finally, a stretcher was handed down to waiting hands, the occupant cocooned in bright orange and strapped on securely. The stretcher was carried away in a different direction and Marion Quinn collapsed into the arms of a person nearby.

Ann's first instinct to offer comfort was arrested as Peter grasped her arm and shook his head. They retreated to the sidelines, and in a daze of uncertainty, Ann watched the scene unfold. Among the assembled rescuers, medics and other personnel an atmosphere of joy and sadness mingled. Owen Wyatt was there with others Ann didn't recognise but who appeared to be connected with the film company. They ushered Marion out of the building to a waiting car. A couple of uniformed police officers on the gate held back a small crowd, some with cameras, yelling questions at no one in particular – the press had caught up with the situation.

*

Ann and Peter sat quietly in the aftermath of a hectic situation. Most onlookers had dispersed, only a few members of the press still wandered around outside the main car park. Angelo and other staff at the rescue centre were back at their posts, continuing with their business.

Peter's phone rang, making them both jump. He answered, stood and once again strode the length of the room whilst listening. At last slipping the phone into a pocket he sat beside Ann and covered his face with his hands.

Ann put a hand on his back. 'What is it?'

He sat straight and inhaled deeply, his voice thick with emotion. 'That was Matthew, he's at the hospital with Lizzie. She's come out of it, she's going to be okay.'

Ann had rarely seen her father-in-law as emotional as he again covered his face. 'She was with me, I can't help feeling—'

'It wasn't your fault. We all know how susceptible she is—'

'Exactly, that's why I—'

'Stop it, Peter. You did everything you should. She's going to be fine and that's all that matters.' Still fit and suffering few of the ailments of old age, Ann noted how he had aged. He'd suffered numerous traumas not of his own making and, despite maybe a few failings, had been a rock for the family. 'It's good news, Peter. Perhaps it's an omen that everything is going to be alright.'

'Oh Ann.' Peter patted her knee. 'You're not usually one for omens, but yes, we should take heart that at least Lizzie will be okay.'

CHAPTER 55

Again in Inspector Varma's office, Nathan watched as the policeman shifted some files to a pile at the side of his desk and rested his arms on the clear space.

'I understand,' Varma said, 'there's been further news of your father and your adoptive mother is travelling to Italy.'

'They may have located my dad and some of the other crew members. It seems they split up – I don't know why. I told Mum to go so she'll be there when they're brought in. Dad suffers from aplastic anaemia, and if he's run out of medication, he might need hospital treatment. He's had it for years and ...' Nathan fell silent, aware he was waffling and the inspector obviously had other news.

'And your cousin has gone home, also?'

'His sister had a seizure. There were problems at her birth and she's prone to convulsions ...' His words again trailed off and he waited with mounting trepidation.

'I understand your girlfriend and her father are still here.'

Nathan wondered if Jessica really was his 'girlfriend' but nodded anyway wishing the inspector would get on with it.

'The river police have recovered two bodies downstream of the weir. A man and a woman. We believe the man is Leo Montague/Thompson and the woman ... Lisa Brookes.'

After a moment, Nathan said, 'Mum told me once that your mind always expects the worst, so what actually happens is not as bad – but that's not always the case, is it?'

'No, son. Not always.'

'Are you sure ... it's ... it's her?'

Inspector Varma drew a photograph from one of the buff folders and pushed it, face down, across the desk. 'You don't need to look, Nathan, if you don't want to.'

Did he? Would he believe unless he saw evidence? Nathan bit his lower lip and gazed at the square of glossy paper. He stretched out a shaky hand and flipped the photo over. She looked relaxed, at ease, death stripping away the hard edge to her features.

'Nathan.'

He became aware of someone calling his name and looked up.

'I said, there's a car waiting to take you to the hotel where Mr Foster and his daughter are waiting. We might need to speak to you again, to clear up some details, but we have the flash drive so there's no reason you can't go home.'

Nathan stood, and after a lingering look at the photograph of his mother, tore his gaze away and followed the inspector out of the building.

*

A member of the office staff brought in yet another pot of coffee, but this time Ann noticed three cups. The young man placed the tray on a low table, smiled and left. He was followed by the head of rescue services, Angelo Russo who pulled up a chair and proceeded to pour hot dark liquid into the cups.

A chill ran down Ann's spine. This is it – the crunch. She shot a glance at Peter and saw he also had tensed, his colour draining.

A buzzing in her head drowned Angelo's words. She pressed fingers to her temple, waited for the noise to subside and, with an effort, gathered her wits. 'I'm sorry, Angelo, can you tell me again?'

Calmly, he repeated, 'The ground team located your husband, but there have been some injuries, so we've dispatched a second helicopter from another base. They'll fly Stephen straight to the nearest hospital for emergency treatment.'

'I was told the medic sent with the team had been briefed on Stephen's anaemia – I don't understand. What injuries?'

'We don't know exactly what happened, but the hospital is preparing for emergency surgery for a gunshot wound.'

Whilst Ann tried to assimilate this information, Angelo went on, 'The hospital is about 40 minutes by road.'

As Angelo spoke, Owen Wyatt entered, Angelo giving a brief nod, obviously confirming he had passed on up-to-date information.

Owen said, 'Ann, Peter, I have a car outside.'

*

Sergeant Varma walked with Nathan from the police car to the lobby of a hotel where Jessica and her father waited in the vestibule. 'Mr Foster has agreed to make sure you and Jessica get home. We'll be in touch in a few days.' He nodded at Brian Foster and left.

Jessica anxiously bit her lip and rubbed her hands down her jeans before stepping forward. 'They told us … about … Lisa.' She placed a hesitant hand on Nathan's arm.

216

Nathan, unsure how to react, swallowed hard as his throat constricted.

Brian put a hand on his shoulder. 'C'mon, lad. Jessica has bought you some clothes. We've a room where you can change.'

Nathan allowed them to lead him to a room on the first floor where Brian tossed him a carrier bag. 'There's a shower in the en-suite. The inspector told us there's news about your dad, so get changed, then there'll be just time for something to eat before we take you to the airport.'

Nathan stood in a daze, holding the carrier bag of clothes.

'They're only from Primark,' Jessica told him. 'Same as mine.'

Of course, Nathan remembered, Jessica had been soaked. As had Lisa. Lisa … He saw the photo again. She was his mother – what should he feel?

His 'Thank you' a hoarse whisper.

After allowing the shower to run as hot as he could bear, Nathan raised his head so needles of water stung his eyes.

*

'Do they fit?' Jessica asked as he stepped into the sitting area wearing the new underwear, jeans and sweatshirt. She held out a laundry bag. 'Throw the tracksuit in here, the police will collect them from downstairs.'

Nathan stuffed the police-issue clothing into the bag. 'Thank you.'

Jessica stacked the bag near the door and turning back seemed embarrassed. She said, 'I'm sure the clothes aren't what you're used to

'They're great. I like them. I'll pay you back,' added hastily.'

'All in good time,' Brian commented. 'There's a meal waiting downstairs.'

*

A waiter showed them to the dining room where a table had been set aside. Nathan watched a portion of cottage pie appear on his plate and sides of vegetables in stainless steel dishes.

'C'on, lad,' Brian urged. 'Get something down you.'

Nathan picked up a fork before laying it down again. 'Mr Foster, I don't—'

'Nonsense. Eat something—' Brian Foster nodded at the waiter as a serving bowl of chips was placed on the table. 'Now your dad's been found, Jessica here has booked you on a flight in—?'

217

'An hour and fifty minutes,' Jessica told him. 'Your cousin Matthew gave us your passport.' She put the passport and a printout on the table. 'I asked them to arrange for a car to meet you and take you to the hospital.'

'They've definitely found him?' Nathan queried. 'Is he okay? No one has told me.'

Brian helped himself to a serving of chips. 'The message that inspector chappie passed on just said he'll be taken to hospital, which is what you expected given the illness you told us about. We thought you'd like to be there, with your mum …'

'Yes, of course, I must go.' He gestured to the passport and enclosed papers. 'Who's paid for all this?'

'Dad used his credit card,' Jessica confessed.

'I'll get in touch with my grandfather, he'll arrange for money to be transferred … but I've lost my phone.'

'We bought a couple of cheap basic phones and put £20 on a pay-as-you-go sim.' Jessica placed a box next to the passport. 'And I understand from your cousin that your grandad went to Italy when your mum came here.'

'Then Dad's agent, Lynn, she can arrange it ... but all the numbers were on my phone …'

'Calm down, lad. As long as it's sorted within the next six weeks 'cos I'm up to the limit on my card.'

'I put my number in this,' Jessica tapped the phone. 'And the number Inspector Varma gave us for the mountain rescue people in Italy.'

Overwhelmed by their kindness, Nathan felt the sting of tears for the first time since hearing of Lisa's death. A hand to his forehead, he covered his eyes and clamped his jaw, hard.

He sensed murmurings between Brian and Jessica and after a shuddering breath he raised his head and said huskily, 'Thank you.'

'Good lad,' Brian grinned. 'Now eat something and we'll get you to the airport.'

Nathan nodded at Brian and exchanged a smile with Jessica. He lifted his fork and forced several mouthfuls of cottage pie past the lump in his throat.

*

The flight was called; people collected at the departure gate, moving slowly onto the tarmac after showing tickets and boarding cards. Nathan shook hands with Brian Foster who gripped his shoulder, 'There'll be

218

time to mourn later, lad. Your mum, your proper mum is waiting for you, and your dad.'

Nathan nodded before turning to Jessica. They reached for each other and embraced until a final call over the PA system tore them apart.

CHAPTER 56

Nathan settled in a window seat, fastened the safety belt, leaned back and closed his eyes. His throat constricted, eyes burning, he longed for a dark room and his own bed. He vaguely sensed someone sit down in the seat beside him, felt them fidget and speak to a companion in the aisle seat. He prayed they wouldn't speak to him – he doubted he could answer.

*

'Are you going back?'

Nathan fought to surface from a swirling mist.

'I said, are you staying on and going back?'

'What?'

'You must have been tired.' A woman was standing in the aisle pulling a bag from the overhead luggage compartment. 'We've landed,' she went on. 'Better get your things.'

Nathan wondered where he was. Realisation hit within a moment. He forced a thank you smile to the helpful lady and, following her into the aisle, lifted a rucksack from the overhead storage and joined the queue waiting to disembark.

Squinting into bright spring sunlight, Nathan descended to the tarmac and, almost in a dream, walked with other passengers to the terminal.

At the immigration desk a customs officer studied his passport. The officer murmured a few words to a colleague before handing the document back and saying, 'Come with me please.'

Before Nathan had time to think, a man stepped forward. 'I'm Owen Wyatt. I have a car outside. I'll take you to the hospital; your mother's waiting.'

In the back seat, beside the film company's representative, Nathan locked his gaze on the back of the driver's seat. They were on the main strada before he plucked up courage to say, 'How is my dad?'

'I'm not sure about the present situation but your mother will explain.'

What is he not telling me? Nathan bit his lip and continued his detailed examination of the stitching on the rear of the driver's seat until it blurred. Emotion see-sawed between longing to see Ann and his dad and dread at what he might find. He shut out thoughts of Lisa, Jessica and

Brian – he'd deal with those later. And Lizzie. He should text Matthew – *the number ends with 378* but he'd forgotten the rest – would Jessica have given Matthew the number of the new phone? The phone pinged and after a search through his pockets Nathan saw a text from that very number. "Lizzie will be okay, Nath. Speak soon."

He must have groaned with relief, prompting Owen to ask, 'You okay, Nathan?'

'Yes. Good news, about my little cousin.'

'I'm pleased to hear that. Your mum mentioned there was a problem.'

Nathan managed a quick smile and wondered if he should press for more information about his dad, but the vehicle pulled into the grounds of a large hospital. The driver found a space to park and Owen led Nathan through reception and spoke to a woman at the desk who pushed buttons on a switchboard. After a few words into a handset, she nodded and pointed along a corridor.

At the end of the corridor, they took a lift to the second floor where Owen pushed open a heavy door and indicated Nathan should enter.

The door swung closed behind and Nathan was alone facing another desk. A nurse, young and rosy cheeked, smiled and said, 'You must be Nathan. This way.'

Another corridor, another door; a narrow room, and standing there, Ann, head down, a hand covering her mouth.

She looked up and after a heartbeat, spread her arms.

Casting off the rucksack Nathan took long strides to enfold her in his arms. He pressed his face into her neck, wallowing in her comforting embrace.

When he stood back, Ann reached up, brushed his hair from his forehead and said quietly, 'I know about Lisa.'

Emotion, held in check, erupted and again hugging his mum, Nathan sobbed into her neck. 'Mum, I'm sorry ... I shouldn't have tried to find her ...'

'It's not your fault, darling. Lisa made her own decisions.'

Nathan felt a firm hand on his shoulder and turned from his mum to be embraced by his grandfather.

Feeling safe in the heart of his family, Nathan took a deep, calming breath. He took a step back and dragged the back of his hand across his face.

'Here.' Ann handed him a box of tissues.

Cleaned up, Nathan tossed soggy tissues into a bin. 'Sorry,' he mumbled. 'Where's Dad? Is he okay?'

'Sit down,' Peter insisted, and indicated chairs lining a side wall.

He and Ann dragged up a chair each. Ann reached across to grip her adopted son's hand. 'Your dad's very ill.'

'He wasn't long without his medication,' Nathan interrupted. 'Surely there can't be that much damage.'

'It's not merely the anaemia. For his own perverse reasons, men were hired by that man Leo to keep your dad and the rest of the crew out of the way, but when Leo's crime boss discovered he'd been using the gang's money – the money Lisa must have known was being laundered … I'm not explaining this very well – but when the two men hired who were with your dad and the crew found out they wouldn't get paid, they had a falling out and in their desperation to get away there were … they had firearms, guns and in the melee Dad was hit.'

'He's been shot?' Nathan looked from Ann to Peter. 'How … how serious? He'll be alright, won't he?'

From a door opposite, a young woman clad in the blue cotton tunic and trousers of medical staff approached. 'Signora Bryce?'

Ann shot to her feet, Nathan and Peter rose more slowly.

She spoke English with hardly an accent. 'We have stabilised your husband and he will be going into theatre immediately the surgeon is ready. It will be at least a couple of hours before we can tell you anything more. I think perhaps you should get coffee and come back in two hours.'

Nathan saw Ann was about to protest but she halted as someone else entered from the corridor behind. A youth, about his own age stood nearby.

Turning back to the theatre nurse, Ann said, 'Thank you.'

The nurse put a hand on her arm. 'We'll take care of him.'

Ann nodded her appreciation.

Peter stepped forward. 'Nathan, this is Francesco. He helped your father down from the mountain village, was there when … when he was … injured.'

The boys solemnly shook hands.

'Come along.' Peter ushered them all into the corridor and out of the ward. A silent journey in the lift and they stood in reception.

'Oh, shit.' Ann turned her back to the entrance. 'Press.'

'Okay,' Peter assessed the situation. 'There's a coffee shop on site.'

As Peter and Ann headed towards a sign, *La Trattoria*, Nathan felt a touch on his arm. Francesco called to Peter, 'Signor Bryce, is it okay if Nathan and I go outside?'

Nathan noticed a look pass between the young man and his grandfather.

'Yes, of course,' Peter agreed. He fumbled in his pockets for his wallet and drew out a couple of euro notes. 'Get something to eat and we'll see you back here in a couple hours.'

Suspecting some collusion, Nathan asked, 'Is that okay, Mum?'

'Yes, love. I have your new number … but don't be too long …'

*

Ann and Peter sat either side of a table at the la trattoria.

'I suppose we should count our blessings,' Ann mused. 'Lizzie is better, Nathan is safe, and Stephen is still alive.' She hugged herself as if chilled. 'I remember being in a similar situation ten years ago.'

'He survived then and will now,' Peter assured her.

'Yes, of course he will.' Ann dug deep and found a smile. It faded as she said, 'How long has it been?'

'Ninety minutes.'

'I wish Nathan would come back.'

'He'll be back soon enough.'

'Francesco seems like a nice lad.'

'He is. I believe he's genuinely fond of Stephen. It'll be better for him to tell Nathan what's happened.'

CHAPTER 57

The boys walked from the entrance of the hospital and into the street, unrecognised by the half-dozen press photographers. Lights in shop windows began to glow in gathering twilight. Nathan shivered – shock catching up.

'Let's go in here.' Francesco led the way to a nearby bar, and they slipped onto chairs either side of a table. Several people perched on bar stools lining the counter and a couple of tables were occupied.

Francesco spoke to a waiter.

Nathan detected the words 'cola' and 'caffè corretto' among the rapid Italian that passed between them.

To Nathan, Francesco said, 'You know there was a landslide?'

'Yes.'

'The guide from the film company brought your father and the others to the village where my grandpapa and grandmamma live. I often stay with them.

'Nonna, she believed Signor Stephen was one of the soldiers her family sheltered during the war when she was a little girl. Your father was very good to her.'

The waiter set two glasses of cola and two cups of coffee on the table.

Nathan gazed at the dark, treacly liquid in the cup. 'If I drink that, I'll be bouncing off the walls.'

'Try it,' Francesco encouraged. 'It has added herbs and spices. Nonna makes coffee like this; it's supposed to help when you're stressed—' he took a sip and pulled a face. 'Well, maybe not quite like this.'

Nathan joined him in pushing the cup away before saying, 'You spent time with my dad?'

'The crew stayed with people in the village. Signor Stephen stayed with us. The power line to the village had been put out of action by the storms, and there is no internet or mobile phone signal. They planned, after a night's rest, that Arturo would lead everyone down the mountain. Next morning, we found Arturo and the man who was the director, Cavendish, had already left, and one of the other men, an older man who was staying with Cavendish and Arturo in one of the empty houses ... he was dead.

'Signor Stephen, the lady and the other man suspected Arturo and Cavendish were not going to fetch help, so I said I'd lead them down the mountain.'

'Was Dad alright then? I mean, he wasn't ill?'

'He seemed fine, but when the other man, Yash, slipped and hurt his leg, they decided that as your dad had run out of medication, it would be better for him to carry on with me and the other two go back to the village.

'He spoke of you and your mamma – the lady who is Ann. He said he missed and loved you both and felt he'd let you down because he had made you a promise.'

Nathan pushed his fingers into the fair curls which tumbled over his forehead and stared at the table top until it blurred. 'I persuaded him to promise to take me on a trekking holiday in the Grand Canyon. Mum wasn't pleased: she told me he ... wasn't fit ... it would be too much ... and when I found out he wouldn't be back in time, I wondered if he'd dallied on purpose. I was angry.

'Ann has always been my mum, but I began to think about Lisa. I can barely remember her, except that she always seemed to be pushing me away or shouting at me. I don't know why I went after her ... and now she's dead and Dad ... Dad—' Nathan clamped his jaw, determined not to cry in the presence of this young stranger.

'My dad was killed in an accident at his work and my mamma died soon after, when I was still a bambino,' Francesco told him. 'I have also seen men die this day, and Signor Stephen is my friend.'

When Nathan glanced up, Francesco's face was wet with tears – sealing a bond between them.

CHAPTER 58

Ann looked up from stirring yet another coffee to see Nathan and Francesco approach. The boys slipped into the chairs beside Ann and Peter.

'Mr Wyatt is speaking to the journalists,' Nathan told his mum and grandfather. 'I heard him say there would be a statement in the morning.'

'Yes. Let's hope there's some good news to tell them,' Ann assured her stepson. She stood. 'I know it's not quite two hours, but shall we find out what's happening?'

*

Ann distractedly thumbed a magazine before pacing the floor of a waiting room situated off an intensive care ward. Nathan and Francesco, heads together, were obviously exchanging experiences. She heard Lisa's name mentioned, and it gave her comfort to think that, in the absence of his cousin Matthew, his usual confidante, Nathan had someone his own age with whom to talk through the events of the day. Francesco, too, would benefit.

A door opened and all heads shot up.

A figure in blue scrubs swiped off the cap covering her hair and wiped it across her forehead.

A stream of rapid Italian created blank faces until Francesco stepped forward. 'Professor De Luca says Signor Stephen is stable and in the recovery room.' He listened again. 'He is out of danger for the moment but there are issues, other issues, which need to be addressed.'

Ann fought tears of relief. 'Grazie, Professor,' she croaked. Her sentiment echoed by the others.

'Prego.' Professor De Luca held up a hand and spread fingers and thumb. 'Five minutes,' she conceded. 'One person.'

*

Ann followed a nurse to the recovery room. How long had it been since she'd kissed her husband goodbye and left for home, leaving him for what should have been a couple of days' filming?

On a trolley, metal side rails raised, he lay on his side and appeared to sleep. Assured he was breathing unaided, Ann assumed the tube taped across his face supplied supplementary oxygen. She stretched a hand between the bars of the rail and touched his arm. Warm and dry, soft fair hairs smooth against his skin. Bending close she whispered, 'Hello, my darling. You're safe now. We've been waiting for you. Me, Nathan, your dad. Francesco's safe. He's here too.'

A nurse bustled in and began fiddling with equipment. She tapped her watch and held up eight fingers before indicating Ann should leave.

Ann took a moment to whisper, 'I'll be back in the morning,' to her husband before thanking the nurse and leaving.

She was met in the corridor by Owen Wyatt who said, 'I've prepared a statement. Would you like to look it over?'

Ann skimmed through the document. 'Thank you, Owen, that doesn't give too much away. Will it satisfy the hungry hordes?'

'Until the Guardia have completed their investigation, that's all we know.'

Though Stephen's prognosis was upbeat, Ann noticed the phrase, 'still remains in a serious condition'.

'Will you read it out?' she asked.

'If you'd like me to.'

'Please.'

'Okay, I'll do that,' he assured her. 'In the meantime, there's a small hotel around the corner. I've taken an option on three rooms for you and the family?'

'You're an angel, Owen.'

'It's the least we can do as it happened in the company's time, though I must point out they may have a different view of things if it turns out the initial emails were fraudulent and were not instigated by the company.'

'I'm aware of that, but I hope you'll forgive me if I take advantage of your generosity and sort out who pays for what later.'

Owen gave her a smile. 'You should be able to get out of the side entrance without being noticed.'

Ann met with Peter and the boys and, when safely out of the side entrance of the hospital, they found the small hotel around the corner.

Before going to their rooms, Ann tasked her father-in-law and the boys with bringing the family up to date and, when alone in her room, rang her sons from her previous marriage.

'I should have sent him home with a flea in his ear,' was Richard's outburst.

227

'He's seventeen,' Ann reiterated. 'Besides, I believed that if he saw Lisa, he'd get it out of his system and be back home in a couple of days. I didn't know what the silly woman was mixed up in, though she didn't deserve—' Ann could feel exhaustion catching up.

'I only know the bits I've heard on the news,' Richard admitted. 'But it sounded pretty horrific.'

'Yes. I don't suppose we'll know all the circumstances until the police have finished their investigation. But Nathan is safe and Stephen is out of danger for the moment.'

After a similar conversation with Chris, Ann lay on the bed and, without bothering to get undressed, slept.

*

'Lizzie is much better,' Peter's elder son, Julian, told him. 'We can take her home tomorrow.'

Peter, unable to express his relief, was confident Julian understood. His son went on, 'Take care, Dad. Let us know how things go.'

*

'Hey, Nath,' Matthew's voice chirped from Nathan's phone.

'Hi Matt, I'm glad Lizzie's okay.'

'Yeah. I heard they found Uncle Stephen. How is he? They don't say on the news.'

'He was shot, Matt. They've had to operate; then there's the anaemia ...'

'Yeah.' After a moment Matt said, 'I'm sorry about Lisa.'

Nathan could only say, 'Yeah.' Then, 'Thanks for bringing Mum to Birmingham. I was glad she was there ... and you.'

'It's the farthest I've ever driven.' Another period of silence. 'Come home soon, kid. All of you.'

Nathan switched off the phone and sat wearily on the end of one of the single beds in the room.

Francesco looked up from the end of the other bed. 'Your family is very close,' he observed.

After a moment's thought, Nathan said, 'I'm sorry about your parents. Do you live with your grandparents?'

'I hardly remember my parents. I was very young. I live with an aunt, but it is a small apartment, and she has many children, so when I am not at school I stay with my grandparents in the mountains.'

'Where you met Dad?'

228

'Si.'

'I'd like to see it some time.'

'I'd like to take you and Signor Stephen. The scenery there is as beautiful as any Grand Canyon. Maybe different, but more beautiful.'

'Okay,' Nathan agreed. 'It's a deal.'

CHAPTER 59

Awake at six and showered and dressed before seven, Ann waited for Peter to join her.

'The boys are still asleep,' he told her. 'The hospital hasn't informed us of any change, so let them rest. I'll leave a message for them to join us later.'

Ann and Peter walked the short distance to the hospital. The streets were wet but a glow in the eastern sky promised a fine day.

A couple of reporters slouched on chairs in the reception area but weren't quick enough to bother Ann and Peter. Ann spotted *Unita ad alta dipendenza* on a sign and headed that way.

After making themselves known, they were allowed into a room where Stephen remained imprisoned behind the rails of a hospital bed.

Again, he seemed to sleep, but as Ann put a hand through the rails and touched his arm, his eyes flickered open.

'Hello, darling. How do you feel?'

His 'Better for seeing you' was barely audible.

She repeated her message of the previous evening. 'You're safe now.'

His brow creased. 'Francesco ... Nathan?'

'Francesco is safe and Nathan will be here soon.'

'Sorry ...'

'Hush. No one could foresee what happened.'

Peter and Ann maintained their vigil, Peter saying, 'While ever he sleeps he's gaining strength. I'll stay, you have a break, get a coffee ... and ring Nathan. He should be up and about by now.'

Later, Ann handed a carton of coffee to Peter. 'I can't get a reply from Nathan. I rang the hotel and they say he and Francesco left almost an hour ago.'

CHAPTER 60

On the street outside the hotel, Nathan passed Francesco a croissant stolen from the breakfast table. The boys were grinning at each other and brushing crumbs from their clothes when Nathan halted outside a small supermarket. A rack of newspapers stood beside the open door. He reached down and extracted one, fished in his pockets for his cash card and entered the shop, newspaper in hand.

The main headline shouted DUE TEMUTI MORTI DOPO IL SOCCORSO ALPINO

Again on the street, Nathan folded the paper so he could read an article below the main headline, 'FitzGilbert Rubini.' After a moment he showed his friend. 'What does it say about the FitzGilbert rubies?'

Francesco scanned the text. 'They were stolen from a museum in Birmingham, Inghilterra, and it says authorities around the world have been asked to look out for them being offered for sale. The jewellery was previously owned by the family of Stephen Bryce. Bryce was found in the foothills of the Abruzzo Mountains after he and other members of a film crew had been missing for four days following a major landslide.' Francesco folded the paper and passed it back.

'I was there,' Nathan said, 'at the museum. I remember Mum and Dad talking about the jewellery before they gave it to the museum, and I wanted to see it.'

A short way from the hospital they came to a piazza and, eager to tell the story, Nathan gestured to a bench beside a small fountain. 'My great-grandfather was a captain in the army during World War Two. He liked to gamble, and to cover a debt from a fellow officer, who was a lord or an earl or something, he accepted the jewellery. Grandad made sure it was returned to the family, but Lady Matilda gave them back to Mum and Dad when they got married. I think Mum only wore them once. She said they always seemed to cause trouble, so she and Dad arranged for the museum to have them.'

'You think this gang stole the jewellery?'

'The rubies are worth a lot of money, and the police believe Leo had already programmed the alarm system to fail before the gang discovered what he was up to, so the robbery went ahead. It was just bad luck we were there. They still believed I had a flash drive with information on it, so they took us to this … place … and then left us – Leo, Jessica, Lisa and me – to drown.' Nathan covered his face. 'Lisa pushed past me. If she'd waited, we could have all got out. I hate water. Why didn't she wait?' He bit down a sob. 'I can't lose my dad …'

Nathan felt a firm grip on his arm and heard Francesco's 'He will be good. We will go, now, to see him, and he will be good.'

'Yeah.' He wiped an arm over his face. 'Let's go.'   Nathan stood, dropped the newspaper in a nearby bin and together the boys headed for the hospital.

'You speak very good English,' Nathan remarked as they walked along.

'One of the teachers at my school is married to an English lady. She took pity on me when my parents died and taught me from being very small.'

'Wait.' Nathan halted some way from the entrance to the hospital. Two policemen stood either side of the gate.

'Carabinieri,' Francesco muttered.

'And reporters inside the gate,' Nathan noted. 'Let's go round the side.'

The streets in this area were deserted but another carabiniere was in attendance at the side gate. Francesco said, 'Tell him who you are; he will let you in.'

'There's bound to be more press inside. Dad always says to smile at the photographers and walk on. They'll be after you as well,' Nathan reminded his friend.

'So,' Francesco grinned, 'I'll distract them, police and press, whilst you sneak inside.'

'No,' Nathan laughed. 'We'll go together. Just walk in and smile when they throw questions at you.'

Their jostling of each other took them into a dark, narrow alley where building work was taking place.   Francesco halted to look at a half-demolished building supported by scaffolding, the area protected by loosely fastened boarding which cast deep shadows across the alley.

'Come on,' Nathan encouraged. 'I want to see my dad.'

'I'll be right there, but I thought I saw something – someone.' Francesco took a few more strides into the shadows.

Nathan looked anxiously towards the side entrance of the hospital, though now out of his direct line of sight, he imagined reporters pressing in on him, shouting questions. He turned back to Francesco but the alley appeared empty. 'Hey, come on.' Nathan jogged to where he last saw his friend. 'We'll go in together ... Francesco?'

CHAPTER 61

A push caught Francesco off balance. A lower crosspiece, to which boarding should have been nailed, caught the back of his ankles; he grabbed the clothing of his assailant – they both fell.

Francesco scrabbled at exposed brickwork, felt the downward motion lift his jacket and scrape his ribs on the jagged edges. As he landed, a piece of loose scaffolding pole shot from under his foot twisting his ankle, his legs folded and he hit his head. Something heavy thudded beside him.

*

The sound of a crash sent Nathan scampering further along the narrow road. He peered through a gap in boarding where excavation work had revealed deep cellars. Planks rested on scaffolding stretching over an abyss where ledges, all that was left of the lower floors, protruded.

Nathan scanned the chasm. Francesco lay near the edge of a shelf of broken concrete, perhaps four metres below. Obviously stunned by the fall, he set off an avalanche of debris each time he stirred.

Nathan yelled, 'Francesco, keep still,' before looking around for help. The alley was deserted. Again, a trickle of rubble crashed into the pit. 'Keep still. I'm coming down.'

Down a ladder secured to scaffolding, Nathan edged along a plank, steadying himself with a hand on one of the horizontal poles. 'Keep still,' he called again to Francesco. 'You're near the edge. Keep still.'

Nathan gazed at a gap of about one and a half metres which stretched between where he stood and the ledge where Francesco lay. An easy leap, but at a peek over the edge, Nathan tightened his grip on the scaffolding. A drop of at least two storeys yawned below.

Francesco moaned, rolled over, an arm flopping over the edge of the shelf.

'For Christ's sake, Francesco, keep still.'

'Cosa sta succedendo,' Francesco muttered, pushing himself into a sitting position.

'You're near the edge, keep still.'

'Mio Dio!' Francesco shuffled into a safer position and touched a hand to his head.

Nathan called, 'How did you manage to fall down here?' He fished into his jacket pocket for his phone. About to press 999 he faltered. 'What's the emergency number? 911?'

'I didn't fall—'

'Drop the phone.'

Nathan looked up from his phone. A man, who must have been hidden in the shadows of jagged masonry overhanging the shelf, gripped Francesco's shoulder.

'Drop the phone.' The man jerked his head to indicate the gaping excavations of the building site.

Nathan let go of the phone and a second later, heard it hit bedrock below.

'Nathan,' Francesco gasped. 'This is Signor Cavendish.'

Nathan gazed with loathing at the man who had murdered the mountain guide Arturo and had shot his father. Younger than Nathan expected, mid-thirties perhaps, but looking haggard, unshaven with hollow eyes that oozed desperation.

'He pushed me,' Francesco called. 'Nathan, run.'

Nathan glanced across the planking to the ladder. He could hardly run. He called back, 'What do you want?'

'I've not been paid. I need money to get me out of here.'

'I can get money.'

'How much?'

'£500 on my card, or,' he amended, '€500.'

'Ha, nice try, lad, but ... you're Stephen Bryce's boy. I hear he's still alive. If the boss won't pay me, I'll get it from Stephen Bryce.' Cavendish shifted position, he took a better hold of Francesco's shoulder and shuffled to the edge of the shelf. 'You ask your daddy for, say, £50,000. Bring it back here or your friend goes over.'

Nathan's mind raced. Where would anyone get that sort of money in cash? He noticed that whilst Cavendish had one hand gripping Francesco's shoulder, his other arm was clasped across his ribs. Francesco had told him about the Land Rover crashing into a tree. Cavendish was injured.

'Okay,' Nathan hastily reassured him. 'I need to know if Francesco is hurt.'

'I banged my head and twisted my ankle.'

'Never mind about him,' Cavendish gasped and again shook the boy.

Nathan heard the man's rasping breath. He assessed the gap from the plank where he stood to the narrow ledge. Could he make the jump and barge into a weakened Cavendish? – perhaps, but would Francesco be able to make the leap back before Cavendish recovered? And … did he still have a gun?

CHAPTER 62

Nathan's question was answered when Cavendish retrieved a weapon from the depth of his tattered jacket.

A distraction needed. 'Mr Cavendish,' he called. 'I'll get as much money as I can.'

Cavendish put the gun against Francesco's head. 'You'd better get enough to get me out of here.'

'Okay,' Nathan was quick to say. 'I'm going.' A meaningful glance from his friend flicked towards the short piece of scaffolding on the ledge and forced Nathan's mind into overdrive. 'What about a doctor?'

'What?'

'You're injured. Do you need a doctor?'

Waving the gun towards Nathan, Cavendish yelled, 'I'm not waiting any longer.'

Whilst Cavendish was distracted, Francesco picked up the scaffolding pole and, from his sitting position, landed a blow across the shins of the man standing over him.

Cavendish screamed and staggered forward – the gun discharged. Ignoring a shower of masonry from above his head, Nathan leapt the yawning gap to the shelf, his shoulder connected with a body – another blast sounded close to his ear, splinters of stone raked his face. His legs tangled with someone else's limbs and he fell to his knees. A THUMP sounded vaguely in the distance, somewhere below.

Nathan felt someone shake him – his name called as if from a distance.

Francesco's mouth moved.

Nathan shook his head. 'What?'

'Are you okay?'

Nathan nodded. 'I think so. Where is he?'

Francesco glanced over the edge. 'Don't worry about him; let's get out of here.'

Nathan and Francesco struggled to stand and Nathan prepared to jump across the gap – the landing place this time was the narrow plank. The loud report from the gun still echoing in his skull, he leapt ... landed, grabbed the horizontal pole, clung tight, heart racing. He shuffled further along before turning, 'Come on, Francesco.'

237

Francesco hobbled to the edge of the shelf.

'Come on,' Nathan encouraged. 'Push off with your good foot. I'll catch you.'

Francesco backed off a pace – Nathan had second thoughts and yelled across, 'Stay there, I'll fetch help.'

'I'm not staying here. Just make sure you grab hold of me.' With no more hesitation, Francesco launched himself across the gap. Obviously not his natural lead foot, he fell short with only his upper body on the plank, legs dangling.

Nathan grabbed his friend's jacket collar, scrabbled to get leverage under his arms and shuffled back.

Francesco kicked and inched onto the plank until both boys sat astride, heads resting together. They took a moment to savour the relief before Nathan stood and helped Francesco to his feet.

Nathan assisted Francesco along the plank and up the ladder. They clambered through the gap in the protective boarding and stood in the narrow alley – no one in sight, it was as if nothing had happened.

Francesco dabbed at a cut on his scalp with a corner of his jacket. 'How's your ankle?'

Francesco tested it with his weight. 'It's not bad. We should tell the Carabinieri what's happened.'

'No need,' Nathan told him. A siren sounded in the distance. 'I pressed the call button before I dropped my phone. I assumed they'd be able to trace it. But—' he turned to face Francesco 'let's not wait around. It will take time to explain and I need to see my dad.'

Francesco looked doubtful.

'I want to make sure he's okay, then we can speak to the police and tell them what happened.'

'Yeah, sure. I want to see him too but—' he surveyed Nathan's face. 'Perhaps we should get cleaned up first.'

Nathan pulled up his T-shirt to wipe specks of blood from the nicks and scratches on his face before ruffling his hair, creating a cloud of brick dust.

The boys exited the alley and headed towards the side entrance of the hospital. The policeman on duty at the gate, who, with a couple of reporters, was distracted by the nearing wail of sirens, didn't notice Nathan and his limping friend enter the building.

*

238

Stephen surfaced from darkness through grey to a brightness that forced him to delay opening his eyes. He rifled through memories culminating in the terrific thump in his back.

A soft touch and soothing voice filtered through and from beneath heavy lids he saw a familiar dear face. He knew she'd be there and curled his fingers around her hand.   Content, he slept.

Morning found Ann nearby. Sitting in a chair by the bed, she sipped coffee from a paper cup. Stephen asked about Francesco and sighed with relief when told he was safe.

'And has Nathan forgiven me?'

'Nathan has been having his own adventure, but I'll leave him to tell you about it. He should be here soon with Francesco.'

Stephen noticed how her gaze slipped away as she spoke and wondered what she wasn't telling him. He was too tired to enquire, and said, 'Will you help me to the bathroom? I'd like to shave and freshen up.'

Exhausted by the effort, Stephen accepted Ann's help to pull on a dressing gown and leaned heavily on her arm to return to his room. He put a hand on the back of an easy chair, but before he could lower himself carefully into it, noticed movement through the window which looked out into a corridor.

A tap on the door and a moment later Nathan and Francesco entered and stood just inside the door.

'Nathan,' Ann exclaimed. 'Where have you been? We were worried.'

Stephen was alert enough to notice Nathan glance at the floor before giving Ann a tentative smile. *What has Nathan been up to whilst I was out of action?*

*

The tension and emotional turmoil of the last few days swelled and at the sight of his dad looking tired, almost haggard, Nathan was overwhelmed and unselfconsciously flung himself into his dad's arms.

'Whoa,' Stephen flinched as the weight of his son almost toppled him.

'Dad. You okay?'

'Yeah, just ease up a little.'

Nathan took a step back to make way for Francesco whose embrace of Stephen was a little more restrained.

239

When released, Stephen put a hand under his son's chin to examine his face. 'What happened to you?'

'Well—' Nathan looked towards Francesco who put a hand to his head where blood had dried in his hair.

Before either boy could speak, there was a disturbance in the corridor and two uniformed policemen stood at the door.

The boys exchanged a glance, Francesco saying, 'Stay here, Nathan, talk to your father. I'll explain to the police what happened.'

Nathan acquiesced, saying, 'I'll follow soon.'

*

Ann had watched the exchange between Stephen and the boys. She noted the resemblance between father and son, keener now they were of a height, though Nathan's loosely curled hair still retained its childhood fairness. Francesco, in contrast, olive skinned and dark haired, there was an obvious mutual feeling of affection, a strong bond between them all.

Ann followed Francesco into the corridor, surprised to see Inspector Varma there with his Italian counterpart.

'We need to go to the police station and get Francesco's statement,' Varma told her. 'I'll come back for Nathan later.'

Ann felt a responsibility to Francesco – he was, after all, only 17 – and asked him, 'Have you heard from your family?'

'It will take days to get news to my grandparents,' Francesco told her, 'And my aunt, she has young children …'

'Then I'll come with you.' Before following Francesco and the policemen, Ann glanced towards the door of the side ward, and wondered what Lisa's death would mean to Stephen.

CHAPTER 63

With Nathan left to tell his dad about Lisa, Ann sat with Francesco in an office at the local police station. The cut on his head cleaned and stitched, Francesco related, in rapid Italian, the events resulting in Max Cavendish lying at the bottom of a building excavation with multiple injuries.

Ann bit her lip and held back tears as she and Inspector Varma listened to a translation of what Francesco and Nathan had endured.

Ninety minutes later, Francesco's statement recorded and signed, he and Ann, with Inspector Varma, headed back to the hospital.

Stephen lay on the bed, apparently asleep. Nathan, sitting in the armchair, leaned on the bed, his head resting on his arms.

Ann was loath to disturb him but Inspector Varma was at her shoulder; Francesco, on his heels.

Nathan raised his head, saw them, stood and, with a tired smile at his mum and a nod at his friend, followed the inspector from the room.

'Can I stay with Signor Stephen until you get back?' Francesco asked quietly.

'Of course,' Ann confirmed. 'And then, I think you should see your aunt.'

'They know I'm okay.'

'It's not the same as actually *seeing* you.'

'Okay, and then I'll go to see Nonna and Nonno. Very little news reaches them.'

Ann planted a kiss on his cheek and turned to follow Varma and Nathan. At the door she glanced back and smiled when Francesco took up position in the chair Nathan had vacated.

After the same procedure at the station, Nathan told the story from his point of view.

'Your son has a knack of attracting trouble,' the inspector commented.

Ann winced. She'd used a similar phrase when speaking of Lisa. *Please don't let Nathan have inherited this trait.*

CHAPTER 64

Nathan's heart sank as he, his dad and Ann were ushered into the front seats of a chapel in the crematorium near Thresingham; their intention of sitting, unobtrusively, at the back in tatters. Representatives of the film industry and half a dozen fellow actors occupied the other seats, whilst beside them stood a distant cousin of Lisa's and an elderly aunt and uncle – her only relatives. Nathan looked past the coffin resting between velvet curtains and focused on a single lit candle, its flame apparently growing to fill his vision before receding.

The town was Lisa's former home and where Nathan had spent the first two years of his life in the care of her parents, his visits to Stephen and Ann growing more frequent and longer as Lisa's mother became too ill to cope.

The service was short. There was no eulogy, despite offers to speak from Stephen and others, and no wake.

A small contingent of photographers snapped and clicked at them as they left. Nathan stood close to his dad and Ann, still trembling despite warm spring sunshine. He watched as Jennifer Bentley cocked an eyebrow at Stephen from beneath a short black net veil and heard her say, 'I had little time for her, but she deserved better.'

His dad grimaced. 'It's not what she would have wanted.'

To Nathan, Jennifer said, 'I'm so sorry, dear.'

He tried to answer her sympathetic smile but failed.

Again addressing Stephen, she said, 'Some of us are going back to town to have a drink … or something. Are you coming?' Her gesture included Ann and Nathan.

Nathan was pleased to hear his dad say, 'No, thank you, Jennifer.'

She touched Stephen's arm. 'How are you?'

'I'm fine, Jen.'

'You don't look all that fine.'

Ann stepped forward. 'Thank you, Jennifer, he's supposed to be resting. We'll catch up with you in a couple of weeks.'

Following handshakes and kissed cheeks, Stephen, Ann and Nathan returned to their car, and Ann drove home.

Nathan immediately went to his room, pulled off his tie and hung his suit jacket on the back of a chair. He rolled onto the bed and gazed at the ceiling.

He must have slept: it was dark. Realising he was still wearing his suit trousers and white shirt, Nathan changed into comfortable jeans and sweatshirt before going downstairs.

The stove in the inglenook fireplace in the empty lounge glowed dimly, taking the chill from evening air. He found Ann sitting at the table in the kitchen.

'Hello, Mum, have I missed tea?'

'I didn't want to disturb you, so I've saved you a sandwich.'

Nathan pulled out a chair and sat at the table whilst Ann fetched a plate of ham sandwiches from the pantry.

'How do you feel?' she asked Nathan. 'Apart from hungry?'

He grinned at the family joke. 'I'm still growing.' Slim and youthfully gangly, it was a guessing game for when he'd stop growing upwards and fill out a little.

The humour died. He shrugged and said, 'I'm not sure how I feel. If I hadn't tried to find her, perhaps she would still be alive.'

'Lisa was in a lot of trouble before you went anywhere near her,' Ann told him.

'She didn't want me around anyway, she never did.'

'She had so many problems of her own.' Ann made coffee and placed a mug on the table with the sandwiches. 'You know Grandma Peggy and Grandpa Reg loved you, but the first time your dad brought you to Elliston … he walked in carrying you in a car seat … and I so wished you were mine. Reg and Peggy were well into middle age when they had Lisa and we knew they were struggling even before Peggy had a stroke.'

'I enjoyed seeing them when I was little,' Nathan said. 'But I'm so happy you're my mum.' He put his arms around her waist and held on whilst she embraced him.

Noise from upstairs prompted them to part, Ann pulling a tissue from her sleeve and Nathan brushing a hand across his eyes.

'How much does Dad know about what happened?'

'Only what you've told him.'

The kitchen door opened and Nathan noticed how tired his dad looked, even after a couple of hours resting. Even so he managed a grin and looping an arm around Ann's neck, he kissed her. It gave Nathan pleasure to see them.

Stephen reached over his son's shoulder and stole a sandwich. 'Hey, you've had tea.'

'I wasn't hungry then,' Stephen told him. 'I'm sure there'll be cake to fill up on. Is the kettle still hot?' He made coffee and leaned back on the countertop.

Ann gave them both a knowing smile and left the room.

Nathan felt a smidgen of tension. This was the first time he and Stephen had been alone since their emotional reunion in the hospital in Italy.

'Dad, I shouldn't have made a fuss about not going on holiday. I should have realised you're too old … I mean not well enough … to be scrambling about in the Grand Canyon—'

'Hey, I'm not that old.' Stephen pulled out a chair and sat next to his son. 'I'm sorry, Nathan. I would love for us to have an exciting holiday together. I didn't want to disappoint you. Six months ago when we first talked about it, I was fine, I didn't know this blasted illness would catch up with me. Perhaps I thought the couple of days' extra work would postpone me having to tell you. I didn't know I was going to be sucked into a whole lot of trouble by that … man, and now people have died because I was so gullible.'

'It's not your fault, Dad. Inspector Varma said he took a whole lot of people in, and I let him manipulate me into looking for … Lisa.' As always, Nathan fumbled over what name he should call his birth mother. 'I put Jessica in danger, and she could have got into real trouble for taking her dad's car—' Nathan bit his tongue. In response to his dad's frown, he glanced at the floor before saying, 'I wasn't going to tell you. Grandad has already given me hell.'

Stephen gave a wry smile. 'I bet he has.'

Ann appeared at the kitchen door and waggled a phone. 'Nathan, come and speak to Francesco.'

CHAPTER 65

'We've time for a break,' Francesco threw down his long handled pitchfork.

Nathan let his own fork fall to the ground and looked back along the row of cut hay he had just turned.

The boys sat in the shade of a single stunted tree and shared bread, baked that morning, and a chunk of cheese.

Nathan took a swig from a bottle of cola, one of the half-dozen bottles carried up the mountain with other supplies he and Francesco had brought from the village in the foothills. Nathan wiped his mouth with the back of his hand before scrambling to his feet. Picking up the pitchfork he skewered a forkful of green hay. 'I'm getting the hang of this. It's just a matter of flicking it over.'

'That is good,' Francesco laughed. 'We'll get the rest of the meadow done before dark.'

*

In gathering twilight, the boys propped the pitchforks with other tools stored inside a small stone hut at the edge of the meadow and, squinting against the setting sun, strolled towards the village.

'You will go to university after the summer?' Francesco asked.

'Yes. Lincoln. Film, media and journalism.'

'Did you say journalism?'

'I mean serious journalism, not the crap those people outside the hospital wrote about us. I know what it's like to be on the other side. What about you?'

'I have a place at the Politecnico di Milano.'

'That's great.'

'Maybe not so great.'

'Why?'

Francesco grimaced. 'Since my grandfather died, I don't believe Nonna can survive alone another winter in the mountain village. My aunt is a widow with young children. There is no room for my grandmother.' Into the sombre silence, Francesco said, 'Signor Stephen, he is good now?'

'Dad's doing fine. Uncle Julian was the best bone marrow match for him. There was a deal of preparation before the transplant and a pretty tense time after but, yeah, he's doing fine.'

*

Nathan and Francesco sat at the scrubbed olivewood table in Nonna's sparsely furnished kitchen. The boys mopped up gravy from a mutton stew with more bread.

Nathan drained a tumbler of watered wine and said, 'Grazie, Nonna.'

The old lady collected the plates and shuffled towards the sink.

Quickly on his feet, Nathan took the dishes from her. 'I'll see to these.'

Nonna's 'No, no' was followed by a tirade of rapid Italian Nathan couldn't follow.

Francesco put an arm around his grandmother. 'No, lo faremo. Per favore, riposati. Ti porterò da bere.' He guided her to one of the quilt-covered chairs by the stove before reaching into a cupboard and withdrawing a bottle of cognac. He poured a drop into a glass. 'Sorseggialo lentamente, Nonna.'

The boys heated water in a pan on the stove and used it to wash the dishes.

*

'Hey!'

Nathan jerked awake.

'You're as bad as Nonna, sleeping by the stove.'

'Sorry, Francesco, I didn't realise …'

'She has gone to bed and so should we. There is much work to do tomorrow.'

Nathan lay on the narrow bed and tried to pin down his feelings for Lisa. *Had Dad ever loved her? Did she love me or was I merely a tool to manipulate others?* His emotions raced around his mind until he was exhausted. He glanced across the room to where Francesco slept and considered his friend's dilemma. Around twenty people left in the village, most approaching eighty or beyond. No solution sprang to mind, and Nathan drifted into a troubled sleep.

*

Still drowsy, a splash of cold water at the sink in the kitchen shocked Nathan awake. He sat at the table beside Francesco. 'Buongiorno, Nonna.' Francesco's grandmother poured thick coffee into his cup.

246

Early morning sunshine spilled into the room as Nonna opened the door to greet a neighbour who rested a basket on the table and handed over three good-sized loaves of bread. Nathan had trouble following the conversation but gathered the lady, perhaps only slightly younger than Nonna, and her husband did most of the baking for the village.

Leaving Nonna to potter around the kitchen, Nathan and Francesco strolled through the village towards the barn where the day's tasks awaited them. Chickens scratched in the dust, and behind drystone walls, women worked with hoes in the vegetable plot whilst others harvested early crops. On the lower slopes, rows of vines were being tended. Nathan surmised the scene wouldn't have differed much over the last couple of hundred years.

'Where are the men?' Nathan commented.

'Out of the twenty-one residents of the village, there are sixteen women. Two of the men have gone into the mountains where the sheep graze in summer. One will check the flock on the high slopes, the other will bring back a sheep to be butchered. Today we must help Giuseppe: he is a metal worker … blacksmith. The blades on the reaping machine need attention before the second crop of hay can be mown, and the iron bands on the barrel of the winepress need to be replaced and some of the wood is rotten. My grandfather was a carpenter, so he is greatly missed.'

*

Nathan dusted cinders from his branded T-shirt and contemplated a scattering of singed holes. He had helped to dismantle machinery and laboured in the smithy whilst Francesco replaced staves in the barrel of the winepress.

'Tomorrow,' Francesco said, 'Giuseppe will repair the iron hoops. They need to be heated and hammered into place. Did Nonna tell you about the English soldiers?'

'No.'

'She was a small girl when escaped prisoners of war came to the village. The people of the village hid them in the winepress, screwed down the lid and covered it with turnips. The Germans searched but did not find them.'

'Did they get away?'

'They left the village when a German patrol came. This and many villages were burnt.'

'And Nonna believed my dad was one of the soldiers.'

247

'She sometimes becomes confused, but she and others were proud that they had helped.'

'What a price to pay.'

'Many villages were never rebuilt. You see the ruins of the little church? Many people left, but some of the houses were re-roofed. The children of the people you see now have also left for the cities.'

'Shame. It's a beautiful place.'

'In the summer it is good, not so in the winter.'

Francesco pointed across the meadows towards a wooded area where the heavy piebald horse dragged logs towards the village. 'The logs need to be cut and dried.'

'I can see there's plenty of work. I hope you'll have time to stay with me at Elliston for a couple of weeks later in the summer?'

Francesco shrugged.

*

A couple of miles below the village, a stream gurgled over rocks beneath the peaks of the Abruzzo mountains and into a crystal clear pool before it tumbled over a ridge, onto more rocks and wound its way through grassy meadows.

Nathan watched Francesco cast off his clothes and jump, naked, into the water. His friend surfaced, shook hair from his eyes and gestured for Nathan to join him.

Despite the warm sun Nathan shivered. Even the gentle trickle of water over the rocks unnerved him. The roar and rush of another river sounded loud. He felt it tugging at him, dragging him under.

'Come on,' Francesco called.

Nathan shook his head and stepped back.

Francesco heaved himself from the pool, droplets of water glistening on his olive skin. 'Scusi, my friend. I forgot you have trouble with water.'

Nathan forced a laugh. 'Only when there's more than in a bathtub.'

'You can swim?'

'Yes, I can swim. There's a hell of a difference between a warm swimming pool and a cold fast-flowing river. I believed I'd overcome it but when ... I told you ... Lisa, my mother ...' Nathan stepped back from the rocks and onto the soft, springy, meadow grass. 'I thought I would be dragged down by the current. That Jessica and I would ...'

'We have both had bad experiences.'

248

'Yes. I'm sorry,' Nathan said more brightly. 'I'm being a wimp.' He went over to where water trickled from the pool over the ridge and onto the rocks below. He kicked off his trainers and sitting on a rock, dangled his feet in the water.

Francesco joined him. 'You were very brave. It seems to me there was nothing you could have done to save your mother or the other man. If it helps,' Francesco sounded indignant. 'I believe they could have easily pulled you and Jessica to your deaths as well.'

That thought had also occurred to Nathan. He looked at his hands. His palms not actually callused but showing signs of three weeks hard work.

Into the silence Francesco said, 'I brought your father this way. Snowmelt and storms caused the water to cover these rocks and it was there—' he pointed further along, 'where the young man slipped and hurt his leg. He and the lady went back to the village, and from then it was just me and Signor Stephen.'

'Thank you for looking after him.'

Francesco grinned. 'We looked after each other.' After a moment's silence, he said, 'We mustn't be late back, there is a special supper to thank you for your help. Tonight, my friend, we are on full-strength wine.'

CHAPTER 66

Lizzie giggled, bouncing in the saddle as Brownie trotted around the paddock, Matthew at the pony's head. Nathan and Francesco jogged either side, each with a hand on the girl's knees, ensuring she stayed safely on board.

'That's enough for today,' Matthew called, slowing Brownie to a walk.

At the stable block, Nathan took Brownie's head while Matthew lifted his sister from the saddle and placed her into her wheelchair. 'Francesco and I will see to the horse, Matt, if you need to take care of Lizzie.'

'Thanks, I'd like to get her cleaned up before Mum gets back.'

The pony unsaddled and rubbed down, Nathan and Francesco took the gear to the tack room.

'Thanks, boys,' Gill, the stable manager, smiled. 'I'll take Brownie back to the paddock.'

Francesco grinned at Nathan. 'You have a good life here, my friend.' With a nod to Gill, he added, 'And some pretty girls.'

His head down, Nathan muttered, 'Yeah, I know how lucky I am.' After a moment, he nudged Francesco with an elbow and said, 'We'll see if there's anything more we can do to help Matthew then go home. My stepbrothers and their partners are coming over this evening. They'll be staying overnight. If Uncle Julian, Fiona and Lizzie stay as well, it might be a lads' dorm in the attic.'

Francesco laughed at Nathan's public school mentality.

They found Matthew in the kitchen of The Barn. Lizzie on his knee, he threaded her arms into a fluffy cardigan before settling her into a special comfy chair.

'I can manage now. Mum and Dad are on their way home,' Matthew told his cousin and Francesco.

'We had better go, Nathan said. 'Chris and Richard will arrive soon and my mum might need help. And, with any luck, Matthew, you and I can go out tonight. There's a new place opened in Bridgford.'

*

Nathan and Francesco waited for the electric gates at Holly Cottage to open before cycling through to the garage where they secured the bikes in a rack.

Francesco looked around at the parked cars. 'Which one is yours?'

'Guess.'

'Not the BMW or the Audi. How about the red MX5?'

'I wish,' Nathan laughed. 'Try the little Fiat outside.'

The boys made a fuss of the black and tan mongrel that ran to meet them. It scampered back to the annex, while Nathan and Francesco went into the kitchen.

'Hey, Mum, something smells good.'

'Ham, pork and beef roasting,' she mused. 'There are plenty of cobs—'

'She means bread rolls – panini,' Nathan told Francesco.

'Salad and other bits in case anyone has turned vegetarian and hasn't told me. You're just in time. Yvonne and I have made the bedrooms ready, but there are the mattresses to make up in the attic.' Ann scooped up a pile of bed linen and plonked it into Nathan's arms. 'And then you can help Grandad set out chairs in the garden.' She turned to Francesco. 'I hope you don't mind making do for one night.'

'Of course not.'

'Oh.' Ann put a hand on Francesco's arm. 'Stephen would like to see you. He's in the dining room.' She pushed open a door from the kitchen.

*

Holly Cottage was beautiful and Ann had worked hard to make it a home, but Stephen occasionally still mourned the loss of his childhood home. He gazed at papers set out on the table. The dining suite, inherited through his mother's family, had been rescued and restored following the fire that gutted Elliston House. The room was used only at Christmas and a few family occasions and now served as his office.

He noticed Francesco hovering at the door and picking out a printed copy of an agreement from a file, called, 'Come in, Francesco. I hope you're making yourself at home.'

'Si, Signor Stephen. Everyone is very good to me. We went to see Matthew and took Lizzie for a pony ride.'

'She loves that pony.'

'It is very sad that she is …'

251

'Yes, Francesco, perhaps it's sad for us, but she's happy.'

'Yes, Signor, she is happy.'

'And what about you, Francesco? I hear your grandmother is refusing to leave the village.'

'Si. Everyone in the village tells me they will look after her – they all look after each other.'

'And are you happy with that?'

Francesco shrugged. 'She is happy.'

'Are you accepting the place at Politecnico di Milano?'

Francesco looked at his feet. 'My family is poor and I have nowhere to live in Milano.'

*

'Francesco seems happy,' Ann told Stephen.

'The least I can do.' Stephen slipped his arms around her and kissed her hair, savouring her reciprocating hug. 'I've set up a trust for Francesco, to be administered independently should I not be around.'

Did he detect a slight increase in the pressure of her arms around his waist? When she pulled away, he decided she either didn't hear or ignored the statement.

She said, 'I'll give you a hand to file these, then Yvonne and I must set the table.

*

Francesco burst into the attic room and almost fell over a mattress Nathan was dragging across the floor.

'Did you know?'

'Know what?' Nathan feigned surprise.

'Signor Stephen, your dad, is sponsoring me through college.'

'Oh, is that all?' Nathan barely contained a grin.

'You knew.'

The grin widened. 'Of course I knew.'

The boys threw themselves at each other, hugged and slapped each other on the back.

The make-do sleeping arrangements sorted, Nathan said, 'I'll show you Grandad's section of the house.'

They rattled down the stairs and into the garden where Peter was setting out chairs on the lawn.

'I'm pleased to see you again, Signor Bryce.'

'And you Francesco. How is your family?'

252

Nathan let his friend and grandfather catch up whilst he fetched more garden chairs.

*

With the arrival of Ann's sons, together with Julian and Fiona, family chaos continued into the evening.

Matthew beckoned to Nathan. 'Do you think we can slip away to that new club in Bridgford?'

'I don't see why not.' Nathan in turn caught Francesco's attention. 'I'll see if I can get us a lift into Bridgford.'

CHAPTER 67

Nathan stirred and opened his eyes a crack. His angle of view was low. A long room, slanted ceiling. Yes, he remembered, he was on a mattress on the floor of the attic. By light filtering through blinds at the skylights, he made out the shape of a body sprawled on another mattress nearby, legs tangled in a bedsheet.

Raised on an elbow he located another similar shape further on.

He heard a clink of crockery and his mum's voice. 'I've brought coffee and orange juice.'

Nathan humphed and pulled the sheet over his head.

'Did you have a good night?'

'Ummm. What time is it?'

'Gone midday. Richard and Chris will be leaving soon. You can use the showers in the bedrooms then you should come down to say goodbye.' On her way out, Ann called, 'And open the skylights to let some fresh air in here.'

*

The family gathered on the forecourt of Holly Cottage to say farewell to Ann's sons, Richard and Chris.

'Richard hugged his mother, his lips close to her ear. 'I hope it's still okay for us to use the flat?'

'We don't use it, you just pay expenses.'

'I wondered if you might need to sell, you know, if Stephen isn't working.'

Ann looked around to make sure other members of the family weren't close by. 'He's done voice-overs and narrations and there are other projects lined up, so there should be no need to sell.'

Richard nodded. 'But you will give us plenty of warning if—'

'Yes,' Ann snapped. Aware the couple's occupation of the London flat had far exceeded the original arrangement she reminded him, 'It was only meant to be a temporary arrangement until you found a place of your own.' She moved on to kiss the cheek of his girlfriend. 'I hope you'll come to see us again soon.'

Ann moved to where Chris was loading overnight bags into the boot of his car.

Another hug, another promise to visit again. Chris said, 'How's Stephen doing?'

'It's a long haul but he's getting there.'

Having said goodbye to Richard, Stephen joined Ann for her farewell to Chris and, together with the rest of the family, waved them off.

Fiona said, 'We should go home too. Lizzie has physiotherapy this afternoon. 'What about you, Matthew? Gill has some rides booked and one of the RDA volunteers couldn't make it so she could use some help.'

'Okay, I'll go home with you.' Matthew turned to Francesco. 'Would you like to come too? Nathan is meeting Jessica at the station later, and we don't want to be gooseberries.'

'Gooseberries?' Francesco queried.

'It's not like that,' Nathan protested, then said seriously. 'But it is the first time I've seen her since the inquest.'

'Is that okay, Francesco?' Matthew persisted.

'Si. I would love to help but what is gooseberries?'

'I'll explain later.' To his cousin, Matt said, 'Good luck Nath.'

*

Nathan gave his grandad a hand folding and stacking garden chairs.

Peter said, 'You'd better see if your mum needs a hand with anything. Kathy and I will take Toby for a walk, then we may have a little nap to recover from all this excitement.'

Nathan smiled. It was only in recent months his grandad had taken to having 'a little nap' during the afternoon.

In the kitchen of Holly Cottage, Nathan came across Ann and housekeeper Yvonne stacking the dishwasher and covering leftover food for storage.

'If there's nothing else for me to do, Mum, I should get ready to meet Jessica.'

'Okay. Wait.'

'What?'

'You're not driving.'

'Why not?'

'You were drinking until the early hours, you might still be over the limit.'

'No, I won't, I'll be fine.'

255

'It's not worth taking the chance.'

'Oh Mum …' Nathan slammed the kitchen door behind him and ran upstairs to his room.

CHAPTER 68

In a clean shirt and jeans, Nathan stopped to glance through a mirror and ruffled his hair into some sort of style. He looked again into the mirror. That he might still be over the drink-drive limit after last night's outing had not occurred to him. The last thing he wanted was his mum driving him to the station to collect Jessica. Driving test passed a little over a month ago, was it worth the risk?

Nathan went downstairs, lifted his car key from a hook in the hall and slipped out the front door. Did someone call his name? He continued towards the garage at the side of the cottage.

*

'Nathan!'

'What's wrong?' Stephen appeared from the sitting room and joined Ann at the open front door.

'I need to stop Nathan: it's only been a few hours since they came home.'

'I know. I heard the taxi drop them off this morning.'

'He shouldn't be driving.' Ann wondered how her husband could be so calm.

'Don't worry. I noticed yesterday his front driver's side tyre is flat. He must have picked up a nail the other day.'

Keeping out of sight, Ann watched Nathan return from the garage. Visibly agitated, he had obviously discovered the flat tyre. At the same time, their BMW was driven up to the gate and Nathan conversed with James, the family chauffeur, finally climbing into the front passenger seat.

'Did you know?' Ann queried.

'I asked James to get the car ready for tomorrow so I guess he's going to top up with fuel, but I'd forgotten Nathan was meeting Jessica.'

'I'm not sure he'll be any the less embarrassed at having James drive him than he would his mum.'

'He'll get over it.'

Ann turned to her husband and put her arms around his waist, savouring his reciprocating embrace. She could tell he had lost weight. She took a step back and examined his every feature, the silver threads mingling among the loose curls of his mid brown hair. A vision of the

257

first time she met his mother came to mind, her faded beauty lingering despite her struggle with ill health. A chill rippled through her.

*

Nathan walked the length of the station platform and let his gaze follow the tracks into the distance. He took out his phone and checked the time before glancing at a screen hanging under the station canopy. The train, due in another three minutes, was on time.

He remembered his last meeting with Jessica. The inquest into Lisa's death had been traumatic for them both, they'd had little time to spend together.

The roar of the train into the station prompted Nathan to take a step back. For a moment it seemed to be hurtling through, non-stop, on its way to London but finally, with the last few carriages adjacent to the platform, it screeched to a halt.

Doors hissed open, a couple stepped onto the platform, another man followed. And just beyond, trundling a small wheeled suitcase, Jessica.

Nathan closed the distance between them and answered her broad smile with one of his own. They exchanged a hug. 'It's good to see you. How was your journey?' He took charge of the suitcase. 'I've had to get a lift,' he explained when leading her towards the chauffeur-driven BMW.

James was out of the car, had stowed the suitcase in the boot and was holding open the rear door before they had drawn breath.

'I had a flat tyre.' At a twinge of conscience, Nathan added, 'And I might still be over the limit after going out with my cousin and Francesco last night.'

'Very sensible, the police are pretty keen around our way.'

'I don't normally drink much, it was just that …'

'You don't need to explain. Good heavens, we own a pub, but my dad has no qualms about telling the police if someone leaves intending to drive. You're lucky to have a chauffeur.'

He couldn't tell if she spoke with sarcasm but at her wide grin said, 'I'm sorry I haven't introduced you. This is James.'

James glanced through the rear view mirror and raised a hand in acknowledgment.

On the outskirts of the village of Elliston, James turned right into an unmade high-hedged road. A hundred yards further, the tall electric gates of Holly Cottage slid open and he pulled onto the forecourt.

258

Determined not to be outdone, Nathan hopped out of the car and raced around to open the rear passenger door before James had switched off the engine.

Jessica stepped out onto the drive, her attention on the frontage of Holly Cottage. 'It's beautiful.'

Nathan took in the red brick building, the lattice porch, colourful and fragrant with late summer roses, and saw it as if for the first time. 'Yes, it is.'

The front door opened. 'Hello, Jessica,' Ann greeted. 'Come inside.'

Nathan dropped the suitcase in the hall and followed in time to hear his mum say, 'Yvonne has made sandwiches for lunch but I'm sure you'd like to freshen up first. Nathan will show you to your room.'

Nathan inclined his head towards the stairs and collecting Jessica's bag led the way to a guest bedroom where Jessica took the case and said, 'Wait for me, I'll never find my way down.'

A few minutes later she emerged. 'I'm so pleased it's en-suite, I hate asking where the loo is. Is your dad here? What shall I say to him?'

'Just say, hello. He doesn't bite. It's Grandad you'll need to watch out for.'

'What?'

'Only kidding.'

*

In the lounge Nathan, sitting beside Jessica, helped himself to another sandwich.

'Leave some for your dad,' Ann told him.

'Last one,' he promised. 'Where is he?'

'Conference call with Linda and some interested parties for a film next year.'

A moment later the door opened. 'Well, that's settled,' Stephen told them. 'You must be Jessica.' He took her hand, leaned forward and kissed her cheek. 'I'm very pleased to meet you.'

Nathan noticed Jessica's eyes widen as she sat, tongue tied, and he wondered at the universal reaction to his dad's smile. He offered Stephen a plate. 'We saved you a sandwich.'

Stephen gazed at the solitary triangle of bread and ham. 'Generous, as usual.'

The alarm on the outer gate sounded. 'You won't starve,' Ann told her husband. 'Matthew and Francesco are here, so I'll make more.'

259

Stephen looked through the window 'And who else?'

Ann joined her husband. Nathan, at her shoulder, said, 'I know who that is.'

Ann led Inspector Varma and his sergeant into the lounge where Nathan, Jessica, Francesco and Matthew stood in a group. Peter, fresh from his afternoon nap, joined them.

'You know my husband, Stephen,' Ann said to the inspector.

'Yes, of course.'

Stephen stretched out a hand. 'May I ask what brings you here, Inspector?'

Varma smiled, shook Stephen's hand and nodded at Nathan, Jessica and Peter. 'I have news.'

Looks passed between the family. Stephen said, 'What sort of news?'

'Well.' The inspector rubbed a hand over his chin. 'Good and bad I suppose.'

Ann sensed Nathan step forward and stand close behind her.

'It's about the jewellery,' Varma explained.

'It's not ours any more, Inspector,' Ann pointed out. 'It was donated to the museum.'

'I know, but previously it was in your family for four generations, and I thought you'd like to know.'

Ann heard a sigh from over her shoulder.

'As we feared,' Varma said, 'one or two stones have turned up on the continental markets, so we must assume most of the pieces have been broken up, the gold melted down.'

'That's a shame,' Ann said. 'Though, perhaps it's for the best; the rubies have never brought us any good.'

'Mum!' Nathan objected. 'You told me how they were a gift. I don't understand why you gave them to the museum.'

Ann turned to face her son. 'Nathan, you know well— Oh, never mind, it's too late now.'

'Ah.' Inspector Varma delved into his jacket pocket and withdrew a padded envelope. 'We have managed to recover this—' He tipped out the contents. In the palm of his hand sparkled eight diamonds surrounding a smouldering ruby, set flush into the face of a thick gold band.

CHAPTER 69

Nathan watched Matthew examine the ring, turning it this way and that. The sparkle of diamonds, the glow of ruby. Ice and fire.

Matthew handed the ring to Francesco. He touched the tip of his finger to the stones before passing it to Jessica who slipped it on to first one finger and then another until it rested on the fourth finger of her left hand.

'You'll be the fourth generation of your family to own it, Nathan. Or rather your wife will.' She quickly pulled off the ring and handed it to Nathan.

Someday, Nathan thought. Maybe someday. He slipped the ring into a black velvet box they'd found for its safekeeping.

*

Stephen tidied some papers spread on the dining table and slipped them into a folder. Was he right to accept more work if—?

Nathan came into the room and held out the ring box. 'We *are* going to keep it, aren't we?'

Stephen accepted the box. 'The insurance company doesn't want it nor does the museum.' He opened it and gazed at the contents. 'I remember my mother, Granny Susan, wearing it until she lost so much weight it became loose and would slip from her finger. It fitted Ann perfectly,' he mused. 'I remember the panic when she thought she'd lost it. Somehow it always finds its way back.' He snapped the box shut.

'We're walking to the park for a game of tennis,' Nathan told him, 'but we'll be back in plenty of time to go to the Red Lion this evening.' Nathan made to leave but turned back. 'You *are* all right now, Dad?'

'I'm fine,' Stephen said automatically, before adding, 'but I don't think I could manage a hike along the Grand Canyon.'

'I'm not bothered about going now,' Nathan grinned sheepishly. Then, seriously, said, 'I did love her, sort of. Lisa, I mean.'

Stephen detected a slight crack in his son's voice and was hit by a stab of anxiety when Nathan asked, 'Did you? I mean once, when …'

A question Stephen had often asked himself, and after a moment's thought, he said, 'Sort of.'

At the door, Nathan again turned. 'But I'm not like her. I want to be like you.'

EPILOGUE

On the landing at Holly Cottage, Ann took a moment to compose herself before carrying a tray into the main bedroom. Nathan, seated by the bed, closed the book he was reading aloud. 'I think that's enough Dickens for today.'

Ann set the tray on a bedside table, touched Stephen's hand, and said briskly, 'Hello, sweetheart.' Noticing he had slipped down the bed, she motioned for Nathan to help and with an arm under each of Stephen's, they levered him up the bed, and adjusted the pillows so his head was raised. A hand on her son's arm, Ann said, 'Thanks, Nathan. Why don't you go to see Matthew for an hour?'

Nathan looked doubtful.

Go on,' Ann insisted. 'Have a break.'

'Okay. Just for an hour.' He closed the door quietly.

Stephen's breathing was shallow; he groaned with each exhalation.

Ann brushed back his hair. It was dull and in need of a wash, but still curled. He quietened at her touch. Ann stirred semolina in the bowl on the tray. 'You should try to eat just a little, Stephen.' Placing her hand in his, she felt a weak squeeze accompanied by the slightest shake of his head.

'Perhaps later,' she conceded. 'I'll put jam in it, or golden syrup.'

Again she felt him tense, the lines between his brows deepening. She continued, 'I'd better get you washed; your dad will be up shortly.' Ann half filled a bowl from the tap in the bathroom and, squeezing excess water from a flannel, wiped Stephen's face and neck. She was drying between his fingers when Peter came in to take his turn sitting by the bed.

They'd been through the disbelief, anger, despair, even blame, and emerged closer, stronger. Stephen had completed a film and agreed to read some stories for audiobooks. He had good days and bad, the bad days becoming more frequent until, six weeks ago, a mug of coffee slipped from his grasp. It smashed on the kitchen floor, hot liquid splashing up cupboards, running under the fridge and forming a pool under the table...

263

'Oh Stephen,' Ann sighed. 'That was a best china mug.' She stooped to pick up the pieces but immediately let them fall, calling, 'Nathan, Peter, come quickly.'

They helped Stephen upstairs. He had difficulty lifting his legs high enough to put a foot on the steps, but they managed to put him to bed, and there he stayed.

Ann took the cereal bowl and mug downstairs and let them clatter in the sink.

'Steady, you'll break those.'

'Oh,' Ann spun around. 'Julian!'

'Sorry, Ann. I thought you'd heard me come in.'

Ann shook her head before clamping a hand to her mouth. After a moment she relaxed and took a few deep calming breaths. 'Damn tears keep sneaking up on me. It's just ... I could manage to move him when he was able to help himself a little, but now ... I'm afraid of hurting him.'

'She must have left it in the sitting room.'

Ann realised Julian was speaking and stepped back. 'What?'

'Fiona's handbag. If she didn't leave it here, I've a good deal of telephoning to do, cancelling credit cards and the like.' Julian went into the sitting room, returning within a few moments with a black leather handbag.

Ann made an effort to collect her thoughts. 'Oh, yes. She must have left it when she was here earlier.'

'I'll buy her a bag she can tie around her neck,' Julian grinned.

'Hey, you.' Ann pointed a finger at him. 'I don't know what I'd do without her help. I don't know what I'd do without support from you all.'

Julian gave her a hug; something he wouldn't have done a few months ago. She reflected on past disagreements and was glad their relationship had improved. She stepped back and patted his chest. 'I was about to put the kettle on. Will you stay for a drink?'

'Yes please. And I'd like to see Stephen if that's okay.'

'Of course it is.' Ann filled the kettle whilst Julian set out the cups on a tray. 'Put some pineapple juice in Stephen's mug, will you please? He's not wanted tea or coffee for a while now.'

Ann followed Julian, who carried the tray upstairs; he placed it on a table near the window and handed a cup to his father.

Peter stood back to allow Julian access to the bed.

'How're you doing kid? Julian touched Stephen's shoulder. 'I've come to annoy you for a few minutes.'

In the absence of any reaction, Ann took Stephen's hand. 'Stephen? Julian's here.'

Stephen opened his eyes a fraction. His mouth moved. It could have been, 'Hi, Jules.'

She caught a faint clicking, deep within Stephen's throat and knew instinctively. Julian had also heard. She went downstairs allowing father and sons a few moments alone.

*

On his return, Nathan set the alarm on the perimeter of Holly Cottage before he and Matthew headed for the kitchen. 'Hello, Mum, we've brought fish and chips for everyone. I didn't know if Yvonne had left anything, and I'm sure you don't want to be cooking … What's wrong?'

'Nothing.' Ann, convinced she had overreacted, continued to load the dishwasher. 'Grandad and Uncle Jules are with your dad. They'll be down soon; pop the food in the oven to keep warm.'

*

Later in the evening, Peter and Nathan climbed the stairs at Holly Cottage. Knees creaking, Peter muttered thanks that his rooms in the extension were on the ground floor. He gently pushed open the bedroom door. Ann, bathed in dim light and swaddled in her white towelling dressing gown, dozed in the chair beside Stephen's bed. She stirred and putting a finger to her lips, beckoned them in. 'Will you both stay with me tonight?' she whispered.

Peter took a moment to touch Stephen's hand and brow before moving to the bed by the far wall, usually occupied by whoever's turn it was to stay with Stephen. He eased off his shoes and propped a pillow behind his head. He watched Ann arrange herself on the bed beside her husband, their fingers intertwined, and waited whilst Nathan made himself comfortable in the easy chair beside the bed.

Peter listened to Stephen's shallow irregular breaths and waited for Ann's breathing to become deep and even before he allowed his own eyes to close.

Something woke him. Peter listened intently before sitting up and putting his feet to the floor. The nightlight bathed the room in a rosy

265

glow; the pair on the bed lying undisturbed, Nathan, slumped sideways, slept, a book open on his lap. *Must have been dreaming.* The image of the first time Stephen brought Ann to Elliston House still vivid. 'Mum, this is Ann,' Stephen had said, holding out his hand to draw Ann into the sitting room. Susan, his beautiful mother, moved, disturbing her perfume of Spring Flowers. The scent overwhelming, Peter almost blacked out, a shadow passed over the room. Recovering, Peter padded over to the bed to look down on Stephen and Ann, their hands still intertwined. It wasn't a sound that had woken him, but the ceasing of quiet breath.

Also by Patricia Greasby

Second Take
First in the series of Bryce romantic mysteries.
Past relationships threaten future happiness and lives are at
risk when family heirlooms attract criminal interest.

First Time
Second in the series of romantic mysteries.
Wedding guests each have a story to tell. First love,
betrayals and a disappearance lead to an underground
nightmare.

Thrice Shy
Third in the series of romantic mysteries.
Whilst Stephen's life hangs in the balance, Ann seeks
shelter in a remote cottage where she is at the mercy of an
old adversary.

Fourth Generation
Fourth in the series of romantic mysteries.
Stephen and a film crew are stranded on a mountain in Italy.
Nathan seeks his birth mother, Lisa, who, he discovers, has
become involved with a gang of ruthless criminals.
*****

Lavender Blue
Are Ellen's enquiries into the disappearance of her
childhood friend twenty years ago responsible for at least
two untimely deaths?